Atlas' Flight
By J. Channing

Book 2 of the Atlas Carter Saga

ISBN: 978-0-9984881-5-8

Title: Atlas' Flight
Description: First Edition

Chapter 1

The Great Orion Nebula planetary system G-1726 - Nicknamed "The Swordbelt"
Capitol planet G-1726-3RT "Gertie"
1,340 light years away from Sol

Colonial Administrator Sickyl Tannin's skull slammed into the dirt. Dazed, he stared at the drop ships streaking like molten knives through Gertie's sky. Bullets whined overhead as the colony's rebellious farmers rejoined their assault on his militia. For a moment he felt disoriented, unsure of where he was or what was going on.

His mind was a fuzzy haze. As he struggled to clear his thoughts, he realized he had somehow gotten outside the administration compound. He'd been communing within the Bwainsong, which was made possible by his ingestion of the strange yellowish mushrooms that grew on the planet's surface. These sessions were becoming more and more draining, both mentally and physically, and he was having difficulty separating reality from the telepathic hum of the collective alien minds of the Bwain.

"Phuri? Where are you?" he called hoarsely, but his assistant was nowhere to be found.

Tannin had been deep in the endless golden knot that allowed him to communicate with the aliens. Earlier, Phuri had tried to rouse the administrator as he writhed in his sweat-soaked sheets in a state of tangled mental agony. At first he was stunned, and then furious when Phuri advised him that the farmers and other colonists had begun revolting after learning of their administrator's secret alliance with the alien creatures. He had promised the Bwain a home on Gertie in exchange for granting him safe passage back to Earth. To make matters worse, the colonists had been fighting with such ferocity, that they'd driven his militiamen back incrementally, until the fighting finally reached the area outside of his private quarters.

Using his militiamen as human shields, he ran from the house and attempted to escape, only to be knocked to the ground by one of his own men who attempted to save his life when he saw one of the farmers taking aim at him. Unfortunately, the man took the bullet that was meant for Tannin, right in the side of the head.

As Tannin lay there, stunned by the sudden impact, he glanced over and saw his savior's lifeless eyes staring at him blankly, as a pool of blood collected on the ground around his head.

Tannin's vision blurred for a moment, and then came back into focus. His men were yelling at him to get up and run, but he couldn't seem to do it. A sudden vision, or delusion, or whatever it was suddenly filled his mind. He'd been captured by Captain Mephista and Lt. Danny Xiao. There'd been a trial of sorts in which he was found guilty of crimes against humanity, and was sentenced to death. A sentence he quickly served when Mephista blew a hole through his chest with a plasma pistol. The vision finished with him lying on the ground with the crowd howling and cheering all around him.

Tannin instinctively reached a hand up to check himself. He could feel his heart pounding with fear, but he was in fact still alive and physically whole. It had all been nothing more than a cruel trick that his mind had played on him as he stumbled out into the courtyard and become enmeshed in the chaos, still in a mushroom induced haze.

More men screamed and fell around him, snapping his focus back to the here and now. This was all Carter's doing. Captain Atlas Carter had destroyed his plan, and now Mephista, the pirate captain Tannin had kept under his thumb for so long, had also betrayed him by sending troops from her ship to aid the rebels.

The administrator rolled over, trying to rise and flee back to his compound, but the barrel of a pistol suddenly appeared right in front of his face, and as Tannin looked upward, his eyes suddenly locked with the man at the other end of the pistol.

"It's all over for you Tannin," Lieutenant Danny Xiao said. Blood trickled from the young officer's ears, and his face was slicked with trails of sweat soaked dust. Xiao had been one of Tannin's operatives, though back then he was just an impressionable young supply officer who would have handed over the *Fate's Winds* antimatter fuel in exchange for the life of his sister. Carter had gotten to Xiao, and somehow turned the lieutenant into some sort of moral crusader who had helped to organize the rebels. Where the boy had once been youthful in appearance, a man's hardness had now managed to seep in under the grime of rebellion.

Behind Xiao, the first of the marines grappled with Tannin's militia, and it was very likely that the battle would be over in a matter of minutes. Tannin had envisioned negotiating with the Bwain, and using them to flee this pathetic, backwater planet so that he could get back home to Earth and punish those who'd abandoned him. Now his return to Earth was no longer possible. His plan, and in fact his very existence on Gertie was now as desolate and hopeless as it was for those on the penal planet, Judgment. Now that they'd been attacked, the aliens would destroy the colony and take the planet for themselves.

"You've killed us all Danny, you just don't know it yet," Tannin wailed.

"Captain Carter's beaten the Bwain," Danny replied, and then he gestured at the wretched creature beside Tannin with the barrel of his pistol. "Go on, ask your friend here if you don't believe me."

Tannin twisted to find the alien that he'd brought to Gertie crawling toward the colonial administration building's steps. The bird-like alien shuddered at each plasma bolt that sizzled overhead, and when its talons reached the plaza's stone, the Bwain's feathers changed from their natural deep black to a mottled white and gray. The alien looked like a cross between a sentient bird and a scaled reptile. It had three clawed fingers and a thumb at the end of muscular arms. Chameleon-like feathers covered its body and limbs, ending at the scaled waddle of its buzzard neck.

"Is it true?" Tannin demanded.

The creature's marbled eyelids fluttered in agony.

"Swarm gone! Swarm gone!" it squawked.

"That's not possible," Tannin whispered, a look of disbelief taking over his features.

"You underestimated Captain Carter. He knew what you were planning the whole time. I only wish that I'd have helped him sooner," Danny said as he narrowed his eyes at the Bwain for a moment and then quickly fixed his gaze steadily on Tannin once again.

"You and your pathetic ship are nothing, and your sister isn't the only Xiao who's gonna die!" Tannin raged.

For a moment Danny's face seemed to dissolve back to its sullen youth, but then a calm firmness settled over him.

"Tell the militia to stand down," Danny ordered him.

Tannin scanned the street. Most of his men were pinned down, huddled behind overturned hovercarts and supply barrels, while plasma bolts scorched the colonist's low pre-fab homes. His plan wasn't finished. If he could just get back inside the administration compound and contact the Bwain, they would help him stop Carter, and he'd still be able to get off this miserable prison of a planet.

An explosion suddenly caused the ground to shake as it showered them both with dirt and stone. Danny ducked, and Tannin saw his opportunity. He quickly seized a fist sized rock and swung it at the weapon in Danny's hand, knocking it away. A second swing caught the surprised supply officer right in the temple, sending him to the ground in an unconscious heap.

Scrambling to his feet, the administrator sprinted through the fighting toward the steps that led to the three-story stone mansion that had been the first structure that he'd ordered built on the planet. It had been specifically designed to hide him from away from misery of his existence on that Sol-blasted planet, and that same design would aid him now.

A claw hooked Tannin's pant leg, pulling him back down the steps.

"And we?" the cowering Bwain croaked.

The disgusting alien's dark marble eyes rolled wide in its skull, while the crest of feathers above its beak shivered in fear. The Bwain should have been Tannin's greatest triumph. They would have paved the way for his return to Sol from his exile to the Swordbelt, but instead the aliens had shown only weakness.

He stomped on the creature's claw, then sprinted up the stairs as the Bwain screeched in pain. He was going to escape Gertie and return to Earth to exact his revenge, and as such, there was no longer time for mercy.

*   *   *

Tannin swung the compound's heavy brass doors shut behind him and leaned against the metal, gasping for breath. His residence had largely emptied when the rebellion started, and yet a lone set of footsteps echoed from the corridor.

"Administrator, how may I assist you?" Phuri asked. His aide had belted a plasma pistol awkwardly over his age-thickened waist, and the Nepali man's brown eyes darted to the locked doors as bullets ricocheted off the metal. Phuri was a man once accustomed to luxury, but his silk suit from Earth was now patched and threadbare, and his fleshy face drooped with an expression of constant disappointment. Gertie had been hard on him as well, but he'd always done his utmost to serve.

"Quick, I need the mushrooms. I have to find out what happened to the Bwain," Tannin replied, his tone laced with urgency.

An explosion rattled the locked doors. Phuri nodded, following Tannin in a panting jog up the stairs to the administrator's quarters.

"The colony?" Phuri gasped as they climbed.

Atlas' Flight

"In open revolt."

"And Carter?"

"Carter…," Tannin growled as they left the stairs and jogged down another
corridor. Windows that had been opened to allow in the pleasant weather,
now showed flames crawling from Landfall's buildings, and the flashes of
plasma weapons streaking back and forth between opposing forces.

"He can still be beaten," Tannin said as he threw open the door to his
quarters, headed straight toward the small wooden box that sat askew on
his nightstand, and pulled one of the small fungi from the case.

"The rebels may gain entry before you wake," Phuri cautioned anxiously as
Tannin laid down on the bed, facing the ceiling.

"When the Senate sent us to this godforsaken planet, was it what we
deserved?"

"No, we didn't deserve it," Phuri replied tentatively.

"Then we need to do everything we can to get back there, no matter what
the cost. I won't let Carter, or anyone else for that matter, stand in my way,"
he said, and then he popped the mushroom into his mouth and chewed it
quickly, letting the familiar sour-sweetness coat his mouth before he
swallowed.

Every native fruit and vegetable on Gertie carried the same saccharine
flavor. Of them all however, only the mushrooms allowed humans to
commune mentally with the Bwainsong, and only Tannin had been brave
enough to stare into that abyss, and listen to the voices that spoke back.

The mushroom's drizzle ran down the back of his throat. Distantly, the
sounds of battle floated through the building's walls. He had a vague sense
of Phuri saying something. Was it a question? The words all seemed to blur
together as his consciousness freed itself from the tether that connected it to
his body, and became one with the alien voices that had somehow become

so much more real to him than his own human perceptions of reality. In a way, it was a release for him from the hell he'd been forced into, and sometimes he almost wished he could just remain in the Bwainsong forever.

* * *

The Bwain were telepathic aliens that had been traveling the galaxy when homo-sapiens' ancestors were still scavenging the savannah, and the Bwainsong was the collective consciousness of their entire race. Millions of alien voices surrounded Tannin like a golden net, each thread an individual's thoughts and sensations wrapping around another, forming thicker and thicker strands that bound together every Bwain throughout the galaxy, and allowed them to communicate with one another instantaneously, regardless of their physical or geographic separation.

For a time, Tannin had thought the Bwain would bring him infinite knowledge and power. He had used their need for a planetary home as a bargaining chip, and had planned to use their power to restore his own power and position back on Sol, but now that he knew how little strength the aliens truly held, he could not stomach their craven cowardice.

"Where is your fleet?" Tannin demanded.

"Swarm gone," the voices answered. *"The Bwainslayer has come."*

"Speak sense!" Tannin thought as he tried to navigate through all the voices in his head.

In response, an image appeared in Tannin's mind. It was the collective vision of dozens of individual Bwain, that stood in a fearful ring around a burning knot of sentient light twenty feet high. It shone more brightly than any sun's plasma, and the chain writhed like joined snakes at the center of an alien chamber. The room seemed as though it had been designed to be some sort of a massive altar, and every aspect of it seemed to dwarf the diminutive Bwain. Tannin focused, trying to understand the pattern in the liquid metal. He wondered for a moment how such a light could give no heat, but then his mind suddenly reared back in anger.

Atlas' Flight

At the ring's base stood a human in a torn EVO suit. The astronaut had lost his helmet, allowing Tannin to recognize the tanned skin and broad shoulders of Captain Atlas Carter.

"Carter! What have you done?" Tannin screamed in his thoughts.

Tannin's fury generated shockwaves within the Bwainsong. The aliens did not understand a mind that could close off parts of its own emotions, and the administrator felt their fearful probing of his emotions like electricity across his skin. Lit with the knot's light, Carter's glowing eyes swiveled toward the administrator.

"I've stopped them, Tannin. The Bwain won't follow your orders any longer," Carter thought back to him. His face was a mixture of triumph and impudence.

The final memories of millions of Bwain suddenly flowed into Tannin's mind. Traveling too quickly to change course, inexperienced in warfare and unaware of what lay before them, ship after ship left the Great Orion Nebula, only to burn in the fury of the gigantic plasma array that Carter had set for them as a trap. He could feel their feathers and skin turn to ash, their lungs explode, and their weak caws for help snuffed out without response.

"You killed them," Tannin accused.

"No, Tannin, you did by bringing them here. I saved them from extinction," Carter though back to him.

"I was fulfilling my duty to the colony..."

"You didn't care about the colony. You only wanted revenge, and millions died because of your selfishness."

"Who are you to judge me? I know what you did in Belize."

The barb struck Carter. The Captain had been exiled to the Swordbelt after he'd stood by and let the *Narcos* kill his beloved wife, and take over the city he'd grown up in. Once Tannin had thought that Carter would be the perfect tool to bend to his will, but out at the edge of human-occupied space, the man had somehow found a conscience.

A surge of mental pressure rose, trying to push Tannin and Carter's consciousness more tightly together in the way the Bwain used to resolve a dispute among their own. Tannin felt Carter's earnestness, his contrition, his devotion to ideals. He saw Carter's wife's face, smiling and drifting into bed with him. Such weakness had no place in the harsh void of the universe. The visions disgusted him.

"And you!" Tannin screamed at the Bwain. *"If you abandon me, you'll* never *gain the home I promised you. You'll wander the universe until the last of your race starves, forgotten and tormented!"*

Fear writhed through the Bwainsong. They had lived hundreds of generations on their ships, long enough to forget all memory of what it had been like to breathe the air of a planet, to till its soil, to scour its lands for food. Now the great vessels that had sustained them for so long were breaking down. They had little food remaining and knew nothing of how to grow more. Once there had been others who had known, others who had fed and housed them, but they were long gone.

The shining knot in the room where Carter stood brightened. Its pattern wound endlessly, but somehow seemed terrifyingly familiar. The Bwain were trying to tell him something, a deep secret they locked away even from themselves. If only he could figure out what it was.

*   *   *

"Phuri," Tannin moaned, his body twisting in the sweat-soaked sheets. He needed to free himself from the Bwainsong. Something was coming; something horrible that he wouldn't survive. He could feel the terror rendered their racial memories, and suddenly he saw in all with startling clarity. In the instant between one synapse and the next, the Bwain revealed the true source of their fear.

Tannin gazed upon the Bwain's nightmare, but the mushroom's effects left him unable to flee the horrible vision. Somewhere within the Bwainsong he could feel Carter weeping. He tried to escape back into his body, but there was no release. He would only be able to return once the mushroom's effects had subsided, but the damage had been done, and the horrible truth had been revealed to him. Every intelligent creature in the galaxy would be consumed, and the knowledge of what was coming tore through Tannin's mind, along with the collective horror of what was left of the Bwain.

* * *

Phuri alternated between hovering at the administrator's bedside while Tannin writhed in the grip of the mushrooms' strange dreams, and checking the battle's progress from the corridor's window. Though the rebel farmers had taken heavy losses, Mephista's marines were trained soldiers and had turned the tide against the colonial militia. A small group of Tannin's soldiers still fought to defend the compound, but they would last only minutes longer.

On Earth, Phuri had aided Tannin's rise through Sol's parliament in ways that were both legal, and not so legal. Though he had long ago pledged his loyalty to the man who had plucked him from Kathmandu's slums, he was starting to feel that maybe it was time to reconsider his options.

A muffled thump and cry sounded from the administrator's chamber. Phuri ran from the corridor and found Tannin shuddering on the cold stone floor.

"They're coming! Phuri, they're coming!" he shouted wildly.

The administrator's eyes flew open. His pupils had widened to swallow the whites of his eyes, and yellow froth from the mushrooms was bubbling down Tannin's matted beard. Phuri stepped back, rather than making any attempt to help. He was all too familiar with the mushroom's unpredictable after-effects, and he didn't want to get too close while the mushroom induced spasms jerked and twisted Tannin's body.

"Oh my god, they're coming!" the administrator panted again.

Who's coming?" Phuri asked.

Tannin's hands flopped onto his chest, clenching his skin as if he wanted to dig into his own heart. Standing beside him, Phuri could smell the decaying sweetness from the administrator's breath. Screams floated from the window, followed by a battering against the compound's doors.

"The rebels haven't made it inside yet. We still have the hovercar in the basement," Phuri said as he glanced nervously down the corridor. The sounds of combat were drawing nearer, and they didn't have much time left before it was upon them.

As soon as the words left his mouth they felt like a reflex of loyalty. He'd been in Tannin's service for nearly two decades, and old habits were hard to break. The man who had once been considered a rival to President Kidewange back on Earth, was now little more than a failed addict.

"Of course," Phuri added. "Then again, if you're in no condition to leave…"

The administrator's eyes fell closed. His breathing came faster and faster, and his hands rose to the sides of his head and tore at his hair.

"Leave? They'll leave no one! No one at all!" The administrator shouted as he rolled onto his side and grasped at the shins of Phuri's pants. The aide backed further out of reach as a variety of scenarios played through his mind.

Tannin's plan had been to steal Carter's antimatter and use it to fuel the ship the administrator and Mephista had built in secret. Using the faster-than-light Alcubierre jump, they would have returned to Earth and revealed Tannin's ability to control the Bwain. All of humanity would have bowed to him, and Kidewange would have been forced to bow down to him.

Carter had destroyed Tannin's ship, so there was little hope of returning to Earth without antimatter. These were challenges, to be sure, but one of the reasons Tannin had picked Phuri from the streets all those years ago was that he had always been a problem solver.

The Nepali spun and left the administrator's chamber. Tannin's moans quickly faded as his aide ran down the corridor. He had to hurry to the compound's satellite communications center before the rebels broke through the residence's heavy, metal doors. The hovercar would take him out of the city, but he would still need to get off the planet. There was still one ship capable of faster-than-light travel that no one seemed to have accounted for.

Tannin had always been far too focused on revenge for his own good. Raised in poverty, Phuri was far more practical in his thinking. He simply did what was necessary, and what was necessary for him right now was to get back to Earth by any means possible.

*   *   *

Once Tannin would have noticed Phuri's absence and grown angry at his aide's betrayal, but the man who paced his bedroom in an arcane pattern was no longer capable of conscious thought. His steps grew faster and faster, carving the same pattern as the flaming knot he had seen on board the Bwain ship. Perhaps some part of his mind still functioned rationally, telling him that he could banish the terrible vision that had consumed him simply by repeating a shape that did not make sense in three dimensions.

"It's ending. Everything I've worked for all this time...it's all ending!" Tannin muttered to himself.

He tore fistfuls of hair from his head but felt little pain. He was running now, trying to weave to and fro randomly for his own protection. Unfortunately, all it resulted in was a painful fall that he barely felt, and a bit of dizziness that forced him to stop. He only half-saw the physical objects before him. The remainder of his vision was filled with glimpses of the terrible beings that had found the Bwain before the Earth's surface had even cooled. He saw the universe as they did; weak, glistening, and ready to be consumed.

Finally, he stumbled out into the corridor, and then staggered over to the window at the end of the hall. Below him, countless bodies were splayed out in the dirt, their blood working as an attraction for Gertie's native insects. Smoke billowed through the streets, and a sudden breeze poured over his skin like acid. He let out an anguished howl, as a look of horror crossed his face. They were all dead. Not just dead, but consumed.

For just a brief moment, the last rational piece of his mind rose to the surface. Some of the colonists were still alive, and several faces lifted toward him.

"I always knew you were a traitor Mephista! You could have had everything you wanted, and now we're all stuck here!" he screeched out the window. The effects of the mushroom were finally starting to subside, and he could feel his senses returning. "You don't even know what's coming, but I do. You all could have been on the right side. I gave you your chance, but now...aaaaagh!"

Tannin stumbled backward, trying to beat out the flames from the plasma bolt that struck him in the chest. Below him in the street, the Bwain he had called The Voice lowered its smoking pistol.

Tannin collapsed once more onto the cold stone as a feeling relief flowed through him. The Bwain's masters were returning, and it was a mercy to be spared the horrors to come.

Chapter 2

The Bwainhome
Two million kilometers from Gertie, drifting toward the wreckage of the
Fate's Winds

The Endless Knot spoke, and Captain Atlas Carter listened.

When he had first reached the massive ship that served as the alien Bwain's home among the stars, Carter had been barely alive. His EVO suit's visor had been damaged, and the vacuum of space was tearing at his face and chilling his lungs. He had wanted nothing more than to die, to shed his pain and join the wife he had betrayed, and to face whatever afterlife awaited him.

He had thought about his crew on the *Fate's Winds*, though, and his responsibility for them. They needed time to escape the aliens if they were going to survive, and so he had forced his way into the Bwainhome, determined to postpone the reunion with his beloved Aida – and to kill whoever or whatever stood in his way.

Rather than resist, the creatures had taken him to the cathedral-like room in which he now stood, and had placed him in front of a writhing coil of light that could have been the physical manifestation of the universe's creator. It was a living, pulsing thing that seemed to be composed of pure energy and intelligence, and even being in its presence filled him with an uneasy sensation of infinite depth.

The Knot's diamond brilliance had laid bare his grief and guilt. He bore this, just as he'd done with all the beatings he took in the concrete boxing rings of Belize City. The revelations continued to worsen however. It began showing him those who were depending on him, namely his crew, the colonists on Gertie, and Captain Mephista, as well as Threed and all the other prisoners on Judgment...and now the Bwain.

It showed him that he wasn't alone, that he wasn't just free to pass into the next world for his own selfish reasons. Furious, he had thrust his hand into the Knot, hoping to strangle the alien vision that had dared to force its lies into his mind. Within the Knot however, there were no truths or lies. There were only memories.

Where before Carter had been one solitary mind, now he was a part of the collective consciousness of countless numbers of alien beings. Every living Bwain's consciousness joined into one collective within the Knot, flooding him with alien sensations, concepts, memories he could not possibly comprehend.

Within the Bwainsong, he was able to see them as the primitive, forest dwelling creatures they once were, concealing themselves and peering through the foliage as a massive vessel descended from the sky. The Bwain's masters had come and taken the aliens from their home planet, binding them to the Knot in a way that increased their intelligence and longevity. They had become slaves, and at the same time they had suddenly become intelligent enough to understand the horror of their fate.

"Bwainslayer," the creatures called to him.

A scene from what looked like Earth swelled in front of him. It was a jungled beachfront viewed from a half-dozen different angles. Men's bodies bled into the surf line while a group of African slaves sprinted away down the beach. One slave stayed, however, rummaging through the supplies in a crude skiff looking for food. The man wore little more than a loincloth and a few scraps of leather jewelry. His once-powerful torso was wasted by whatever hard march his captors had imposed on him, and blisters bubbled along his feet.

The Bwain stepped out of the jungle, their camouflage feathers fading from the greens and browns that they remembered from their long-lost forests, to a deep blue. Carter heard the slave scream in fear and shock, felt the Bwain's curiosity turn to fear as the slave lifted a heavy oar from the boat. Charging into the shocked aliens, the man pummeled them to death before they could react.

They had no idea how he had arrived on their ship, and yet here was a Bwainslayer who had mindlessly killed them when they meant him no harm. Here inside the Knot, each one of their billions of connected minds felt his burning self-hatred, and interpreted it as an emotion that was being directed at them.

The Bwainsong shifted then to a mixture of both curiosity and fear. A vision of himself in his helicopter over Belize City suddenly filled his mind. While in reality he had given in to Cazador and the *Narcos* and let them take the city in exchange for what he thought would be his wife's safety, in the vision the Knot was showing him, he'd shoved his helicopter's stick forward and rained destruction down upon them. The drug lords who had threatened the city were decimated, and the grateful citizens poured out of their homes to give thanks as he flew overhead.

Tears rushed down Carter's face as he recognized *Calle Boxer* and his home back on Earth. The street had been decimated, and his beloved Aida had perished in the destruction. In the Knot's version however, the house still stood. He pushed the throttle to its stops, and flew faster and faster toward the rooftop where he had once planted tomatoes with his wife, and sipped on chicory with her while they enjoyed the salt breeze.

A single Bwain stood on the rooftop in the place where he had last seen Aida. A pathetic, bedraggled, and exhausted creature. A traveler of many miles, and yet a prisoner at the end of its chain.

"Save," the creature pleaded.

Carter realized in that moment that whether they be human or alien, they had all come to the Swordbelt to be freed.

* * *

After they had been taken from their home planet, the Bwain did their masters' scut work for them. Things like repairing ships, visiting new worlds, exploring for arcane materials and data that they did not understand, and which their masters would not explain. It was on one of these expeditions that the Bwain had first encountered humans, which they found to be a barbaric race that lived in caves and threatened them with unintelligible sounds and wooden spears. However, the Bwain recognized the level of intelligence that these creatures possessed from when they themselves had lived in the jungles and forests. When their masters weren't looking, the Bwain had returned often to examine humanity's evolution. That is, until their first encounter with a Bwainslayer.

"Why one slave fight another? How we make mad?" they had wondered, even as their brethren on Earth were slain.

The Bwain had pondered these questions for centuries, but had forgot them and so much more on the day their masters disappeared. Many thousands of years passed in which the Bwain wandered through space with no direction...no purpose. Their knowledge of how to maintain their ships faded, as did so many of the other skills they'd once known. The great Bwainhomes faltered and died, and their numbers dwindled. Their swarms had spent countless years searching the galaxy for habitable planets that were like the one from whence they came, but their search had come up empty. That is, until one day a strange voice that was separate from the rest appeared in the Bwainsong. The voice had called itself Tannin. It remembered the planet that they had visited so long ago, and it led them to what they had hoped could be a new home on Gertie.

The Bwain remembered the humans, remembered Earth, but the vision was dim. In a few thousand years, humans had lifted themselves from the caves to the stars with no masters at their backs. The humans had planets, ships, engineering, and everything else that the Bwain needed, and wanted. As a result, the Bwain had allowed this voice to lead them. Rather than leading them home however, the promises it had made only led them to their doom.

The humans fought them, just as the original Bwainslayer had, and one by one their swarms were defeated. Exhausted, and now more desperate than ever, the aliens had nearly been on the point of extinction when Atlas Carter cut his way into the Bwainhome, and thrust his hand into the Endless Knot.

Now, rather than wanting a home to share with the humans, they simply asked to be spared.

Carter stumbled away from the eldritch plasma before him. He slumped backward against the deck, his head spinning with the sensory input from hundreds of alien eyes. The Bwain were cowering creatures, a cross between humanoid dinosaurs and buzzards, and they scratched at the decking almost in shame. No, not shame. It was fear.

"Bwainslayer..."

Carter was their master now. He held their life or death in his hands, and they made no move to resist him.

"I've destroyed everything I ever had. Everything I ever loved," Carter said to the echoes of the Bwainsong in his mind. *"I came here to destroy myself."*

The aliens huddled more tightly against each other. In a way they seemed like children, lost and alone. They knew the pain of loss.

"I can't. It's too much."

It was then that a new vision filled his mind. It was of a warm, spring morning. The sky was a clear blue, and the sun gliding overhead filtered down through the brilliant emerald leaves on the trees.

This was the morning of the last day before the Bwain had been taken, and it was a view that they longed to see again. This vision came with a certainty that they would see if again, but only if they survived and persevered.

Carter tried to sit up but the encounter had weakened him. A dizzy ringing battered his ears, and his mind felt too large for his skull.

"Save?" one of the creatures asked. It shuffled toward him, holding out a scaled arm to try and help him.

"Forgive me, Aida," Carter whispered as he reached out to take the creature's hand.

*   *   *

Gertie

Captain Mephista leaned forward in the hoverchair that kept her ruined body held above Landfall's streets, and studied the Bwain that was standing before her. It seemed more animal than intelligent creature, a cross between a chicken that would rather scratch in the dirt, and a dull reptile returning her gaze through its oversized eyes. The creature had the vague smell of dry earth, and the hard chitin on its beak and claws reflected the reddish color of Gertie's sky. Mephista would prefer to be halfway across the galaxy, and away from this thing that had murdered so many of her crew on two different ships, but right now the alien's telepathic connection with the others on its Bwainhome was the only way she could communicate with Captain Carter, and man for whom she'd discovered she could do just about anything.

"What does it feel like?" she asked him.

"It's hard to describe," the Bwain squawked. The creature's voice sounded nothing like Carter, and it whistled where a human's lips would have come together, but the words were unmistakably his. "It's like my mind is so much bigger. They've got some kind of a collective consciousness, so everything they've ever learned or experienced is stored in the Bwainsong's memory. They've got so many thousands more years of cultural reference points than we do, and they're so…I dunno. Strange, I guess? Yeah, that's as good of a word to describe them as any I suppose."

"So you know how they think?" an exhausted Danny Xiao asked from beside her. The young lieutenant was supervising Hal Yellowknife's clean-up of the aftermath of the colonists' successful rebellion against Tannin, and Mephista had been quite surprised at both his stamina, and his willpower. Carter's inspiration had changed more than just Mephista's perspective. The whole Swordbelt seemed to have come to the realization that it now had a chance at something better, now that he had come.

"I'm working on it. Some of what they're trying to show me doesn't even seem possible. I'm gonna need to ask Granger or Pandith for some help in interpreting what I'm seeing. I don't know how long I've been on the Bwainhome either. Time seems to be different here somehow. Has the *Fate's Winds* reached orbit yet?"

Mephista's stomach lurched. She had been so caught up in events on Gertie and the novelty of a talking Bwain that she hadn't checked in with her crew on the *Tranquility* in hours.

"This is Captain Mephista to *Tranquility* bridge," she called. The microphone that all SSC officers had surgically implanted into their jawbones picked up her voice, transmitting the broadcast through the communications array built into the administrative compound and relayed it up into orbit where her crew would be listening.

"Aye Captain," a voice replied.

"Nav, what's the status on the *Fate's Winds*? They should be in sensor range."

A voice in her ear answered after a few moments, "I'm sorry, ma'am, but we don't seem to be able to see the corvette."

"My orders were to make repairs to weapons, propulsion, and sensor modules as soon as possible," she snapped.

"It's not damage, Captain. There's some kind of interference in the region of space where the *Fate's Winds* was last reported. Infrared, spectrometry, telescopes...nothing is returning a reading."

"Mephista, what is it?" the Bwain asked. The creature flashed a strange mixture of agitated orange and purple, snapping its short wings and tossing its head from side to side. With surprise, she realized the alien was channeling Carter's anxiety. She had never seen him reveal anything other than a hard sense of purpose, but now she realized he genuinely cared about the well-being of his crew. If she had to deliver the news to him that they were gone, she didn't know if she'd ever be able to forgive herself.

"Look...Captain...," she started.

The bird twisted one eye toward her, and then another.

"What is it?" the creature trilled.

"It could just be a minor issue, sir. We're still in a distant sector in the galaxy," Danny Xiao interjected. He'd been listening to the exchange on his own cochlear implant, and Mephista was grateful for his intervention.

"I can't see anything here. The Bwain don't use sensors like we do. There's no holoscreen, or anything like that. Hell, they don't even have a radio, so I'm pretty much flying blind here. What are you tryin' to tell me?" Carter asked through the Bwain.

"Look...Carter, I'm really sorry to have to tell you this, but I think something might have gone wrong," Mephista said quietly.

*   *   *

The Wreckage of the Fate's Winds
One million kilometers from Gertie, drifting near the Greater Orion Nebula

"You were ostracized. You were abandoned," the voice groaned like a leviathan from the blackness.

"No," Aric Keith mumbled. He didn't know if he was alive or dead. He wasn't even sure if he was speaking the words aloud, or if they were nothing more than his own delusional thoughts. The last thing he remembered was his body collapsing against the cargo bay's manual controls. The ship had been crippled, and its crew were left wounded and dying. The Bwain were coming, but with no power the only chance any of them had to survive was to escape in the *Fate's Winds'* orbiter.

When the Bwainswarm had first arrived, Aric hadn't yet been fully healed from a previous injury sustained in a Bwain attack, where a small portion of his body had been pulled through a breach in the ship's hull into the vacuum of space. He had nearly passed out trying to fit himself into an EVO suit in the med bay, but his fellow crewmen had needed him. Though he had loathed the other crew members for so long because he hadn't felt adequate in the face of their expectations, their new captain had managed to show Aric how to accept his past failings, to learn from them, and then to move on with his life. For that, he would always be eternally grateful to the man who'd offered him some semblance of redemption.

The ship had lost power. The orbiter couldn't escape the cargo bay unless someone remained behind to open the bay door manually. Each twist of the control had torn Aric's wounds wider, until a spray of blood coated his visor. He had collapsed, split open, just as the orbiter escaped into the safety of space.

When Aric's eyes had fallen closed, he hadn't expected anything other than death to cradle him in its arms. What he was experiencing now however, felt like someone's dark version of what Hell would be like.

"You gave up your fellow humans to death," the voice cried. It sounded like stones scraping against each other, as if the words it used were emanating from some sort of blunt machinery.

"Danny...," Aric whispered. No, Captain Carter had rescued Danny from Judgment's surface. The crew had fought the Bwain until the aliens' massive ship appeared and crippled the *Fate's Winds*...and then...what? Had they escaped?

"No, wait. I saved them," Aric croaked.

"You are with us now. There is no saving. All will be ours."

Aric coughed, and then started gagging. A cold liquid tasting of sour copper spilled from his lips. It must have been more of his blood, but he could see only a golden glow. He tried to lift his arms so he could unseal his helmet, but his extremities had no feeling at all. More memory came to him then.

He saw Danny Xiao's selfish, disinterested face while Aric had lectured him on his responsibilities; Danielle's hostile flirting with the other members of the crew; Julie's constantly fluctuating weight, and the irritability and self-doubt she had failed to mask; Pandith's gentle calmness, and Granger's incessant curiosity. One by one their faces drifted before him, and then broke apart in the amber haze.

He'd hated them all to some degree for various reasons. He was an engineer, and far more comfortable with physics and material science, than he was with the pettiness and quirks of others. He hadn't been ready for his elevation to acting captain, and dealing with the pressure of a system that was quickly falling apart had made him angry. That's why he was so quick to court martial Danny when he'd been insubordinate, and essentially sentenced him to death on the desert planet, Judgment. He'd done the right thing in exacting his vengeance...hadn't it?

No. No, it hadn't. Captain Carter had taken Aric to Judgment's surface, and had forced him to see the consequences of treating people as if they were simply parts in a machine that could be replaced when they were judged to be somehow defective. Captain Carter had changed him...given him a new perspective on things, and in doing so, he had given him his life back.

"What is Carter?" the heavy voice roared.

"He's my captain. Who, or what are you exactly?" Aric gasped.

The cold glow surrounding him forced its way down his throat, trying to choke him and pull him back down into the emptiness, but Aric clung desperately to his last thread of consciousness, feeling that if he were to let it go, nothing would ever be the same.

"There is no Carter. There will be no Carter. There will be no hope," the voice said to Aric, and then the brittle light consumed him.

*   *   *

The Fate's Winds Orbiter
Four thousand kilometers from the Fate's Winds

Kaylee Wyatoshi was screaming. Pandith's heart broke to hear her curdled howl, but he had no time to check on her and whatever problem she was wrestling with. The rest of the crew was dying.

A mangled stump of bone and flesh jutted from the shin of Danielle's EVO suit. Her suit's nanobots glowed as they tried to repair her suit, performing the programming they calculated would save her life. As they trekked back and forth in their mindless repairs, they mingled the new carbyne thread with Danielle's blood and flesh, tearing and fouling the wound. Pandith jabbed at the keypad on Danielle's chest, fumbling with the code that would shut down the unconscious navigation officer's suit. As the *Fate's Winds'* environmental engineer, he had been cross-trained in medicine and psychology. He knew he was panicking and needed to regain his calm to be effective. He was normally so steady. A part of his mind wondered what the other crew would think of him sweating and fumbling over them the way he'd been doing, but if he didn't help them, there would be no crew left to think much of anything.

Granger had been knocked unconscious by the explosion when the Bwain laser had sheared off the front of the *Fate's Winds* and superheated the bridge atmosphere. His brainwaves were scattered but stable. Bryon on the other hand was in far worse shape. His helmet had a deep dent from a piece of debris striking it at hypersonic speeds, and the weapons officer twitched and jittered with the effects of what must have been a severe brain injury. Pandith would need to get his helmet off, perform a molecular scan, and possibly insert a stent to relieve any cranial bleeding. Julie had a severe abdominal laceration that seeped blood, but her nanos had sealed her suit, and the biogel layer on the material's inside would staunch the bleeding enough to keep her alive as he tended to Danielle.

Then there was Kaylee, who continued to cry as though she were dying, but there wasn't a scratch on her. She stared out the orbiter's portholes as she keened, swaying and clutching at herself. She had been telepathically connected to the Bwain once when the aliens had taken mental control of the crew on board her old ship, and Pandith hoped the creatures were not trying to do so again. They all wore the latticed cowls that Granger had constructed to block the Bwain's Majorana particle-based thought waves from reaching their minds; but if the aliens had found a way around the protection, it wouldn't matter if Pandith saved them or not. The only question would be, which death would be the fastest, and least traumatic?

Danielle's chest controls flashed red. Finally, his shaking fingers had keyed the right sequence. Her suit's carbyne mesh darkened as the nanobots powered down, and its magnetic seals unlocked. He undid the waist skirt that protected the seam at her hips, then opened the trouser flap. The biogel layer that reprocessed exhaled carbon dioxide into oxygen peeled away from her flight suit. He unwound the zipper to reveal flesh pallid from blood loss.

"Pandith!" Kaylee sobbed.

"Not now!" he responded more harshly than he'd intended.

Warnings from the orbiter's medical programs pinged in his cochlear implant. Bryon's boot heels bounced spasmodically on the deck plates as Pandith worked the EVO suit pants away from Danielle's limp legs.

"Mr. Pandith-san!" Kaylee screamed.

"Kaylee, I have to help Danielle first."

Threads of carbyne steel pulled away from Danielle's shredded calf muscle. A piece of shrapnel had severed her foot a few inches above her ankle, and the wound would not be easily sealed. He could use a torch from the toolkit to cauterize it, or the biofoam from the first aid kit to use her own body's cells to form a scar. From the way the bright blood pumped from Danielle's torn arteries, though, there wasn't time even for accelerated biology.

"Please!" Kaylee howled. "Please!"

Pandith raced to a supply locker and pulled a short length of spider steel from the repair components. Touching his thumb and pinky finger together, he triggered a brief electrical current from the finger of his own EVO suit, and the steel wire slackened so it could be manipulated. He wrapped the cable as tightly as he could around Danielle's calf above the wound, then triggered the current again. The steel hardened, biting into her flesh and sealing off the bleeding.

Pandith slumped back, exhausted. The tourniquet had staunched Danielle's bleeding, and he could turn to the rest of the crew. Kaylee stepped in front of him when he rose. A blush mottled her face, and her eyes were red from crying. He tried to push past her but she clung to him and would not be separated.

"Kaylee, Bryon is hurt. I need to...," Pandith said, trying desperately to keep the impatience out of his voice.

"You need to look!" she exclaimed as she pulled him toward the porthole.

Sighing, Pandith went with the girl. If she could only just calm herself, he could really use the former comfort girl's help. She had been a great aid to him during Aric's recovery.

"I don't see any...," he said, but then he trailed off when he suddenly realized that Kaylee had been right to be afraid.

"What do we do, Mr. Pandith?" she asked.

Pandith gaped at the foreign object that hung just off the bow of the *Fates' Winds* for a moment longer. Then he sprang for the pilot's station.

"We have to get to the *Tranquility*! It's our only chance. Kaylee, come here. Hurry now. I'm gonna need your help!" Pandith cried. The horror she'd been feeling in the aftermath of the attack has now been replaced by an urgent fear, and a new purpose, and as such, she was at his side in an instant, awaiting his orders.

*   *   *

The Fate's Winds

When Aric woke up again, his chest expanded as if gasping for breath, but no air entered his lungs. He lay on his back with the bright light of the *Fate's Winds'* cargo bay shining through a dried brown film that smeared his EVO helmet's electroglass visor. Studying the spray's pattern, Aric wondered how the ship's power had been restored. He was also wondering how he was still alive, when every logical thought told him that he should be dead.

He patted his gloved hands over his stomach. There was no pain. In fact, there was barely any feeling at all. When he reached up and unsealed his helmet, the sensation of his fingers curling around the handles felt distant, almost like a memory. Aric's diaphragm dragged inward in reflex, but he could not tell if his lungs inflated or not since there was no feeling at all in his chest.

Gathering himself, he sat up in the empty cargo bay. Somehow the bay doors he had struggled to open manually had closed. Floodlights shone over the gleaming metal. There was oxygen here, and the bay's status indicators all showed green, but the *Fate's Winds* had been crippled. What had happened while he had been unconscious?

Aric stood without thinking, considering the dim memory of his wounds only after he reached his feet. His first thought was to check engineering to see if the ship's fusion reactor was still stable. The Bwain attack had destroyed the bridge, but if there was power, he would be able to control the ship from his old duty station.

He started aft but immediately stumbled over an obstruction at his feet. He had nearly tripped over his helmet, and he bent to pick up this last piece of his suit. He spat into the visor and swept the glowing glass clean with a glove. Then he twisted the helmet back over his head and resumed his journey. Much of the ship was exposed to space now, and he needed to be careful not to put himself in danger. He had the vague notion of a duty to perform…some task that needed his attention. More than anything though, he needed to understand what had happened.

The cargo bay opened onto a supply storage corridor filled with rows of stowed crates. This had been Danny's Xiao's station, where the lieutenant had spent his time tampering with the signal array in his insubordinate attempt to conspire with Administrator Tannin. Xiao had always been worthless, a pathetic excuse for an officer whom Aric should have spaced at the first sign of disloyalty. It was what the entire crew had deserved, and what everyone on Gertie deserved if they rebelled.

Aric paused in front of the airlock that led to engineering. Those hadn't been his thoughts. That wasn't how he felt any longer, but it would be easy to slip into old habits. He puzzled over his conflicting impulses.

He triggered the double-doored airlock as he puzzled over the conflicting impulses he was feeling. Carefully he stepped through the opened hatch, and then sealed it once again. In front of him, the hull breach warning indicator flashed a bloody red. As long as he was secured in his EVO suit, he had little to fear from a depressurized compartment, so he unsealed the sequential hatch.

An incredibly loud battering poured through the opening. Aric clamped his gloves over his helmet in reflex, though it did little good. The port side of the hull had been peeled open in a long jagged tear, and a series of flashes from what must have been a damaged conduit left afterimages across his retinas.

Worried that the reactor had destabilized, Aric scanned the instruments for any sign of damage or malfunction. The antimatter fuel had been depleted by the crew's ignition of the laser array that had stopped the Bwain. The ship's starboard inducers were still online, but the holocontrols for the port side of the ship were dark. He checked the fusion reactor's containment fields, expecting to see the reactor operating on reserve capacity, and hoping what he was witnessing wasn't the beginning of a meltdown, but as he examined the readings on the holodisplays, he suddenly stilled in shock. The reactor was dark. The emergency batteries and backup generator were both offline.

The *Fate's Winds* should have been dead in space, but somehow it lived. Aric tried to concentrate on the readings he was seeing as he rerouted navigation and sensor output to his station, but the arcing around the hull breach distracted him. It was growing worse, but what was causing it? Had the nanobots tasked with repairing the hull somehow malfunctioned? Aric clambered over a section of damaged decking, gritting his teeth as he climbed toward the hull's gaping wound.

As he got closer and was able to see outside the ship, it felt as if all the pain that had fled his body, quickly returned in one brutal wave.

A massive white pillar hung in space a few kilometers from the ship, shimmering and arcing like some electromagnetic reaction. The column stretched so far above and below the *Fate's Winds* that Aric had to lean out of the hull and crane his neck to see where it ended in a swollen capital. It seemed to be made of porous white material, almost limestone in appearance, and its brightness pulsed in a throbbing rhythm. A rope of what looked like pure energy ran from the object to the *Fate's Winds'* hull. Not quite a laser, the channel seemed more like a branch, or a thread of web in the familiar white-gold of the nanobots.

This was the source of the arcing he was seeing, and as the beam from the strange vessel crawled toward him, he found that he could no longer move his limbs, and the task the he had vaguely recalled earlier took on a deeper clarity. The energy bore its way into his mind, and he could no longer look away from the structure.

"Aric Keith," a voice said in his thoughts.

Clumsy in his suit, Aric tried to turn and run, but his numb limbs wouldn't obey. The stream of energy continued to writhe closer, carving a glowing pattern over the hull. Its undulations spoke to parts of him that hadn't existed before he had opened the cargo bay, sensations that seemed to hover within and outside of his consciousness.

Atlas' Flight

"Aric Keith."

"What do you want?" he screamed into his helmet.

The rope of light curled over the gash in the hull, fluttering through the torn metal, and casting molten shadows across what had once been the engineering room.

"Leave me alone!" Aric cried, but his words were ignored. Suddenly, he felt his heart shudder, and then stop as his lungs shriveled within him.

"It is time to serve us," the voice intoned.

The white fury of the beam struck Aric then, bathing him in its destruction.

Chapter 3

Gertie

Bored, Phuri tossed a stone at the earthen wall in front of him. He had hidden for three days in a small cave dug into one of Gertie's endless hills, surviving on whatever food that Vartan had been able to smuggle to him, and waiting for a change in the maddening wash of static that poured from his radio. Before fleeing Landfall, he had made a small change to the administrative compound's communication system that would forward certain off-planet frequencies directly to his receiver, but he had no way of knowing when those transmissions would come. He had food, water, and a shovel if he felt so inclined; but if there was one thing that Phuri had run out of on Gertie, it was patience.

He lifted another stone and hurled it through the lamplight. It bounced and landed near his boot. What would Mephista think of him using one of her crew's abandoned hideouts for cover? The erstwhile pirate captain had been ready and willing to raid both Landfall and Judgment in the name of striking back at those in Sol Space Command who had so callously tried to sacrifice her and her crew, but then she met Atlas Carter, the man who had destroyed Tannin's plan and left his chances of returning to Earth hanging by a thread.

One of the scaled nematodes that passed for earthworms on Gertie wriggled from the wall and dropped among Phuri's stones. The creature squirmed to get its bearings, and then scuttled off into the cobwebbed darkness. He preferred the shadows as well. True power was to make the powerful come to you, and the longer he spent in his cave, the more he came to realize that Atlas Carter would be his key.

Imagine what Sol Space Command would give to the man who brought word of the greatest racial betrayal in human history. The man who claimed to know exactly what Atlas Carter would do now that he had joined forces with the Bwain to threaten the very core of human space. There would be public panic, senatorial inquisitions, jockeying among the SSC officers for the prestige of eliminating Carter's barbaric threat...and he would be right there at the center of it all, more valuable than President Kidewange, or any of those self-important senators.

Phuri had memorized the messages he would write to certain members of the Sol Space Command who still responded to Tannin's communications. The key was to gauge their intentions as quickly as possible, so he could identify those who were dissatisfied, and give the rest of Sol's government no chance to stand against the tide of history that would sweep them aside.

Phuri continued to throw his rocks and maintain his calm, counting each worm that shied from his strikes as a politician who had voted for his exile. The Senate's cowards had been just as corrupt as he or Tannin, but they had chosen to turn their backs on them. In a way he was glad for the lessons they'd taught him, for now he knew how to return the favor.

Phuri's pile of stones diminished, and after a time he dimmed the light and lay down on his pallet to sleep. It took him a long time to realize that the static had ended, and had been replaced by a voice that was now coming through his radio. For a moment he was confused as to why he wasn't hearing Vartan call with another shipment of food, but then he leaped to the radio and cranked its volume.

"Repeat, this is Capra Falconi of the SSC Messenger Vessel *Mosquito*. I have just arrived in the system via Alcubierre jump and request permission to land at coordinates..."

"Falconi!" Phuri cried into his transmitter. He tried to add the appropriate amounts of shock and sadness to his voice. He needed to be believable when he arrived on Earth, and Capra was his first practice performance.

"Phuri?" the voice answered back.

"Yes, it's me. Capra...something terrible has happened! I need your help." Phuri smiled as he congratulated himself on the tone of concern and sincerity he had managed to convey. Now he just had to continue to make it sound believable.

$*\quad*\quad*$

Landfall

"It's bad enough we have to deal with that...that *thing*, but now we're bringing back the criminals?" one of Landfall's farmers shouted as he pointed to where the Bwain hunched in a corner of the Colony Council chamber.

"Now Dax, you know they don't have enough food on Judgment. There's a hell of a lot of innocent people over there who could really use our help, and since Tannin isn't running things around here anymore, now we've got a chance to help 'em," Hal Yellowknife replied. He needed to be the voice of calm and reason in this already tense situation.

Another voice shouted, "So who is in charge now exactly? We're supposed to let some kid from the navy and a drunk run things now?"

Hal ground his teeth as the roar of the arguing colonists swelled in the room. His shaking hand reached for the tumbler of water on the table in front of him, and he took a swallow from it just to have something to do. He'd been a drunk back on Earth; he'd been a drunk when he'd decided to ship out to the farthest colony he could find to try to build a better life for himself, and he'd been a drunk when he'd looked past Tannin's falsified orders that had directed the colony's manufacturing away from goods that would have helped the colonists, and redirected them toward the ship that he'd been building in secret - a ship to return him and his cronies to Earth, while leaving Gertie for the Bwain.

Initially, he'd been unaware of that last part of the plan. When he finally discovered the truth however, that had been the impetus he needed to get himself off the booze, so he could focus clearly on the matters at hand. Back on Earth, Hal's people had been lied to for generations, shoved into reservations, and told to keep quiet. Here on Gertie however, Hal had been the one that manufactured the guns, and led the rebels who had retaken the colony. Now, because the rebellion had been his idea, he found himself leading a colony that was none too happy that the Bwain were coming anyway. Carter's order to repatriate Judgment's prisoners was simply the last straw. These people had already seen too much upheaval, and change was always hard. If anyone knew how hard change could be, it was him. The whole situation was enough to make him long for the taste of the gin that was made from Gertie's native berries, but instead he sipped his water and tried to maintain his calm.

"You can argue all you want, but Hal's the furthest thing from a problem at this time. If we don't start working together right now, right this very minute, then things are gonna get a hell of a lot worse," Danny Xiao said, addressing the assemblage.

"Not for us they're not!" Dax replied irritably.

Hal let out a heavy sigh. At least he wasn't facing the colonists alone. He had only really gotten to know Xiao in the few days that led up to the rebellion. His first impression had been one of a sullen teenager that had withdrawn into himself, but since Xiao had returned to Gertie as a double agent under orders from Carter to help in Tannin's ouster, the boy had displayed a kind of strength, and an inner peace that Hal envied. Whereas before he'd been bound to Tannin by the administrator's cruel manipulation of paying for his sister's life support, now he seemed to have found a new sense of freedom with the acceptance of her passing.

"The Bwain followed Tannin here because they're starving and homeless," Danny continued. "There are millions of them on that ship. And if we try to turn them away, then what happens?"

"Mephista will fight them off!" someone shouted. The crowd roared at this, having fond memories of *Tranquility's* marines who had come to their aid in their fight against Vartan, and Tannin's militia, while conveniently forgetting how those same soldiers had acted as Tannin's pirates in the system for years beforehand.

"She'd be dead in seconds if she tried. One ship can't hold off a Bwain swarm for long," Danny argued.

"You told us Captain Carter is controlling them with his mind! Why doesn't he just turn them around?" another farmer asked loudly.

"Because they would die. There isn't another habitable planet for dozens of light years."

"That's not our problem," someone called.

"It will be if they kill Carter and attack us anyway. He's the only thing keeping them at bay, but he can't do it if he asks them to commit suicide," Danny said as convincingly as he could.

Grumbling filled the room as the farmers considered their predicament. Hal leaned over toward Danny.

"Is that true?" he whispered.

"I don't know," Danny answered. For a moment, Hal saw once again the deviousness that had let Danny lie straight-faced to him with every order of parts and supplies from the *Fates Winds* that had been destined for Tannin's ship.

"It might just convince them," Hal whispered back.

The room quieted, and Dax rose to speak. He wore muddy boots, a work shirt torn during the fighting, and the wary expression of a man who depended on the uncertainties of rainfall and sun for his survival.

"Hal, I think what the problem here is that you're telling us we don't have any choice. How is this supposed to be different than when Tannin ran things?"

"Now Dax, that's not fair. You of all people know that I've had the factories going full bore since we found out what was goin' on. We're gonna have new plows, new harvesters, new earth movers...and we're finally gonna get a chance to do what we should have been doing when we first landed," Hal said. He wanted to continue, but he couldn't finish over the grousing of the farmers.

"I don't want those devils landing here!" a voice cried out from the crowd.

"We did our job, Hal! You didn't do yours!" another voice called.

"You'd rather drink than help us!"

Hal's temper, never the best, was edging toward breaking loose in the face of the angry insults. If he'd have been drunk, he'd have probably jumped over the table and given the farmers a damn good thrashing. Instead, he reached for his glass. Water slopped over his fingers, and he realized his hand was shaking. Maybe the colonists were right, maybe he wasn't the right person for them. The last thing he'd ever considered when he'd charged down out of the hills with a gun in his hand was that they would actually win. Gulping down the last of the cool water, he slammed the glass back down and then stomped off toward the exit.

"Hal? Hal, where are you going?" Danny called after him, but Hal gave no response. He simply clamped his mouth shut as he pushed through the throng and out of the Council chamber. He didn't want to say anything he would regret, or lash out at anyone and ruin what Carter and Danny were trying to do, so he hurried down the stairs and out into Gertie's cool night air before his anger overtook him.

Most of all, he didn't want to admit that he needed a drink. The truth was that he was afraid. Whenever he had been unsure about what to do, or was sitting around feeling sorry for himself, he'd always had the booze to fall back on. The next day when he would crawl out from under his hangover, whatever had been on his mind would be nothing but a foggy memory. Now the colonists were asking questions. Questions he didn't have the answers for. How was one tiny colony supposed to support millions of aliens? There were only a few thousand farmers at most, and it was a pretty safe guess that the Bwain didn't know how to grow their own food, or they would have done it. What would happen to the humans' own food supplies with such a massive influx of aliens suddenly showing up with rumbling stomachs?

Or an even better question. Why should the colonists help the Bwain at all? Until Carter showed up and made contact with them, the aliens had murdered every other human colony that they'd encountered, right down to the last settler. Every farmer, and even Hal himself had grown up hearing horror stories about the Bwain, and what happened to those who'd been unfortunate enough to encounter them. Now they were just supposed to accept this new reality, all based upon the word of Carter, and their alien guest?

What he wished more than anything at the moment is that he knew what was going on up there in space. Mephista had jetted onto one of the *Tranquility's* orbiters as fast as her hoverchair could take her, and Danny's face had been tense when he'd returned from his powwow with the captain and the talking Bwain. Whatever was going on had the colony's ragged navy scared, but Danny wouldn't talk about it. There was just too damn much happening, and he needed some time to himself so he could gather his thoughts and get things straight in his own mind before he'd be able to go back and deal with it all again.

It was dusk on Gertie. A cool breeze rushed through Landfall's streets, and brushed through the grasslands outside of town. The sky was a blushed rose above the blue-green hills, half-lit by the Orion nebula. Gertie was a beautiful planet, at least in its own way. There were no trees or larger animals. There were just the endless rolling plains that could have been what his ancestors first looked out on when they'd come to North America, thousands of years ago. They had built a people and culture that had been destroyed by the arrival of the Europeans, and he couldn't help but to wonder what misfortunes the Bwain would be bringing along with them, and if they'd end up meeting the same fate as his ancestors.

For a moment he considered heading toward the western edge of town where Leonard ran his stills. A hint of the distillery's sweet exhaust floated through the air, and Hal's mouth watered.

No, he couldn't give in now after he'd come so far. With a heavy sigh, he turned turned south and headed toward his trailer. Gin wouldn't give him any answers, and the most important thing now was for him to figure out

A way to get these fool colonists to accept what had happened, and to go back to doing their jobs. If they didn't, then the rebellion was all for nothing.

A shadow suddenly darted between two buildings. Hal cocked his head, trying to process what he'd just seen. Everyone in town was at the administration compound. The only reason someone would have for being out in the streets right now would be if they were up to no good.

Glass shattered one house away from him.

Hal drew the fusion pistol he had used in the rebellion and swung into a run. At least some decisions were still simple. This was his colony, damn it. He wasn't going to allow anyone to get away with breaking and entering on his watch.

"Whoever you are, you better drop what you took and put your hands up!" Hal yelled as he rounded the corner of the house. A man burst out of the door a few yards in front of him, and then sprinted off toward the grassland. Hal took off after him, pushed his legs as fast as they would go.

The fugitive reached the end of Landfall's dirt roads and knifed into the thigh-high grass. Hal followed the man's bobbing shoulders, catching up to within a few paces. When the man shot a look back over his shoulder however, Hal's pace faltered.

"Vartan?" he called.

The fugitive didn't answer, still streaking through the soft evening light. Instead of following, Hal paused, aimed his pistol, then fired a bolt of plasma that streaked just over the man's head.

"That's enough, Vartan!" he yelled. "I'm a much better shot now that I'm sober."

Tannin's former militia leader skidded to a halt and raised his hands. Puffing for breath, Hal trudged up behind him while he scanned the hills on either side. He was a bit paranoid after finding the pirates' hiding spot a few short kilometers from his own factories, but it appeared that Vartan was alone.

"What the hell are you doin' out here?" Hal demanded.

Vartan said nothing. As Hal drew closer, the white glow from his pistol illuminated a defiant scowl on the man's face.

"You're too late Hal. Your rebellion's already over," Vartan panted.

"Oh, is it now?" Hal asked incredulously.

"You have no idea...," Vartan replied, his scowl giving way to just the hint of a smile that suddenly made his captor feel rather uneasy.

*   *   *

Danny thought it best to let the farmers work through their issues on their own. He'd been pushed and compelled by Tannin's manipulations for so long, that he'd almost let the festering resentment of his predicament cause him to betray his fellow crewmates when Tannin demanded that he steal the *Fate's Winds'* antimatter. Captain Carter had shown him that there was another choice. He showed him what it was like to be part of a group, and how it felt to sacrifice for others. When Danny had been forced to choose between Tannin or the crew, Carter had given him the courage to say goodbye to his damaged sister, and the strength to turn his back on the former administrator and all of his blackmail.

Now that things had been more or less settled however, all he wanted was to know what had happened to the *Fates' Winds*. The thought that his crewmates had died fighting the Bwain while he still lived was almost too much to bear, and he was angry at himself for how much time he'd wasted in trying to betray them.

"We'd need another two million acres under cultivation. Even with whatever Hal can give us, it won't be enough," Dax was saying.

"Dax, you know we're already halfway through the growing season, an it'll be fall before all that equipment's ready," another farmer argued.

"Look, I already know it's gonna take time. That's exactly what I'm saying," Dax replied.

"And time's the one thing we don't have," Hal's voice boomed from the chamber entrance.

Startled out of his reverie, Danny turned to find Hal shoving Vartan into the room with the muzzle of his plasma pistol. The former militia captain had fled during the fighting, and he hadn't been heard from since.

"Hal, what is this?" Danny asked, but his question was lost in the angry roar from the crowd. Vartan had personally arrested many of the colonists' friends and relatives for extradition to Judgment in Tannin's purges, and quite a few of the farmers in the room wanted to see him hung.

"Quiet! Everyone be quiet!" Danny bellowed.

Slowly, the farmers calmed, but their faces seethed with anger, and Danny knew that if he turned Vartan over to them, the man wouldn't last five minutes.

"Where did you find him?" Danny asked.

"Stealing food on the edge of town, but that's not what matters. Tell them what you told me, you piece of garbage," Hal ordered as he roughly shoved the prisoner forward.

Vartan smirked at the gathered farmers. Rather than being remorseful, if anything, the man seemed proud.

"You think what you've done here matters? You think you're all big shots now? Well go ahead and enjoy it while you can. Hal, maybe you should just go settle in with a nice big glass of Nightcrawler...unh!" Vartan groaned as

Hal bashed his pistol against the back of the bigger man's neck.

"I'm gonna bury you alive if you don't start talkin', you piece of crap," he growled. Vartan pressed a hand to his neck, grimacing at the pain.

"Phuri left Gertie on the *Mosquito* earlier today. He's carrying a message back to Earth about the rebellion. He's going to tell them that Carter and this whole colony are working with the Bwain," Vartan informed them as he rubbed his neck and turned to glare at Hal.

Danny's heart sank. He saw at once the perfection of the plan. Captain Carter had already been exiled due to his inaction during the *Narcos'* attack on Belize City, so Sol Space Command would need very little convincing that Carter was so corrupt that he would join with the enemies of humanity.

"What does that mean, Danny? What's the navy gonna do?" Dax asked, concern edging his voice. Danny sighed as he glanced over at the farmer.

"The protocol for any Bwain encounter is clear. They're gonna send a fleet out here and glass us all. They're gonna flatten the whole colony."

"And you can thank Hal's little rebellion for that," Vartan spat. Hal's insides suddenly felt hollow as he looked over at Danny, as though he were asking him what they were going to do. The look he got in return did little to reassure him.

* * *

The Tranquility

Captain Mephista hurtled through the *Tranquility*'s corridors, heading for the bridge as fast as the oxygen bottle she used as a thruster could take her.

Mephista's navigation officer spoke to her through her implant, "I don't know if the *Fate's Winds'* orbiter is gonna make it. Whatever's after 'em…I mean, I've never seen anything like it."

"I need specifics, Ms. Niven," Mephista barked.

The captain's oxygen bottle sputtered and ran out of compressed air. Growling, she left it floating behind her in the ship's zero gravity and hauled herself hand-over-hand toward the elevator. A squad of marines newly returned from Gertie's surface pulled themselves to a stop and offered salutes as she passed, trying not to stare at the withered legs she trailed behind.

She wasn't crippled. Tannin had tried to make her believe she was, but Carter had shown her that she had the power to change her own destiny. She felt a considerable amount of shame over the fact that she'd been more than ready to kill him for his antimatter, and then use the fuel to roar back to Earth with Tannin so she could take out her rage on Sol for betraying her to the Bwain so many years ago.

In just the short time that she'd known him, Carter had changed her life in ways she could have never imagined. It'd been him who showed her how to find herself once again. It was he who inspired everyone around him with the incredible courage he'd shown in joining with the Bwain to save the lives of everyone in the system. It was a selflessness that shamed her, and as she pounded the elevator button, she felt like she had knots tied around her heart. Those few who'd managed to survive the encounter with the Bwain were out there somewhere, and in desperate need of rescue. She just hoped that she could reach them in time, and protect them as well as their own captain would if he were here.

"We're having trouble getting a clean signal, Captain. It looks like there are some kind of...well, I'm not sure what they are exactly. It's like they're holes in space that keep appearing around the orbiter," the ensign replied.

"On-duty science officer to the bridge immediately," Mephista ordered as the elevator whisked her to the cruiser's top deck.

"All crew to battle stations. Helm, prepare to bring us close enough to that orbiter that we can guide it into our bays. EVO teams, stand by your airlocks."

"Ma'am, I need to advise you that whatever's after that orbiter will probably turn on us as well," Niven called from her station once again.

"Understood, Ensign, but that's a chance we'll have to take. We're all in this together now."

The elevator doors opened, and Mephista floated onto the bridge. The *Tranquility* had been a capital cruiser before Mephista had commandeered it for her private mutiny, and its bridge felt incredibly spacious. A ten-meter holoscreen at the bow end served as both the main telescope and viewing station, and the master plotter for mission objectives. Right now, it showed the *Fate's Winds'* scarred orbiter surrounded by what looked like a haze of flickering static. Behind the clouds, she could just see the bright streak of the tiny vessel's inducers pushed to their maximum output.

"Missiles and lasers are hot, Captain, but I've got no target," her weapons officer called.

The elevator whisked open behind her, and science officer Spar sprang through the opening.

"Captain, it appears as if whatever's attacking the orbiter may not be trying to damage it. The disruptions seem as though they're targeting the ship's inducers," he advised after he moved to his station and examined the readings.

"So what are you telling me, Mr. Spar?"

"Inducers generate thrust through quantum vibrations. Whatever's attacking them seems to be *powered* by that same energy. It may not actually exist in any physical sense within this universe."

"Confirmed, ma'am. Any shot I take would have to be manual. The computer still shows no target," her weapons officer added.

"Comms, do we have a channel open yet?" Mephista asked.

"Yes, ma'am."

"*Fate's Winds* orbiter, this is Captain Mephista. What is your...," she started to ask, but she was interrupted by what sounded like a child's scream cutting through the speaker. Carter had told her about a girl he'd rescued. Could that be her?

"Kaylee, please," another voice urged impatiently.

"Identify yourself," Mephista ordered.

"This is Environmental Engineer Dashan Pandith," a strangely gentle voice replied. "I'm the ranking officer on the *Fate's Winds* at the moment, and the only one fit for duty."

"Mr. Pandith, we're gonna get you aboard just as quickly as possible. Can you match our course and speed?" Mephista asked. Suddenly, a burst of static filled Mephista's implant. On the holoscreen, one of the disruptions brightened into a golden-white flare. The orbiter shuddered, and then began to slow down.

"That's most likely a negative, Captain. I'd suggest you retreat. You're not gonna be able to fight whatever this is that's after us. Please include in the logs that I, along with Science Officer Aaron Granger, Lieutenant Bryon Purcell, Ensign Julie Ford, Lieutenant Danielle Hoff, and passenger Kaylee Wyatoshi, survived the encounter with the Bwain. I'm now gonna change course to lead these things away from you. Please do not attempt to follow. You'll put both your ship and its crew in grave danger," Pandith managed to say before his soft voice was replaced with a burst of static.

"My science officer says that whatever's after you may be drawing power from your inducers," Mephista noted.

Silence stretched over the connection. On the holoscreen the orbiter bucked and swayed as if it was fighting its way through a tar pit. Mephista ground her teeth, poised for action but frustrated by her lack of options.

"Mr. Pandith?" Mephista said into the radio after a few tense moments.

"Of course, it makes total sense," Pandith replied thoughtfully.

"I don't understand. What makes total sense?" she asked.

"You know Captain, we may just be able to accept your offer of assistance after all. Just give me a few moments here...."

*   *   *

The Fate's Winds

Aric sat in the ruined day room of the Fate's Winds, shuddering. Once there had been gentle grass here, as well as an artificial stream, a small orchard, and a vegetable garden. Every SSC ship had been equipped with a day room after humanity's psychologists realized that long space confinement was easier if those in the navy had a space on their ships that would make them feel closer to home.

The antimatter laser's malfunction had torn open the ship's hull, exposing the day room to space, and much of what had once come from Earth was gone. A prisoner resurrected by demons, Aric would never again see grass or sky. He stared at the harsh black of space, beyond the glittering debris that surrounded the ship, to where the massive obelisk hung outside the *Fate's Winds.*

The Bwain had been slaves, not masters. Long before any other life had stirred in the universe, the First Ones had claimed it as their own. They had disappeared into higher planes, seeking some purpose lost among themselves, and now they were returning. The obelisk would be their path, and Aric would be their builder.

Reaching up, he unlocked his EVO suit's helmet and set it aside. There was no choking for breath, no pain of skin freezing on contact with open space's bitter cold. His body, reconstructed by the First Ones using a bastardized version of the *Fate's Winds'* own nanobots, felt very little in the way of the human sensations that his mind still remembered. He stood and walked to the jagged hole in the hull. It would be easy to push away from the deformed ship and float through space for eternity, where he'd be unable to cause anyone any further harm.

"You will not disobey," the voice warned him. *"You will hasten our return."*

Sudden pain wracked his body, doubling him over and leaving him clutching a stomach that had been refashioned out of a mishmash of elements by the microscopic robots.

In the distance Aric could see shuddering tendrils lash out at Pandith's fleeing orbiter. He should not have been able to see that distance, but some part of the First Ones was in him as well; growing...building. He could not see them, but he could feel their presence crawling through him. They showed him fractured visions and nauseating geometries that he couldn't even begin to comprehend, and they compelled his body through force and pain.

As they revealed more of themselves, he sensed something that he never would have suspected.

"You're weak," he thought.

Instantly, the feeling of being torn apart returned. Aric collapsed against the frozen deck. He felt the frigid metal bond to his skin, felt his eyes bulge as the vacuum of space tried to rip them from his head. He tried to gasp without air in his lungs, and his whole being was begging for death.

"We will be strong soon. You will make us so," the voice said.

"Yes," Aric whimpered.

Then his body's sensations faded. He felt his legs gather under him, turning him mechanically to do the bidding of masters that had left him with only the pain of what he had once been.

Chapter 4

Earth
Milan, Italy

Lana Delgado was bored. Professor Trimonti's discussion of a new ability to bridge space-time had drawn a packed house to the University of Milan's physics laboratory. Instead of a major news story, she had spent the last seventy minutes listening to him hypothesize about what other dimensions might potentially look like to a human being. The sum total, so far, was nothing at all.

"And so, as we can see, these dimensions could be infinite," he said in his Italian-accented English. "There has been no way to know what lies within them...until today."

Lana shifted in her chair. Her eyepiece was recording, and she prepared her holostylus to take notes. This was what she had come from Madrid for. After a long winded introduction, he was finally getting around to demonstrating his theory.

The professor stepped to the center of the stage. The lights dimmed, and a holoprojector somewhere in the recessed floor sparked on.

"What you are about to see has been created from a series of probes sent out from Sol over the past five years. I think you'll be quite astonished by our findings."

The holoimage showed the eight glowing planets of the Earth's solar system. A series of hexagonal panels descended over the planets, and the solar system rotated until Lana was facing its profile. Where the panels joined together, they grew into crystalline patterns of stark geometry that seemed to overlap and build on each in shapes much more complicated than the simple spheres of Jupiter or Saturn.

"What you are seeing here is my model's representation of amplituhedronal space, which includes nine additional dimensions interacting with the three we can normally observe. You'll note of course that I do not include time in my model, which is commonly thought of as the fourth dimension. In 12-dimensional space, there is no time. A human, or any other creature able to exist in this fashion, would in essence be immortal," he said before pausing to take a drink of water.

Lana leaned forward, studying the strange blobs that appeared to flow like sleet through the solar system. The majority bubbled from Earth and streamed out along the solar system's major travel routes, but her eye wandered to the outskirts of Saturn, where the tiny research and mining presence seemed out of sync with the volume of the Majorana readings. While she was studying it, the professor resumed his lecture, and referred to his model once again.

"So you see, we interact with these particles, and these particles appear in different dimensions. In fact, these dimensions can help explain many of the longstanding questions we've had about our universe, such as the planar nature of much of the galaxy, and..."

"Professor," Lana interrupted.

"Yes?" he asked, as he scanned the audience to see who was speaking.

"If these particles are interacting with us, then what's happening in Saturn's orbit?"

For a moment, she thought her boredom at the topic would lift as he provided her with some intriguing explanation, but Trimonti only glanced at the data and shrugged in that infuriating Italian way.

"Well, we don't know that yet, do we?" he replied simply.

*　*　*

"The story's posted," she said to her editor, Eduardo, on the flight back. "Holovideo with commentary, but there's nothing there. He can basically show that he's observed something, but he can't explain what it might be or what the implications are. He can't even tell me if his data is accurate, because it hasn't been peer reviewed."

"There has to be more to it Lana. Is he the only one with these theories? What are the potential applications?" he asked, a tinge of impatience creeping into his voice.

"As far as I can tell, there are none. None he's thought of anyway. I'm not even sure he knows…"

"I expect better than this," he interrupted. "Do your research. Be a reporter. That's what you're being paid for."

Her cochlear implant clicked off and she stared out the shuttle flight's window, annoyed by his implication that she wasn't doing her job. There was no point spending her time on stories like this when there was so much more to cover. Sol's government was in constant crisis, torn between trying to ensure the proper balance of support for the outer systems, and protecting the prosperity of the inner, older worlds. There were also rumblings of the Senate's dissatisfaction with President Kidewange that just wouldn't go away.

She should have been covering politics, digging into the future of the SSC and its government. Instead, she was reporting on dry scientists who liked to hear themselves talk. Sighing, she realized that Eduardo had been right. She had let boredom overtake her when she'd filed. She'd done her job all right, but she'd half-assed it. Slipping on her holovisor, she did a query for some background information on Majorana particle research.

The results she got back were thin at best, amounting to little more than a few theoretical papers, and discussions at various seminars. As she scrolled through the pieces, one in particular stood out. It was a report brought by an SSC Messenger vessel from one of the outermost systems. The report was a proof of concept of a Majorana probe that a science officer named Aaron Granger had designed. He was stationed on a ship called the *Fate's Winds,* in the Orion Nebula.

Atlas' Flight

This granger person was an Alcubierre jump away however, and there was no way in hell that the Bureau would ever pay for that kind of travel. If she could find the messenger who had carried Granger's initial findings and pay him to transmit an interview message back. With any luck, she would have more details in about a month.

In the days that followed, she would often wonder if it would have been better if Eduardo had never asked her to follow up on the story. What would have happened if she hadn't have called Capra Falconi?

The messenger's face appeared in her hololens. He wore his curled hair swept tightly down over his forehead, and his nervous eyes darted back and forth in front of her.

"Mr. Falconi, my name is…"

"Why are you calling me?" he asked.

"I, uhhh…I was hoping you could take a message to someone in the Swordbelt on your next run out there. I want to get some information from a man named Aaron Granger. He's stationed on a ship out there called *Fate's Winds*," she hurried to explain.

Capra's lips pursed as if he was fighting to hold back a flood of words, but after a few moments of silence he simply shook his head.

"I'm sorry, but there aren't gonna be any more runs out there," he said to her, and then he closed the connection. She tried to call back twice more, but he blocked her. As her plane descended, Lana found herself wondering what kind of story a man like Capra Falconi, who was so clearly under some sort of pressure, had to tell.

* * *

Madrid

At first she didn't notice the men waiting for her when the car from the airport dropped her at the steps of her flat. She lived on *Calle Diego*, a block from a busy intersection filled with restaurants and bars, and there were always people coming and going. When she pressed her palm to the entrance scanner, a hand clamped over hers, while another man swung open the door and pushed her inside.

"Who are you? What are you doing?" she demanded fearfully.

The men said nothing and remained stone-faced as they marched her up the stairs to the second floor.

"*They know where I live*," she thought as they stopped in front of her door.

"Open it, senorita," the man instructed her.

"No," she answered and sucked in a deep breath for a scream just before a hand clamped down on her mouth. The man holding her nodded to his partner, who lifted a small badge from his waist, scanned it in front of her door, and pushed open the entrance.

They tossed her onto the couch in her small living room, and then took up positions on either side of the door.

"Only the police can do that," she said as she tried to scoot back away from them. "The police don't abduct people though, so who the hell are you?"

"We brought you home," one of the men smirked.

"We kept you safe," the other added.

"What do you mean, *safe*?"

"Why did you contact Capra Falconi?" the first man asked.

"I was working on a story. I was hoping to contact the source."

"On the *Fate's Winds*."

Atlas' Flight

"Yes. Now what the hell's this all about?" she demanded as she rubbed her wrist where the man had grabbed her. The men glanced at each other, gauging how much they could trust her. A few moments later, they both relaxed just a bit, and one of them opened the door.

"You're right, we're not the police. Please understand though that we meant what we said about keeping you safe. There are certain elements in the outer planets who do not want to see the Senate succeed, and we have to constantly be on our guard."

As the door slipped shut behind them, Lana gathered herself. Her racing heart finally began to slow down a bit, and she considered for a moment filing a complaint against the two men. The *Global Guardian* had a contact who would be able to run a face recognition program that could pull the data from her holovisor; so it should be a simple matter to identify them. However, something told her to wait. Whoever these men were, they'd given her the story of the decade. The outer planets fomenting a rebellion against Sol was something she could totally sink her teeth into.

"All right, so...what's the story here gentlemen?" she asked as she motioned for them to both have a seat.

* * *

Gertie

Bringing up the holocontrols in the administrative compound's communications station, the first thing Danny did was to eliminate the backdoor that Phuri had used to communicate with the *Mosquito*. Then he tapped the record button.

"Attention all SSC navy craft. This is Lieutenant Danny Xiao of the *Fate's Winds*, currently stationed on Gertie. What you have been told by Phuri Vongsa is a lie. The former administrator, Sickyl Tannin, was plotting with the Bwain to allow them to settle on Gertie so that he could return to Earth. Please contact me, Captain Mephista on the *Tranquility*, or Captain Atlas Carter on the Bwainhome ship before initiating any action against the colony."

He tapped the control, set the transmission to continually broadcast, and then sat back.

"How long do you think we've got?" Hal asked.

Danny closed his eyes, and performed a few quick calculations in his head.

Phuri had left on the *Mosquito* one day ago. Capra Falconi's ship was a messenger vessel, which was humanity's workaround for the physical limitations of communicating across the vast distances of space. Using the Alcubierre drive's faster-than-light travel capabilities, ships like the *Mosquito* carried messages through the network of human-colonized planets, but the jumps weren't instantaneous. The *Mosquito* would reach Earth in just under a week. With the SSC already on high alert due to the Bwain attacks that had been occurring in other systems, there was little doubt that they already had a battle group assembled and waiting for word of the next attack. If that was the case, then the humans and the Bwain within the Swordbelt system had very little time to prepare for their arrival.

"I think we've probably got at the absolute *most* two weeks before the navy shows up," Danny replied.

"Do you think they'll listen?"

"They're gonna be geared up and ready for war, so I seriously doubt they'll be in any mood to listen to reason. The best that message will do for us is to slow them down for five minutes...if that."

The bigger man sighed, shaking his head.

"So what do we do now?" he asked.

"The first thing is that we'll need to tell Mephista, and then we'll find the Bwain and get word to Captain Carter. They'll know what to do...I hope," Danny said as he tapped a control and felt the click of the compound's communications system tapping into his surgically implanted jawbone microphone once more.

"This is Lieutenant Xiao to Captain Mephista. I have an urgent, real-time message. Over."

Danny closed his eyes, waiting for the subtle pressure in his cochlear implant that would indicate the receipt of his message. The seconds dragged on slowly, with no response.

"Maybe she's asleep?" Hal offered.

"Mephista doesn't sleep. Even if she did, there'd be a comms officer on duty. *Tranquility*. *Tranquility*, please respond. This is Lieutenant Xiao on Gertie with an urgent message for Captain Mephista," Danny said once again. His face was a mask of calm as he waited for a reply, but he was starting to get a hollow feeling in his gut. He cupped his ears to make sure he didn't miss the acknowledgement signal, but nothing came back.

"Would the satellite be down?" Hal asked.

Danny brought up another window and ran the same diagnostic he had begun when he first sat down at the console.

"The system is fully functional. At least Phuri didn't sabotage anything on his way out."

"Didn't you say that there had been some problem with the *Fate's Winds*, and that Mephista had been seeing some strange readings?"

Danny's fingers flew over the glowing controls before him, pulling up the feeds from Gertie's few telescopes. The last reported telemetry of the *Tranquility* had been in the direction of the *Fate's Winds*. He saw a note from their helmsman in the logs that they'd been looking for survivors, but after that there was nothing.

Looking for survivors. What had happened to the rest of the *Fate's Winds'*

Crew, and what about the *Tranquility*? Danny focused Gertie's lone orbital telescope on the *Fate's Winds'* last known position, frowning as the telescope's instruments returned conflicting readings.

"What is it kid? What do you see?" Hal asked.

"I'm not sure. It seems like...," he said, but then he trailed off for a moment. Suddenly, he shoved himself back in his chair, got to his feet and started running toward the door.

"Where are you going?" Hal called after him.

"We need to find that Bwain so we can get back into contact with Captain Carter," Danny called back over his shoulder.

* * *

The Fate's Winds Orbiter

"Hang on, Kaylee!" Pandith cried. Beside him, the terrified girl nodded. She'd made sure that each of the wounded crew members was strapped securely in an acceleration couch, and she was just buckling herself into the co-pilot's chair when another of the terrifying, ghost-like streams of energy pierced the hull.

If he by some miracle happened to live through this, Pandith would have to thank the *Tranquility's* science officer for his suggestion about what might be attacking the orbiter. If Granger lived, the two of them might just be able to figure out how to defend themselves against the malevolent bands of energy that had followed them from the alien object that had appeared near the *Fate's Winds*. For right now though, their ability to survive the encounter was very much in doubt.

The shimmering tentacle didn't punch a hole in the hull's steel, or burn any of the crew. There was no sensation of touch as it passed through Pandith's thigh and entered the control console. Oddly enough there was only a smell like dry ash, and a vague feeling of static. It was almost as if the band of light was some ghost intruding from another world. Pandith could sense when the energy reached the bow inducers and overloaded them. The fiber brightened for a brief moment, and the orbiter slowed. The bands of energy were like harpoons fired at the orbiter, trying to break its ability to escape and then reel it back toward the *Fate's Winds*.

"Posit that what is attacking us uses the same intradimensional technology as the Bwain," he thought to himself. *"Posit as well that the bands' lack of effectiveness against solid matter compared to Casimir inducers, which operate by harnessing quantum vibrations, suggests they could not affect the physical universe."*

As his hypothesis developed and solidified in his mind, it allowed him to formulate a plan of action.

"Hold on," Pandith cried, as one of the tentacles brightened where it cut through the shuttle's holoscreen.

First he shut down the orbiter's inducers. Immediately the tentacles recoiled as if shocked. Before they could recover, Pandith reached under the console, and after saying a quick prayer to Ganesha that he only half-remembered, pulled the emergency handle he found.

The cabin darkened, and a grating thump shook the orbiter as its fusion reactor vented into space. The orbiter wouldn't be able to go far with battery power and chemical thrusters, but as the tentacles faded like smoke in the wind, Pandith's confidence grew. Without its inducers and fusion reactor, the orbiter had no more potential interactions with other dimensions. This was the energy's weakness. It was blind to this world, unless those who existed in it gave them eyes to see with.

Safe for the moment, and armed with only rockets and his own navigational skill, Pandith nudged the orbiter toward the distant speck of the *Tranquility*, and now that they were out of any immediate danger at least, it was time to help his crew.

* * *

The Tranquility

Mephista watched the *Fate's Winds'* orbiter settle onto the shuttle deck from behind the bay's observation glass. As soon as the bay door closed and atmosphere was restored, she released her painfully tight grip on the railing and pushed herself through the airlock. Medics rushed beside her, reaching the hatch just as it sighed open in front of them.

She coasted to a hand bar on the orbiter's frosted hull, reluctantly realizing she herself could do little for the wounded other than staying out of the way so the medics could do their work. She searched for any kind of scoring or damage, but the orbiter seemed intact.

Below her, the medical team swept four unconscious bodies from the shuttle to the med bay. Mephista had ordered her ship's psychologist to the shuttle bay as well, and when a young girl with jet black hair drifted out of the shuttle in shock, the psychologist took the girl's hand and led her away from the craft.

"Are you Kaylee?" the psychologist asked. The girl seemed terrified, and offered nothing in the way of a response.

Mephista drifted down in front of the hatch just as a haggard man appeared in the entrance. Pandith had taken off his EVO helmet, revealing a sweat-slicked brown face and eyes that roved as if still searching for danger. They locked on his fellow crew as they drifted through the far hatch, and his face clouded.

"Where are you taking them?" he asked.

"To the med bay. They'll be treated well," Mephista assured him.

Pandith's eyes flicked for a moment toward where the psychologist had wrapped a blanket around Kaylee's suited shoulders, and then they returned to Mephista. His tears bubbled, and she gave him this time to process without saying anything. Carter had taught her that silence could sometimes do more than conversation ever could.

"Captain Mephista," Pandith finally said in a voice so soft it was almost a whisper.

"Yes?" she asked.

"I thought I was gonna lose 'em."

"What you did was incredibly brave," she said consolingly. Pandith simply shook his head.

"I wasn't brave, Captain. I was afraid. There's something else in this system besides the Bwain, and it's coming for us all."

*　*　*

Kaylee walked through the med bay, studying the unfamiliar faces that lay in row after row of beds. One of the doctors had told her that the *Tranquility* had been heavily damaged during the initial battle with the Bwain. The creatures had taken over Kaylee's ship, the *Ichikari*, as its crew roiled in terrified anguish, their minds controlled by the telepathic aliens. Kaylee had been the sole survivor.

While taking care of Aric Keith onboard the *Fate's Winds*, Kaylee had discovered that helping others recover somehow kept the all the horrible visions of her time on the *Ichikari* at bay, so she kept herself busy with changing dressings, and helping to bring food and water to the injured. She used the self-control she had learned in her comfort girl's training to keep the fear of what she had seen from overwhelming her.

Granger had awakened from his concussion hours ago, and had been given a cabin to share with Pandith. Bryon, Julie and Danielle were still unconscious. All three had undergone surgeries, and the doctors were keeping them sedated. Kaylee dabbed sweat from their faces, squeezing each one of their hands to let them know that they weren't alone. Julie's head had slipped from her bed's pillow, so Kaylee fixed the cushion for her and gently nudged her head back up onto it.

Once she had finished, she took a step back as tears began to flow from her eyes. The last thing she had done as a comfort girl on the *Ichikari* had been to fix the futon cushions with Madam Mirabelle. Then the Bwain had come, and her life had changed in an instant.

"Are you all right?" the ship's psychologist asked. Dark circles hung under the man's eyes, and she could see a half-dozen caffeine tabs fixed to his wrists.

"I miss my friends," Kaylee answered.

"They're all going to make it, thank god. I promise you we'll take very good care of them," the doctor said.

Although Kaylee was concerned about her new friends from the *Fate's Winds*, she had been thinking of her other friends, Rika and Atsuko and Madam Mirabelle, from the *Ichikari*. She was the only person left who even knew they had lived, but what if she forgot? What if the Bwain or whatever the other thing was outside the *Fate's Winds* took her mind again, and she lost their memories forever?

The doctor's eyebrows pinched together.

"You don't need to cry. I promise, the worst is over," he said, trying to sound reassuring.

The other thing in space had tried to talk to her as well when it had pushed its glowing arms through her. She had heard pieces of its thoughts, knew it was hungry.

The psychologist squatted before her and set down his tablet.

"Would you like to talk?" he asked.

On the *Fates' Winds* she had always been able to talk with Aric Keith. He had been recovering from his wounds, unable to move, and had been happy for the company of someone who hadn't been a member of the ship's crew when he had been the acting captain. He had answered all of her questions about what life was like in the navy, and soothed her fears when the nightmares of the Bwain returned. He had been the closest thing she'd had to a friend, but now she was worried she would lose Aric's memory too. She thought she'd heard his voice in the orbiter, and it unsettled her to no end. The man who'd been so kind to her was dead, so it couldn't have possibly been him.

Kaylee sighed, and dabbed gently at her eyes. The psychologist had been trying to help her open up...to start expressing herself a bit, but he couldn't help her answer the question that worried her the most.

"I'm sorry. It's late, and I shouldn't keep you," she said to the doctor as she turned to leave the med bay.

The psychologist couldn't explain to Kaylee why she thought she still heard Aric's voice, and why she felt he was still alive even though she knew he couldn't be. People often had their own reasons for believing certain things, so he would just have to continue to work with her once she'd relaxed and had more time to process everything that had happened.

* * *

"This is what you saw outside the *Fate's Winds*?" Mephista asked Pandith as she stepped away from her cabin's holoprojector to show the environmental engineer the image that her science team had collected. The column in the middle of space appeared to be vibrating...pulsing in some unfathomable rhythm. Then the object abruptly disappeared, leaving only the blank afterimage in the air between them.

"It's been doing that ever since we began observations," Mephista explained. "There's something about it that seems to be resisting our instruments. My science team..."

The object reappeared, flickering as the *Tranquility's* telescopes and electromagnetic sensors reestablished its position. Its dimensions seemed largely the same, but the column looked *different* somehow, almost as if its textural pattern had changed.

"That's what we saw," Pandith confirmed. He rubbed his eyes, and his voice was hoarse with exhaustion. "My hypothesis is that it's some sort of an intradimensional rift. I'm not sure if it was caused by the Bwain or not, but whatever it is, it's definitely hostile."

"That's not the real question though, is it? What we need to do is to figure out what we're gonna do about this thing," Mephista said as she continued to stare at the image.

Pandith floated closer to the display, reaching out as if he wanted to touch the white scar that was glowing before him. Mephista studied his face, trying to judge if the calm he displayed was fear, curiosity, or some other inscrutable expression.

A miniature bolt of lightning lifted from the object and crawled toward Pandith's finger. The engineer abruptly pulled back his hand and pushed away from the table.

"We should withdraw to Gertie. We can fashion Majorana probes and send them from a distance," he suggested.

"Why not do that from our current location?"

"Because that object will have capabilities we can't defend against. It was trying to pull us back toward the *Fate's Winds*. If Captain Carter is controlling the Bwain, that means that whatever that thing is out there, it's controlled by another, as yet unknown species that intends to do us harm."

"And if that object suddenly decides to follow us to Gertie? What then?" Mephista asked.

For just a brief moment, Pandith's calm broke, and she saw a flash of anger cloud his face. Then he sighed, and reached up to run his fingers through his dark hair.

"I'm sorry Captain. I just…I wish we were able to speak with Captain Carter, so we could get his thoughts on this whole thing. For right now though, I'll sit down with Granger and your science team so we can discuss our options. Hopefully we'll have something for you in the morning.

"Thank you, Mr. Pandith, but maybe you should get a little rest first. Things always seem clearer when your mind is rested.

"I wish we had that sort of time," he said, giving her an uneasy look for just a brief moment before he turned and floated out into the corridor. After the door shut behind him, she turned and studied the strange object before her. What bothered her the most was that her gut was telling her that Pandith was right. They *should* withdraw to Gertie. Whatever that thing beside the *Fate's Winds* was, it filled her with dread, but with Carter stuck on the other side of the object, she was the only thing standing between it and the colony.

There was only so long she could stare at the object until its gyrations gave her a headache. She powered down the holoprojector, and then floated over to the doorway. Roaming the corridors of her ship always calmed her when she grew restless, and she hoped it would bring her some calm tonight.

Kaylee was floating there in the corridor when Mephista's hatch slid open. The girl's face was streaked with tears, and she swaddled herself in a ship's blanket. In a way she had become a sort of mascot for both crews, like a reminder of what they fought for.

Instinctively, Mephista pushed herself toward Kaylee and gathered the girl in her arms. The captain had never been married, never thought she ever wanted children, but now that she'd been robbed of the ability and a young girl had arrived on her ship, something had shifted in her. She could tell that Kaylee was struggling with something, and the girl collapsed into her.

"I had trouble sleeping. I heard things," the girl murmured into Mephista's collarbone.

Mephista knew from Pandith that Kaylee had barely escaped with her life from the *Ichikari* as its crew tore themselves apart under the imperfect, telepathic control of the Bwain. People suffered nightmares that were caused by far less than the horrors she'd seen. Joining her hand with Kaylee's, Mephista pushed from the wall and floated through the corridor with the girl.

"It's okay kiddo. I have trouble sleeping too. Moving around the ship always seems to calm me though," she replied.

"Why don't you sleep?" Kaylee asked.

"*Because I'm afraid*," Mephista wanted to say, but a captain couldn't admit that. She couldn't say that she had no idea what would happen with the new object that they had discovered, and that she hoped that the Captain Carter that she'd met, who was currently aboard the Bwain ship, was still the same man he'd been when she'd last seen him. If she had to spend the rest of her life marooned in the Swordbelt, it wouldn't be so bad to spend that time with a man like him.

"Because I have a lot to think about," she answered instead, as they made their way to the bridge.

"I understand. I think about Mr. Keith all the time. He still thinks about me too."

"He's in a better place now. He's probably looking down on you from heaven right now," Mephista responded. She was surprised how easily the platitudes she remembered hearing from her parents rose to her lips.

"No, that's not it," Kaylee said.

Mephista glided to a halt against the bulkhead. She tried to meet Kaylee's eyes, but the girl's flat gaze focused on a distant point farther down the corridor.

"Kaylee, it's okay to grieve. It's okay to let go. Sol knows I had a hard time with that, but we can't hold on to the past. In reality we…"

"He's on the *Fate's Winds*," Kaylee said. "He talked to me while we were on the orbiter."

"He...*what*?"

Thoughts flashed through Mephista's mind. Powered by photonic and quantum energy, an EVO suit's water and oxygen recycling would hold out for months; it was possible the ship's engineer had survived. If he did, what could she do for him, and was it worth putting the whole ship at risk?

"What did Aric tell you when he spoke to you?" she asked.

"He asked me to help him. He said he wants to die."

Chapter 5

Earth

Phuri paced back and forth in front of the admiral's secretary. He was aware of how his impatience looked, but he was unable to contain his tense eagerness. His plan had gone better than even he could have predicted. That fool messenger Falconi had broadcast Phuri's warning as soon as the *Mosquito* had arrived in Earth orbit, and the message had spread like wildfire among official and unofficial channels: *Atlas Carter has allied with the Bwain. They're assembling a fleet, and heading for Earth!*

The same planetary senators who had condemned Tannin and Phuri during their exile on Gertie now sought him out through means both official and private. Emissaries bombarded him in person as Phuri took his walks among Cape Canaveral's sun-warmed streets and gardens. His communicator rang constantly, bombarding him with questions. Handwritten notes were slipped under his door overnight. Every move was calculated to build a political advantage and to gather intelligence. Phuri had responded with carefully placed hints and hypothetical scenarios. It had only taken him three days to arrange a meeting with the man who would be the perfect partner for the next phase of his plan.

"Admiral Nico will see you now, sir," the secretary announced.

Phuri nodded, but before entering he closed his eyes and took a deep breath. It was important to be confident and relaxed in this first meeting with the man who would depose Sol's president. Everything depended on having an alternative to Kidewange waiting in the wings. The admiral was the perfect foil.

Standing at a bearish seven feet tall, Nico was a tense boulder of aggression looming behind his desk. The man wore a close-cropped black beard, and the insignia across his uniform sparkled with holograms from dozens of engagements with the Bwain, as well as other rebellious systems that dated back four decades. From what Phuri knew of Nico, many of those battles had been won at high cost. Nico was not a man for subtlety or tricks, which was why he would be the perfect stepping stone in Phuri's plan.

"I have five minutes," Nico said tersely.

"Five minutes hardly seems enough time to discuss the greatest threat Sol Space Command has ever faced," Phuri remarked. Then, without being asked, he sat.

The admiral leaned over the desk, a lip curled at Phuri's insolence.

"I've already sent a preliminary expedition to the Swordbelt. Those ships will tell me everything I need to know," Nico said. He wasn't a man who liked to mince words, and he was already growing tired of this conversation.

"*If* they come back you mean. Some in the president's cabinet would consider it rash to have deployed assets without first gathering the proper intelligence," Phuri said. He watched the man's reaction to his not-so-subtle intimations.

"I know how to run my navy!" the admiral bellowed.

Phuri saw why Nico had advanced to become the head of the SSC's navy. The man was incredibly intimidating, and brooked no subtlety. He would have to manage the man carefully. He couldn't let his confidence waver for a second.

"Yes...and I suppose that's why you sent Atlas Carter to the one system where he could become the most dangerous to you?" Phuri said, still attempting to maneuver the conversation.

"Carter's dirty. We thought we'd get him out of the way."

"You thought wrong, Admiral. He's much more than dirty...he's a genius. So I say again, do you have more than five minutes for me?"

The admiral's coal eyes bored into Phuri. It was clear that this man respected no civilian authority. To even have to take a meeting with someone outside the military was almost offensive to him.

"No," Nico snapped.

"Well…what a pity. I was told by certain senators that you might have been a valuable alternative to a government they fear has grown too weak, but it appears they were mistaken," Phuri said as he stood to leave.

Just as he opened the door, Nico called to him.

"Wait…tell me more about what you have in mind," he said as the admiral motioned for him to sit back down. His tone held more curiosity than arrogance now, and Phuri smiled as he returned to his seat.

*   *   *

"What do you mean, he's been reassigned?" Lana asked the SSC lieutenant who faced her on her holoscreen with a politely bland expression.

"I mean Capra Falconi is no longer with the messenger service. He shipped out on another wing of the navy.

"That's awfully sudden, don't you think?"

The man's brow's creased as if he was confused.

"We're the navy, ma'am. We just follow the orders we're given."

"But you can get a message to him?" Lana persisted.

"Certainly. We're the messenger service for the entire galaxy. Provided, of course, that you have a transmission license and the appropriate fees."

Sighing, Lana pressed her palm to the lower edge of the screen to transfer the credits.

"Thank you ma'am. Now, go ahead please," the man instructed.

"Um, Mr. Falconi, this is Lana Delgado from the Global Guardian's Madrid Bureau. I'm hoping you can get a message to uhhh...," she said, pausing to scan through her noted for a moment until she found the name she was looking for. "Yes, I'm hoping you can get a message to Aaron Granger, the the science officer on the *Fate's Winds*. I'm trying to research a story on Majorana particles, and it looks like he's the only other scientist who's been doing any work on this particular subject. I'd like to discuss his twelve-dimensional space theory in more detail if possible. Thank you for any assistance you can provide to me in this matter."

"Is there anything else, ma'am?" the aide asked.

"Just a question. How quickly will the message be sent?"

"The Swordbelt is on a reduced schedule of one monthly messenger voyage at the moment."

"Once a month? There's no way to speed things up?" she asked.

"I understand you've been trying to reach the *Fate's Winds* for some time. This is the best schedule for both Sol and the colony."

"Ok, I understand. Thanks."

"Thank you for using the SSC messenger service. Our mission is to serve."

The holoscreen darkened in front of her, leaving Lana sitting there completely frustrated. She had searched for Capra Falconi for three days, but had found nothing. Under the guise of her story on Majorana particles, she'd talked to a half-dozen aides who had given her the same story, but there was no record of Falconi being transferred. All SSC orders were public record, and she'd scoured them thoroughly for any mention of him.

It was almost as though the SSC was hiding something. Like a pending coup perhaps? She didn't know, but a desire to find out the truth burned within her.

She drummed her fingers on her desk while she ran it all through her head once again. The messengers were based in Cape Canaveral, Florida, at the SSC's headquarters. It was a relatively short flight, but she needed to develop a source who would give her access to the facility, and so far she was having no luck.

Sighing, she pushed away from the desk, shook out her hair, and lifted a sweater from the hook. She needed caffeine to think through her next steps, and the Etoile Café was three blocks from her flat.

It was November, and the day had been rather overcast, which was unusual for Madrid. She she pulled the sweater tightly around her chest as a chill wind kicked up. It was later than she thought, and there were few people out on the streets.

As she wove her way down the old brick walks, Lana turned over in her mind the precious little she had, trying to unearth a new angle on what she knew could become the story of her life. Eduardo was breathing down her neck for a new story, something meatier, but so far she had nothing.

The two men who had visited her had mentioned revolts on the outer planets, and Capra was somehow involved, but how? The little she had been able to discover about the messenger showed nothing that would indicate any kind of anti-SSC leanings. He had gone into the navy out of high school, like so many other men looking to leave the Earth for a little adventure, and he had been a messenger for three years serving the Swordbelt. There was literally nothing remarkable about him.

The Swordbelt, on the other hand, was full of pirates, mineral smugglers, Bwain attacks, and the home of a penal colony for political prisoners shipped from Earth. If a rebellion were to start against the SSC, a system like the Swordbelt would be the perfect incubator. She wondered how much of a role this Captain Atlas Carter had played in what was happening. The disgraced captain had spent a week in Alcubierre transit with Falconi just before this uprising, but he had been in the system less than a month. What had he done in those few weeks he'd been there, and who could she find to tell her?

The coffee stand was a small cutout window that opened onto the street. Lana made her way over and joined one other man in the queue. The air wafting out of the window warmed her with its bitter aroma and the hint of burnt metal. The man in front of her took his coffee from the barista, but instead of stepping aside to clear room for Lana, he turned directly around to face her.

It was the same thick-browed man who had visited her three days prior to warn her about Capra. The man smiled at her widened eyes, blowing across his steaming coffee so that the blast of his breath curled around her face.

"You're surprised to see me here?" he asked.

"Why are you following me?" she demanded.

"I was in line before you, so who was following who?" he answered, his smile growing even wider.

"You know what I mean."

"Senorita Delgado, I've told you before that I'm protecting you. Earth's government has enemies. They may be mostly on the outer planets, but there are some right here on our home world as well."

"Is that what happened to Capra Falconi?" she asked. The man cocked his head curiously at the mention of Falconi's name.

"I believe you already know what happened to Ensign Falconi, and if you'd like to remain within my protection, you will stop asking about him. Are we clear?"

She studied the steam curling under the man's heavy chin. Behind him, the barista idly flicked his communicator to talk to a friend.

"Of course," she answered.

"Excellent," the man said as he once more pulled his heavy face into a smile. This time however, there was little warmth in it. It was more of a warning. He leaned closer to her, his eyes boring into hers, and the unspoken message made her take an involuntary step back.

"Please enjoy your beverage," he said casually, and then he turned to stroll back in the direction of her flat.

She watched the man until he turned the corner, and then scanned up and down the street. Aside from the rather bored looking barista, she appeared to be alone. She was sure the man's partner was out there somewhere though...watching her every move.

"Can I help you?" the barista asked after she finally made her way up to the window. He was young, with a bristle of beard across his face and the glow of his communicator shining through his shirt pocket.

She reached into his pocket, snatched the communicator, and dialed Eduardo's number.

"Lana? Is everything all right?" he mumbled sleepily.

"I need to drop the story we talked about. I'm burnt out. I need a vacation."

"All right...I guess. Where are you going?"

"I just need to get away. "Look, I gotta go. I'll be in touch," she said before hanging up the call. Ignoring the barista's protests, she then proceeded to use his communicator to search for tickets to Florida.

* * *

The Tranquility

"What's our status, Mr. Spar?" Mephista asked the science officer. Spar was a seasoned spacer, with the pale skin and the meticulously maintained uniform of a career officer. His green eyes flicked to the main holoscreen, where a confusing mishmash of data and imagery presented itself.

"We're just arriving in near-sensor range of the *Fate's Winds'* last known position, Captain, but the interference we noticed before is even more prominent now. So much so that we're having a hard time validating the computer models."

Floating beside him, Mephista tried to make sense of the imagery on the main holoscreen. One moment, the *Fate's Winds* hung in space, and the next it seemed to be bound to the object with cords of white lightning.

"Those tendrils weren't there when we left the ship," Pandith noted.

"That's what attacked us?" Granger asked from beside him.

"It looks the same to me," Mephista answered.

"Comms, any response from the *Fate's Winds*?"

"No ma'am. We're broadcasting, but I'm not sure the transmissions are getting through. We haven't been able to raise Captain Carter either."

Mephista cocked her head, trying to rotate the view. The ship's computer was having extreme difficulty reconciling the various sensory inputs its holo-imaging software was receiving, and the screen kept jittering, as if it were showing different scenes. She squinted at the giant pillar of white stone that hung near the *Fate's Winds*, and studied it for a moment.

"Has the object moved?" she asked.

"Not that we can tell, but the *Fate's Winds* is on a tightly circular trajectory," Spar replied.

"It's orbiting the object," Granger observed.

"Yes, it is, and in spite of us seeing no gravitational readings that would allow an unpowered orbit to be possible," Spar finished his comment.

The holoscreen's view sharpened, and Mephista saw that the corvette was indeed drifting in a slow arc around the obelisk, trailing a tangle of what looked like golden webbing that connected it to the alien object. As she watched, another filament unspooled from the white stone and lashed itself to the damaged ship. The effect was that of a wagon wheel, with the glistening white stone as the central axle. What did it all mean?

"Mr. Pandith, you've seen this thing up close. What do you think is happening?" Mephista asked.

"Without direct observation or probes, it's hard to say. But my guess would be that we're looking at some sort of a dimensional rift. A portal between our physical universe and something else," he replied.

"What would that 'something else' be?" she asked.

"I don't know if we want to find out," Granger said, a hint of nervousness creeping into his voice.

"I'm in complete agreement," Spar added. "The object is definitely hostile, as we saw from what happened with the orbiter. I'd recommend the probe approach as well."

Mephista fell silent for a moment and considered her position. Nothing made her feel more ill at ease than a lack of good intelligence, and if Aric Keith was in fact still alive there on the *Fate's Winds,* then he might have information that they would need. She'd certainly had her differences with Keith during her pirate days, but he had been someone in whom Captain Carter had put a great deal of faith. She felt she owed it to Carter to do everything she could to save his stranded crew member.

"Mr. Pandith's encounter proved that the object is blind to purely physical reactions and technology, as well as chemical thrusters and batteries."

"Captain, what are you proposing?" Spar asked.

"There may be a survivor on board that ship, and if there is, then I intend to rescue him," Mephista responded.

* * *

"Well, I can't say that I'm not terrified, but look on the bright side. This is gonna be a pretty historic scientific expedition, ain't it?" Granger said as he adjusted the holoscreen at his co-pilot's station. "Hell, maybe we'll even make the newsfeeds! How cool would that be?"

"Not very actually, if said newsfeeds are reporting our death," Pandith said dryly.

"Awww, come on now. Don't talk like that. We're stuck in this situation now, so you gotta try to stay positive," Granger said encouragingly as he glanced across the console to his friend. He couldn't see Pandith's face through his darkened visor, but he was pretty sure he'd gotten a smile out of him. He liked to think he did anyway.

Pandith slipped the orbiter out of the *Tranquility's* cargo bay. The craft had been stripped of all technology that relied on radiation or quantum fluctuations, including its fusion reactor, forcing the engineers to sacrifice power for the interior environment so that enough remained for navigation and the scientific instruments. The dozen men on the search and rescue team all wore EVO suits to protect them. After his recent concussion, however, the thin carbyne mesh of the suit and the shimmering outer layer of nanobots did little to make Granger feel more secure.

"Do you think we'll find him?" one of the marines asked.

"Mr. Keith will either be in the cargo or medical bays. Please keep trying to reach him," Pandith urged, not willing to voice his concern that they might not find Aric alive.

"Still no response, but we may be getting interference from the object," Spar reported.

Granger stared at the white smear that lay ahead of the craft. The rift flickered with what looked like an occasional lightning bolt that left him with a queasy sensation in his stomach. The object was easier to see with the naked eye, but the effect of studying it without a computer-interpolated buffer was even more unsettling.

"You know, your description didn't do it justice," Granger commented.

"I'm not sure any description could," Pandith replied. "Initiating thrust in three seconds...two...one...burn."

With the smooth, computer-controlled acceleration and deceleration of the orbiter's inducers removed, the hard shove of antiquated rocket fuel boosters pressing Granger against the back of his acceleration couch was a bit of a shock. This was how the early astronauts felt, pushing into the dark on spears of flame, testing the limits of what the human body could endure.

Beside the rift, the *Fate's Winds* seemed little more than a sewing needle against the blackness of space. Pandith had briefed Granger on Aric's condition once the science officer had recovered consciousness. To Granger, at least, it seemed highly improbable that Aric would have survived, unless his EVO suit's biogel had managed to staunch his bleeding. Even so, the suit couldn't have fixed any internal damage or bleeding.

Granger could have protested Captain Mephista's orders, but in truth a part of him wanted to see the rift up close. What could be the direct observational validation of a lifetime of theory was only a few minutes away.

"You know Granger, if your theory is correct and there are 12 dimensions, what would...I mean, what do you think those living on the other side might look like?"

"I don't know really. It's hard to say. I think they'd probably look like whatever they want to look like. And anything with that level of technical knowledge would most likely have found a way to conquer death at some point, so there's no telling what their life spans could be. Hell, they could even be immortal for all we know," Granger replied. Just then, Mephista's tart voice echoed in Granger's cochlear implant.

"That's enough chatter. I need a report, gentlemen."

"Copy that Captain," Spar acknowledged. "Star field mapping shows inconclusive object dimensions. It's somewhere between five and forty kilometers tall, and between two and ten kilometers wide."

"Inconclusive? That's about as vague as it gets."

"I'm sorry Captain, but the readings are changing all the time. Now it's six wide and and forty-one tall. Spectrometry is all over the map. It's showing some signs of hard regolith, but other readings make it seem as though it isn't even there."

Granger felt his breath growing shallower and shallower. So much so, that a yellow warning rectangle for his heart rate flashed inside his visor. In spite of his assurances to Pandith and the other crew, he had no idea what they would encounter. The thought of the discovery, that moment of new truth that lay just outside the grasp of his gloves, drove him, and like a pinprick in the dark, they glided toward the object.

"Ten kilometers wide, thirty tall," Spar noted.

"Mr. Pandith, any sign of hostile intentions?" Mephista asked.

Granger glanced at his HUD, studying the telemetry.

"We're ten kilometers from the object, ma'am. At this range, I'm sure that if it was gonna attack us, it'd be instantaneous. Since it hasn't, I'd say we're in the clear, at least for now," Pandith reported. "Granger, why don't you go ahead with the probes now. Let's see what we can pick up out there."

"Copy," Granger acknowledged. After he released himself from his restraints, he gathered up the simple probes that Pandith had helped him fashion from spare parts on the *Tranquility*, and then floated to the orbiter's rear airlock.

"I can make out the *Fate's Winds* now. It's another fifteen kilometers beyond the object. The damage appears to be extensive, and...wait a second," Pandith said before his voice trailed off.

"What is it, Pandith?" Spar asked.

Granger cycled into the airlock, pulled the heavy door shut that led to the cabin, and began twisting the manual valve to open the outer door.

"The ship appears to have been *modified,* Captain. Definitely not human construction," Pandith observed.

"Mr. Spar, transmit visuals," Mephista ordered.

"I'll try, Captain. We're having equipment issues over here. The telescopic feed is failing," Spar said, and then he fell silent. The only sounds coming from him were his fingers tapping the various controls on his console.

One of the probes slipped from Granger's gloves and rolled off his boot. He cursed, setting the other two down as he rummaged for the escapee.

"Then *describe* it, Officer Spar."

"It looks like limestone...or maybe even marble, but it's actually some form of plasma. I'm attempting to get a magnification on it. There we go, that's better. Now...oh my god!"

On Granger's helmet visor HUD, the other team members' status indicators flashed orange as their vitals spiked.

"What's going on?" Mephista called, but her voice was garbled, twisted by some sort of ionization.

Granger found the third probe, set it with the other two, and returned to the task of opening the airlock manually. Gray coils of escaping air slipped past his ankles.

"We need to get out of here! Now! Get us back to the *Tranquility*!" Spar shouted urgently.

"Pandith, talk to me," Granger called. The science officer's shoulders burned, but the valve finally spun to its stops, and the door locks fully retracted. He pushed open the hatch and gathered the probes.

"Granger, we shouldn't have come," Pandith replied.

"We can't abandon Aric!" Granger said as he tossed the probes into the vacuum of space.

"Whatever Aric is now, it's not alive," Pandith said, his voice swelling with emotion.

The airlock door swung wide, and Granger was finally staring at the full vastness of the object. Whatever dimensions Spar had recorded were useless. The object pulsed with a malevolent swelling as if it was trying to push through the fabric of space itself. The thing was a boil, a seething mass of infection. As Granger stared, a white-gold shimmer began at the top of the object and spit it open like a lava flow at the bottom of an ocean. Unmistakably, the object grew in size, despite the chaotic readings flashing over Granger's HUD. The molten seam then dribbled downward like a rope and shot out into space, reaching for the orbiter.

"Aric," Granger whispered.

Tawny lightning gathered on the object's hazed surface. The space in front of Granger changed. For a moment Granger saw an infinite number of threads stretched out in crystalline shapes that blurred whenever he tried to grasp them. He tried to draw a breath, but oxygen was only a memory. He tried to reach for the airlock door, but his limbs had fractured into dozens of strands and moved in every direction at once. His mind felt torn and reconstituted, while the pattern of his hands repeated endlessly with no meaning or control.

Words filled his head, language, a screaming like metal shapes grinding together. As tendrils shot from the object to the orbiter, Granger joined their terrified chorus.

Chapter 6

The Bwainhome

The Bwain clustered around him on their ship's bridge were all terrified. Most had turned entirely yellow, trembling and squawking as the Bwainhome closed on the white column that hung like a blasphemous doorway through the slate-black of space.

"The Masters come! The obelisk is their sign!" the Bwainsong screamed in his mind.

The obelisk was the portal the Bwain's former masters, the First Ones, would open to begin their return. Before they had faded from the physical universe millennia ago, the First Ones had ordered the Bwain to prepare for their return. The Bwain, euphoric at being in control of their own destiny, had forgotten their orders as they explored the universe on their own. With the First Ones returning, the Bwain wanted no part of the punishment that would come. Every single mind in their collective consciousness longed to flee the Swordbelt, and Carter had to fight to control their will. If he didn't, whoever was on the orbiter, and on the *Fate's Winds* would be taken by the obelisk.

"If you flee, you'll die. You don't have enough food," Carter thought, focusing his words into the Bwainsong.

"Die is better. Other swarms will live."

"For how long? If not this swarm, then the First Ones will find another, and another. You'll be slaves again no matter what," he reasoned.

Slivers of rational thought crept into the Bwainsong. He felt their panic lessen, and it was soon replaced with a small kernel of resolve. The Bwainhome remained on course toward the fragile dot of the *Fate's Winds*. Carter could see the human ships through whatever the Bwain used as the equivalent of a telescope, but he longed for greater intelligence.

The Bwainhome's bridge was breathtaking. Sheathed almost entirely in the alien's equivalent of humanity's electroglass, it was a spherical bubble jutting out above the vessel's hull a kilometer backward from its enormous bow. Overhead, Carter could see the last orange and pink froth of the Greater Orion Nebula, the faint glimmer of the tiny mirror array he had used to destroy the Bwain's attacking fleet, the endless black of space, and the green disk of Gertie in the distance. There were no stations as there would have been on a human bridge, few pieces of machinery visible. Twenty or so of the creatures bobbed their heads or froze in place, only occasionally hunting and pecking at eldritch controls that flashed in and out of existence in the blink of an eye. They controlled the ship with their minds, and it left Carter frustrated with how little he knew about what was happening with his fellow humans.

He had heard nothing from Mephista since talking to her through the Bwain on Gertie, and now here she was just a few hundred kilometers from the obelisk. Worse, she had sent a low-powered orbiter toward the *Fate's Winds*. If it was a rescue mission, what good would a crippled orbiter do? If it was something else, what had happened to his crew?

On a telepathically controlled ship, there was no radio with which to reach out. There was no way of warning her how great the danger was. Carter was pushing the Bwainhome as fast as he could to try and intercept the ships, but he wasn't sure yet what good he'd be able to do when he arrived.

The Bwainsong's tone changed. Mind by mind, he felt a fragile hope replace the panicked fear. Green streaks of confidence appeared in the yellow feathers around him.

"Carter will save?" the creatures asked.

"I'm gonna try to save you and my friends...if I can," Carter answered.

"Carter save. We help," the creatures chorused.

Carter nodded. The Bwain nearest to him nuzzled against his waist. He felt their shuddering necks and wings press against him for strength and whispered a quick prayer.

"Dios, please give me enough time. Please keep Mephista and my crew safe."

Then he closed his eyes and gave more of his mind to the Bwainsong. There was a ship to command after all, and he had never led aliens into battle against other aliens before. If what he planned was going to work, he had to marshal the Bwain into performing more complex tactics than they'd ever employed before. He could speak to the Bwain with his thoughts, but human command structures and tactical concepts were completely foreign to them. He found himself trying to simplify his plan as best he could, walking the aliens step-by-step through each task.

"Take the ship there," he thought, focusing his mind's eye on a point in space that would allow the Bwainhome to shield the *Fate's Winds* and the tiny orbiter from the obelisk's reach.

"Will be hurt! Will die!"

"No, you won't. Open the shuttle bays on the port side of the ship. Prepare two fighters," Carter instructed.

"What cargo? What fighters do?"

Carter closed his eyes and visualized the next steps of his plan to them. The Knot had showed him so much, giving him hints about the Bwainhome and its original purpose that the Bwain themselves had largely forgotten in the long story of their own enslavement. Though his hope was thin, it was all he had. It had been that way ever since his youth in Belize City's slums, and he had clung to that hope all his life. That is, until Cazador convinced him he had no alternative other than to work with the *Narcos*, and until Aida had died in a rain of their fire. Now he had no other choice than to cling to it once again.

"Bwainslayer will kill us."

"No, you have to trust me," Carter assured them.

In spite of their protests, the Bwain swung into action. Carter had no idea how the Bwain actually executed his commands, or how they showed him the different images of what lay before the ship in his mind, but he felt the gigantic ship shift, and saw the angles of the obelisk changing. They were responding to him. They were believing in themselves.

The obelisk scraped overhead like a chalk streak through the darkness. The First One's portal was massive, seeming larger even than a planet, and it appeared as though it was burning with a white-hot lava. In the Bwainsong, the obelisk seemed like a cracked door, the tendrils that clung to the *Fate's Winds* a part of a turning knob.

Bolts of searing plasma battered the tiny orbiter that had been trying to make its way to Carter's old ship. Carter had no idea who was on the craft, had no way to tell them to hold on. He could only hope they saw him bearing down on them and understood his plan. Or that they knew he was even on the ship, and that hostilities with the Bwain had ended.

"How far are we?" Carter asked through the Bwainsong.

"Not far," came the vague reply.

"Kilometers. Measurements," Carter clarified.

"Close."

Suddenly the bridge lit with a blinding flash of the same consistency and cool touch of the void as the Endless Knot. Only this time, he felt a bottomless hunger with it. There was an angry will to consume and control that the Knot did not possess.

The First Ones had discovered a ship they had left behind thousands of years ago. This was Carter's moment of truth. He closed his eyes and gave himself entirely into the Bwainsong.

A part of him joined the two shuttle pilots who left the Bwainhome on their way toward the crippled orbiter. He showed the pilots how to attach to the orbiter's grapple points, and how to tow the craft back toward the shuttle bay. To a group of other Bwain waiting near the bay, he showed his memories of his naval academy first aid training while praying that they wouldn't be needed.

Then he shifted his thoughts to the obelisk.

The low thunder of the First One's insatiable agony was spreading through the Bwainsong. Its plasma struck the Bwainhome, writhing like tentacles against its ancient hull.

"We are returned," a deep bellowing voice hummed.

"You are not welcome," Carter responded.

"Slaves do not give orders."

"There are no slaves here."

"What speaks?"

"My name is Captain Atlas Carter."

"The one called Aric Keith knew you."

"What happened to Aric?"

"He serves us now, as will you."

Carter felt sweat pour down his body, but he could not give up. In every fight he had ever had, Carter's instinct had carried him. According to the Knot, it had taken 500 years for the First Ones to leave the universe. They could return again with immediate strength. They had built the Bwainhome, but it was stronger than they were. They had enslaved the Bwain, but Carter would show no fear.

"No," Carter replied steadily.

"You have no choice," the First Ones intoned.

"This is not the same universe you left. We are strong now," Carter stood his ground, his thoughts not allowing any room for hesitation or fear.

With that, Carter pushed his mind deeper into the Bwainsong, into the Endless Knot and its memories of the Bwainhome itself. He felt a dim shudder in the ship, an awareness that he knew must have existed in order for it to interact with the Bwain. He felt where the obelisk tried to lash itself to long-forgotten moorings, felt the ship responding to the First One's energy.

Carter pushed as many thoughts of rejection as he could through the Knot and into the Bwainhome: shield, barrier, rejection, escape, barrier, armor, bulwark, fend off, and a variety of other defensive thoughts.

The Bwainhome lurched, pulled off course by the obelisk. The Bwainsong erupted in a terrified chorus.

"The Carter is ours. All is ours," the First Ones thrummed through the Bwainsong.

* * *

The Tranquility

"Why can't I hear the orbiter? I need to know what's happening!" Mephista barked at her comms officer.

"We're getting too much interference from the object, ma'am. I've tried everything I can think of!"

"Well try again, damn it!"

On her holoscreen the orbiter sizzled with shards of energy that poured like flame from the object. It was clear to Mephista that Pandith's strategy had failed. The orbiter was tumbling through space, drifting closer to the object, rather than the *Fate's Winds*, and she had lost all contact with the craft.

"Nav, prepare to get me closer to that ship. We need to bring them home."

"Captain, if we do that, I can't guarantee we'll be able to withdraw," her lieutenant answered.

"Get me the solution," she ordered.

"Ma'am, with due respect, we're the last ship in this system. We'd be putting the entire colony at risk."

Mephista glared at her flickering holoscreens, unable to accept that she had just sent more good crew to die. It had been a stupid risk, something she had known in her heart of hearts would never have worked.

"I'm sorry. You're right," she conceded. "Prepare a withdrawal solution, and prepare to execute it on my...wait a minute. What's that?"

"It's a new signature, ma'am. It's enormous. I think...yes! It's the Bwainhome!" the navigation officer called.

On the main holoscreen the Bwainhome's bulbous hull hurtled into view. The great ship was traveling incredibly fast, and with a start, Mephista saw that Carter had put himself between the *Fate's Winds* and the orbiter.

"What are you doin' Carter?" she whispered as the object's plasma claws burrowed into the Bwainhome. The entire ship's hull lit, showing a patchwork of repairs and modifications prepared over thousands of years, until whatever its original form had been was nearly unrecognizable.

The Bwainhome flickered, jittering closer to the object. Shadows crawled along the hull's protuberances.

"It looks like the object has them, ma'am," her nav officer noted. The woman's voice was flat with disappointment.

The order to withdraw was on the tip of Mephista's tongue, but the words wouldn't come out. She simply couldn't believe that Carter would fail. He was too strong, too smart, and too good of an officer. Regardless, she felt entirely helpless, because she had no idea how to help him.

"Weapons, target the object as best you can. Full battery, nukes authorized," Mephista snapped.

"Yes ma'am. Armed and ready. Awaiting your command."

"Fire," Mephista ordered.

On the holoscreen brilliant blue lasers streaked toward the object, followed by the slower orange burn of nuclear missiles that, had they struck the *Tranquility* itself, would have reduced it to ash in seconds. The magna cannon projectiles streaked unseen through space, accelerated to nearly the same speed as the lasers by her gravity cannons.

"We have laser impact. At least...I think we do," her weapons officer called.

"Status?" Mephista asked.

"I can't be sure. Hold on. Now we have magna cannon impact."

"Weapons, give me a status," she demanded.

"Nuke impact in four, ma'am."

Mephista fell silent and waited. Suddenly, a hard glint of light appeared in front of the object, scattering like glitter raining down from fireworks. Unfortunately, when the explosion cleared, the object remained there in space, apparently unaffected by the impact.

"Prepare to withdraw," Mephista ordered. She hated the choked-off sob in her voice.

"Captain!" her nav officer called.

"Was there an issue with my order?" Mephista demanded.

"Ma'am, the Bwainhome! It's free!"

Blinking away the tears that had gathered in her eyes, Mephista zoomed her holoimage. Nav had been right; the Bwainhome had somehow fought off the object and was continuing toward her.

"It looks like they've got the orbiter in tow! I can't believe it. We did it, ma'am! We did it!" her weapons officer exclaimed.

"Excellent work everyone, but we need to get the hell outta here. Let's get ourselves turned around and prepare to match course and speed with the Bwainhome. A ship that big is gonna need an escort back to Gertie."

*   *   *

Atlas could barely contain his smile as the airlock hatch swung open to reveal Mephista floating just behind her medical staff. At first she didn't see him. She was counting her crew and verifying that both her marines, and Spar's science team, were all intact. When he saw her frown as a result of the two missing crewmen, he stepped out from behind the marines who were patiently submitting to the med team's vital checkups. Mephista's eyes widened in surprise when she saw him.

"I asked Pandith and Granger to stay on the Bwainhome, so everyone's been accounted for," Carter assured her.

"You didn't tell me you were coming," she said as she let out a sigh of relief.

"How could I? The Bwain don't have radios."

"So, what these are for?" she asked, indicating the three Bwain that stood in a nervous cluster at the orbiter's ramp. The aliens were alternating between curious stabs of their heads and clenched camouflage flutterings of nervousness.

"That's right. I brought you a present."

She pushed her chair forward, a half-smile breaking over her face in spite of her attempts at self-control.

"I haven't seen you smile the entire time you've been in this system," she noted.

"You've never seen me rescue anyone from the obelisk and the First Ones either."

"Well that's true. Mr. Spar, give me your report," she said, turning to her science officer.

"Ma'am, it was...well, I'm not sure how to describe it really. It felt as if we were being torn apart. It was almost like we were being consumed, and there was nothing that Mr. Pandith, or any of the rest of us could do to stop it."

"The First Ones' weaponry is one of the things I've got Granger working on at the moment," Carter explained.

"The First Ones? The obelisk? You seem to know a hell of a lot more about all this than I do. Wanna fill me in?" Mephista asked.

Carter's smile slipped from his face. After enjoying being alive for a moment that had been all too brief, he felt the formal mantle of command tighten once more around him.

"Listen, we've got a serious situation here. That object is gonna start leakin' aliens that are much more powerful than the Bwain any time now. Among other things on his list, Pandith is gonna be tryin' to figure out just how soon the First Ones are gonna start showin' up here, and we need to be ready for 'em when they do," Carter explained.

The medical team had finished the exams, and the marines gave a grateful whoop as they were dismissed to their cabins. Spar's team followed, leaving the two captains alone in the corridor.

Mephista's eyes fell closed. She seemed more fragile than he remembered. Her hair was shot with gray, and she seemed to be developing some crow's feet at the corners of her eyes. She also seemed to be forming some frown lines around her mouth. A part of him felt bad for her, but in a way he also found it somewhat striking. They were the marks of someone who bore the burden of command, and they were well earned.

"I'm sorry. I can see you're exhausted," he added after a brief silence.

Her hand fluttered near his. He reached for her but stopped himself, torn between Aida's memory and the thought that he might just live long enough to move past it.

"Did they tell you about Aric?" Mephista asked. His mouth flattened into a line, and he hesitated for just the briefest of moments before he answered.

"I've lost people before."

"I wish I could have done more."

"You took in the rest of my crew, and you could have all gotten yourselves killed trying to help Aric. What more could I have asked for?"

Her face slackened, a measure of relief building within her. He remembered the feeling of grinding away at himself, thinking he was the only one who had felt pain, and that no one understood his suffering. Then he entered the Bwainsong, and learned what true suffering really was.

"Would you like to see your crew?" Mephista asked.

"Of course. I'd..."

Their conversation was interrupted by the *Tranquility's* comms officer with an incoming message channeled through each of their implants. "Captain! Urgent message from the planet, ma'am. It's Lieutenant Xiao."

"What does he need?" she asked.

"I think you should speak with him on the holos, ma'am. It doesn't sound good."

*   *   *

Gertie

The flickering holoimage of Captain Carter rubbed its eyes in front of Danny. What had happened outside the *Fate's Winds* was almost too much information for Danny to process. He could only imagine the thoughts that were racing through his captian's mind. When he'd first seen Carter and Mephista together on the holoscreen, they'd seemed almost happy. He'd felt somewhat guilty delivering the news about Phuri, and the SSC navy's impending arrival, but the truth was a powerful element of change, and Danny would never lie to his captain again.

"Is there anything else, Lieutenant?" Mephista asked.

"That's not the worst of it, ma'am. Falconi left five days ago. We've got maybe nine days tops before the window opens for the SSC's arrival," Danny reported.

"Does the colony know?" Carter asked.

Hal's voice came through as his face appeared on the screen. "Oh indeed they do, and I have to say Captain, we're havin' one hell of a hard time holding people together down here."

"They need to hang on just a little longer. We're a day out from Gertie. If we...," Carter began, but Hal interrupted him.

"With due respect, that's part of the problem. By all means, if you want a full revolt, show up with a boatload of Bwain and land them here," Hal said.

"Now come on Hal, just stop," Danny said, stopping him from spewing out more of his pointless sarcasm.

"The Bwain are gonna starve to death out here," Mephista said. "Now look, I don't like the this either, but they're on our side now, and they can't stay on their ship forever. At some point real soon here we're gonna have to bring 'em to Gertie if we're gonna have any chance of saving 'em."

"With all due respect Captain, none of that matters to the people down here," Hal continued. "They just saw a lot of their friends and family die. They've been told the navy is on their way out here, and that the SSC is mad as hell. Now you want us to tell 'em that we've got even worse aliens on the way. This is a lot to take in, and you're talkin' about farmers here. These ain't people that adapt well to change, must less huge, life-changing changes like the ones we're talkin' about,"

Captain Carter looked off-screen. Danny could just see the head combs of a few Bwain bobbing around behind him. What would it have been like to see what Carter had seen, to connect with billions of alien minds, and to have the responsibility on his shoulders extend beyond anyone's imagination? Even in his short time running the colony with Hal, he'd struggled with carrying the weight of it, so he had no idea how the captain could handle it.

"Hal, listen to me. We don't have a whole lot of choice in what's goin' on at the moment, and...," Mephista began.

"Mephista, wait," Carter interrupted.

The *Tranquility* captain turned toward Carter. Danny studied his captain's face. Carter's hair was streaked with two white blazes at his temples, and the scars and knots from his former boxing days seemed polished to a high sheen against his lightly tanned skin. If anything, Carter looked more himself. The clenched vise of his former bearing had loosened ever so slightly, and Danny wondered what angles he was considering now that he had access to the Bwainsong.

"We're dealing with a morale issue," Carter continued.

"It's not morale. It's discipline, and these farmers had better start learning it," she argued.

"I agree, but you just said exactly what the problem is. They're not soldiers, they're farmers. They're just regular old human beings trying to live their day to day lives. I know this is gonna sound strange, but the Bwain are very much the same. They don't believe in themselves, and they don't have a whole lotta hope. So what can we do to give that to 'em?" Carter asked.

"Keep those aliens in the sky," Hal interjected.

"Destroy the obelisk," Mephista replied at the same time.

Danny's mind was churning. He remembered how beaten down he had felt every minute of his existence while he served Tannin, and how much more alive he had felt when he'd finally shed the burden of servitude, and was able to make his own choices.

"Captain, I think I have an idea," he offered, and then he spent the next few minutes explaining his proposal. When he finished, Hal and the two captains were silent for a long moment. Then suddenly, Captain Carter broke into a grin so broad that it was almost startling.

"I think you've pretty much nailed it Danny. That is, provided that Captain Mephista is open to a brief detour?" Carter asked as he glanced over at her. Mephista nodded thoughtfully in response.

"All right, I'm on board with it. I think the kid here's got as good of a feel for these people as anyone," Hal said as he reached over and mussed up the hair on the back of Danny's head a little. Danny grimaced and shrugged him off, but then returned Hal's grin before looking back at the two captains.

"Well then, the only thing left to do is to figure out what we're gonna do about the SSC."

* * *

The Fate's Winds

"How did the Carter know?" the voice thundered. Its anger was like fingernails clawing through his flesh, and he felt pieces of his body thrum under a vibration that seemed as if it could shake the *Fate's Winds'* deck to atoms. Which, he supposed, given the First One's control over elements at the quantum level, it most likely could.

"I don't know," Aric responded.

He had learned to separate his mind from the body that performed the tasks demanded of it. Tasks like nursing the strange biological crystalloids that had taken root in the sheltered spaces of the ship, and using what remained of the *Fate's Winds'* tools and repair capabilities to fashion materials and components that would never have been possible under human control. Those pieces were then sent out toward the obelisk for them to be consumed and assembled into something that he could not yet quite grasp, or was prevented from understanding.

The separation of his mind allowed him to endure the thought that he was helping to destroy his fellow humans, and that he'd almost taken the life of the man who'd saved him when Pandith's orbiter had strayed too close. It allowed him to hide the hope that his friends had not abandoned him, that Kaylee and the others had somehow heard him in the maelstrom. If he showed disobedience, if he showed anger of any kind, then he would be punished once again, which was a thought more terrible than anything he could imagine.

This time the pain was a reawakening of nerves that opened onto long-frozen skin that had cracked and broken against the vacuum. There was no heat on the *Fate's Winds*. The First Ones' energy came from a deeper place. It was like the frigid bottom of an ocean of hunger, and they would not be denied.

"I DON'T KNOW!" Aric screamed.

"He has our ship. He took it from us."

"You have to ask him. I don't know what he's doing with the Bwain."

"Our slaves could not have done this. They do not understand the Knot. Does the Carter?"

"What is the Knot?" Aric asked.

For a moment, a sliver of understanding passed into him. He saw a brief glimpse of a glowing writhing thing that was not borne of the obelisk, that had come from a much earlier time, when the First Ones had been quite different.

In the part of his mind he kept hidden from the First Ones, the part where he was still Lieutenant Aric Keith of the SSC ship *Fate's Winds* under the command of Captain Atlas Carter, Aric realized that the First Ones needed him. They were growing stronger but were still weak. Carter had somehow known this, had seen into their technology without truly understanding.

Now Aric had seen a key that might undo the First Ones. If only he could warn the man the First Ones wanted to destroy more than any other, he might have a chance to escape this nightmarish torture, and to save all of humanity in the process.

*   *   *

The Bwainhome

When he had first seen the Bwainhome as it had emerged from the The Gates to do battle with the *Fate's Winds,* Granger had assumed it would be an immaculate dreadnought; a feat of engineering unparalleled by humanity. Now, as a cluster of squawking Bwain led him and Pandith through the heart of their artificial world, he saw the true state of their desperation.

The vessel was thousands of years old. Its twenty-foot-high corridors were choked with broken parts, garbage, shed feathers, and awkward nests made out of grimed wood and scavenged insulation. Waste's pungent odor fouled the air, and nearly all of the aliens on the ship's lower levels seemed unhealthy. Their eyes were clouded, and their feathers had fallen out in patches. Many squatted on their haunches or lay collapsed where they'd fallen, listless and exhausted.

"This colony is gonna collapse," Pandith observed.

One of the creatures twisted its neck to face them as it kept pace with its companions.

"Carter save," it croaked.

Granger didn't know if the captain had realized the magnitude of what he had agreed to do for the aliens.

Where the natural assumption had been that the Bwain had built their home ship, Granger knew now that the aliens had simply been using what their masters had left them. They passed through corridors of glowing lavender that seemed to shift position even as Granger entered them, and massive rooms that looked almost like alien aviaries. There was arcane machinery everywhere that was surrounded by jury-rigged tangles of amateur cabling that had long ago fallen into disuse. Much of the technology was clearly dependent on multi-dimensional capabilities and power sources that the Bwain had lacked the skill to maintain.

"What does that do?" Pandith asked when they reached a wide, tall room filled with the garbage of shed feathers, rusted components, and strangely withered organs that looked as if they were fossilized biological growths. At the center of the room, what appeared to be a mirrored bullet the length of two men rose from the deck. Granger leaned down to look at his reflection, but whatever the thing was made of, it reflected nothing back.

"We take you here," one of the Bwain croaked.

"This is what Captain Carter wanted to show us? This is your engine?" Granger asked.

"Many engines. This one Bwainslayer pick," the Bwain responded. Now that they had reached their destination, they had lost interest in their task and were hunting and pecking through the trash.

Granger met Pandith's gaze. He pulled on his beard, and then rang a knuckle against the smooth cylinder in front of him. There was no sound, but the tacticle sensation was similar to that of hitting a soft, liquid surface. A faint ripple spread for a few inches from his touch, and then died.

He straightened, shaking his head as he continued to observe the object.

"I don't know how the Captain expects us to fight the First Ones from a dumpster, but we're gonna have to find a way," Granger said.

"Sure, let me just pull out my tool box full of miracles, and I'll get right on that," Pandith replied dryly. Granger looked at him, and they exchanged an amused glance for just a moment before returning their focus back to the matter at hand.

Chapter 7

Gertie

Hal sat outside of his trailer on the stool where he used to drink away so many of his days on Gertie, just watching his nanofactories hum in Gertie's soft midday light. They stood like sentinels among the rolling hills, working at full capacity in order to make Carter's plan a reality. He had spent the morning reprogramming his nanobots to increase the ratio of iron ore they were bringing into the factories, and had them stockpiling hydrocarbons and sugars that could easily be turned into chemical fuel. He had assigned another cohort to gather proteins, and the two of them had already filled a dozen hovercarts with a fine pinkish powder that he hoped to Sol he wouldn't have to spend the rest of his life eating. The farming equipment he had promised the colony was just going to have to wait a bit longer.

In spite of his sour mood, he had to admit that Danny's plan might just work to set the colony right. There was no arguing with Mephista that they had little choice but to accept the Bwain, but people needed time to heal, and Danny seemed to understand that better than anyone. As a way of saying thanks, Hal had even ginned up a few surprises to fit what the kid had in mind. He was just taking a break from staring at his nanobot interface when two farmers came walking around the corner of his trailer.

"I was wondering if you'd be wantin' to talk," Hal said as he glanced over at them.

Dax and Lisa ran the farmer's market in town...or at least they had up until a few days ago. They had been the first to join Hal in the rebellion against Tannin's cruelty, but now they found themselves pulled toward speaking for the farmers since Hal had become the colonial administrator. Ever since he had put out the announcement about the SSC and the Bwain and everything that Carter had asked him to say, he had been prepared for the moment when things would start to sink in. A part of him wondered if it might be better if the colonists would simply vote him out. At least then he could spend his time worrying about simpler concerns, like what kind of weapons he could possibly make that would hurt an alien that the *Tranquility* hadn't been able to damage, even with the variety of weapons it had on board.

"So, it's true, Hal? The Bwain are coming?" Dax asked.

"It's true."

"And the criminals from Judgment?" Lisa asked.

"A lot of them are our friends and family. They didn't deserve to be over there," Hal responded calmly.

"We both know that, Hal," she acknowledged.

"But there are killers over there too," Dax added.

"We've all had to become something else out here," Hal said as the wind kicked up and rustled the grass against his ankles. The worn patches where he had rested his Nightcrawler glasses night after night were just starting to grow in again.

"Hal, you know what I mean."

"Dax, you know what the captain is gonna ask those people to do...what he's asking all of us to do. The only question is, do you think you can do it? You know what the alternative is. This might not be just the last week we spend on Gertie; it might be the last one we spend alive, so what have we got to lose in trying?"

The tall man glared into the distance and fell silent. Under the sky's orange tint, he seemed even more than usual to be a man of the soil who had been forced to contemplate the end of the only life he'd ever known.

"Look, I'm not gonna lie to you Hal. We're not happy about any of this, but the fact is, we came here to say we're all ready to support you," Lisa said as she placed her hand gently on his arm.

"So what's that mean exactly? Do you mean the farmers are actually okay with everything that's happening, or that you're just gonna swallow all your objections to this plan and support it anyway because you don't really have any other choice?"

"She just said we're gonna support you Hal. There's no need to go splitting hairs and trying to find hidden meanings in it. Just take the support and stop complaining," Dax retorted.

"Look, I know this ain't gonna be easy. Danny and the captains know it too, which is why they've got a nice surprise planned for everyone," Hal said. Dax and Lisa stared at him for a moment.

"Come on Hal, the last thing we need right now is another surprise," Lisa said.

"Oh, I wouldn't be so sure," Hal said, grinning at them both. Dax and Lisa shot each other an uneasy glance, and then listened carefully while Hal explained everything to them.

*　*　*

Alistair Threed unstrapped his restraints and rose from the orbiter's acceleration couch. The air inside the vessel was cold, and gooseflesh tightened on his skin. Two years on Judgment had made him used to blistering desert heat, and the thin rags he wore did little to warm him. Life on the penal planet had been cruel. As the prison planet's mayor, he had tried to organize his fellow prisoners so that they could scratch out some semblance of a living. Despite his efforts however, many had still chosen to either take their own lives, or die in the constant fights that were the colony's only source of entertainment. As a result, a part of him hadn't wanted to believe the crew of the *Tranquility* when they'd arrived on the hardscrabble settlement and told him that the convicts had all been pardoned and were returning to Gertie.

"On whose authority? That bastard, Tannin?" Threed had demanded.

"Captain Atlas Carter. He's running things in the system now," one of the marines had told him.

Despite his shivering, Threed was eager to step out into Gertie's cool evening, so he could find the captain and thank him personally. Carter had shown himself to be honorable in a much deeper way than any of the opposition politicians Threed had dealt with in London. Most notably, he had used the *Fate's Winds* to dig irrigation canals on Judgment that would have helped the prisoners survive the brutal summer heat and still grow crops. Threed would follow a man like that, even if it meant death on a different planet at the hands of either the SSC, or the strange new alien threat. At least before he died he'll have gotten a second chance at life.

Reaching over, he took the hand of the tattooed woman next to him as the hatch opened.

"Are you ready for the next chapter, my dear?" he asked.

"As long as they have food," Jolina replied as they got up and stepped through the hatch together.

The town of Landfall was lit by solar bulbs twinkling above the drab buildings, and backlit by the blush of sunset. Threed had never seen Gertie before, and a combination of the cool wind and the sight of cartloads of food brought tears to his eyes.

"Is this heaven?" one of the other prisoners asked as he spilled off the ramp. A heavier man with long black hair answered as he strode toward them.

"Not quite, but it's a hell of a lot better than Judgment. I'm Hal Yellowknife. I'm the new administrator here."

Threed shook the man's hand, feeling the same roughness as his own palm borne from years of manual labor. Other prisoners tumbled off the ramp, kissing the ground and hugging each other. Sunburned, starving and blistered, many of the once-hard men and women fought back tears of their own as a tall farmer and his wife held out fresh fruits and vegetables.

Another passed out glasses of a clear liquor that made Threed's mouth water. Jolina pulled his arm, but Threed stood his ground, smiling.

"You go ahead, dear. I've got a whole list of stuff that I need to discuss with the administrator," he told her.

She laughed, and then trotted off to a folding table that was piled high with breads and cakes. He watched her for a moment, and then turned his attention back to Hal.

"The first thing on the list of course is restitution for illegal imprisonment. I suppose you know that a lot of us were railroaded, don't you?"

Hal's demeanor didn't change, which surprised Threed. The man seemed to have anticipated this, and possibly even considered what this transition would be like for the prisoners. Being considered a human being again was a welcome change from Tannin and his cruelty, but there was still a part of Threed that didn't trust everything that he had heard on Judgment, and on the orbiter.

"Now, I was told that a condition of you being allowed to come here was that you put the past in the past, otherwise the people here never would have agreed to this. To my knowledge, you agreed to those terms, did you know?" Hal said, meeting Threed's gaze unflinchingly.

Threed let his silence linger, studying the man who at first had seemed soft, but had clearly been hardened from his own experiences in the Swordbelt. Before the tension grew too large, another form stepped out of the shadows.

"I think you'll need to get to know Threed's sense of humor, Hal. He's not the sort of a man who's gonna let an angle go easily," Danny said as he stepped into the dim circle of light.

*   *   *

Atlas Carter paused on the edge of Landfall. He had directed the Bwain landing craft to come down south of the town so as not to scare the colonists during the party. There would be time enough for alien assimilations in the morning. In truth, he relished the chance for a moment of peace. It would be the first time he'd had any since he made his last drawing in his cabin on the *Fate's Winds*. As he trailed his hand through the dew-damp grass he felt a profound sense of peace settle over him. He could hear the music and celebration echoing from the administrator's compound, and all the voices raised in merriment. Danny had been right. The Swordbelt had been under so much stress for so long now, that tonight they were finally going to have a chance to just relax, and to start feeling human again.

The town's lights swelled in front of him. He turned down the main street, joining the clots of farmers that were trickling toward the bonfires and revelry in the square that surrounded the administrator's compound.

The crowd thickened as he reached the festival. There were a large variety of vegetable dishes, roast corn on the cob, fresh-baked breads, fried potatoes, and tangy salsas on display, in addition to the meat that had been harvested from the south continent's herds. Glasses full of Nightcrawler passed hands liberally, and Carter returned dozens of smiles from those who had been celebrating for hours. The colonists didn't know him by sight, but they recognized his uniform and put two and two together.

"Thank you, Captain!" they said to him as he wound his way through the party toward the administrative compound's steps. He smiled, shook their hands and returned their hugs as they pressed food into his hand and pounded him on the back.

"Thank you!"

"You saved us. We couldn't have done this without you."

"We wouldn't be here without you."

"I can't believe you made those Bwain listen to reason!"

Yet as he walked and smiled, keeping his face brave and stoic while a crowd built behind him, his worries returned. In a week's time, what would these people think of him?

In the administrative plaza Danny Xiao was busy talking to Threed while the former mayor of Judgment wolfed down vegetable wraps as quickly as they came off the grill. Threed's woman, Jolina, sat on the steps next to him, leaning against his thigh. There was an overturned bottle of Nightcrawler next to her, and a glassy look in her eyes. Hal Yellowknife stood beside them, laughing and joking with a group of farmers. The colonists were mixing with the prisoners, feeding them, laughing, and sharing in dances and music. For a moment, it was enough to make Carter forget the weight on his mind. Rather than joining those who he knew on the steps, Carter slipped to a shadowed section of courtyard to watch as the colony came together.

"You're gonna have to say hello to 'em eventually," a voice said nearby.

Startled, Carter turned and found Mephista hovering beside him. Her eyes shone in the firelight, and a smile broke across her face.

"How long have you been there?" he asked.

"I just arrived, but I saw a tall, dark, and handsome man slip out of the spotlight, so I thought I'd come over to investigate," she explained. In spite of himself, Carter smiled.

"You're wearing your uniform," he commented. Mephista had been committing acts of piracy on behalf of Tannin before Carter arrived in the system, and every time he'd seen her prior to this, she'd been wearing a black flight suit. Tonight she had dressed in her SSC blues

"Yeah, I am. I guess it just felt more appropriate, especially considering what's gonna happen."

Carter nodded, and then looked back out over the celebrating crowd. A fast-paced dance song was playing in the courtyard, and dancers were swirling around the fires. At the top of the steps, Carter could just make out a small solitary form. The single Bwain who'd been down on the planet was peeking around the stone wall and bobbing its head in time to the music.

"Do you think we can do this, Mephista? Do you really think anyone's gonna listen?"

The hoverchair inched closer to him, and her small hand slipped into his.

"I don't know what's gonna happen, Atlas. I never did to be perfectly honest, but I do know that everyone here, and everyone up in orbit, is gonna do their damnedest to make sure we get through this."

"That's not what I'm worried about," Carter said as a frown played at the corners of his mouth. The Bwain took a hesitant step into the light. One of the prisoners from Judgment saw it, scowled, and hurled a glass jar of Nightcrawler at the creature. The Bwain flashed yellow and ducked back into the shadows.

"You're worried you're gonna fail," Mephista commented.

He came to himself again, realized he was holding hands with another SSC officer against regulation, and gently pulled his hand from hers.

"I should go say hello," he said, his voice tinged with reluctance.

"Look...Atlas. We've both failed, and people have died because of those failures, but you taught me that those mistakes don't have to define us. Maybe...you know...you should just stop for a minute and listen to your own advice," Mephista said as he turned to join the revelers. He stopped and turned back around to look at her.

"Who's this Atlas guy you're talkin' about? He sounds pretty smart," Carter said with a grin.

"Oh he is. That's why I think you should take his advice to heart," she said, smiling gently back at him. He nodded at her, and then turned to join the others.

*   *   *

Later that evening, Mephista spotted him gazing out on the party from the third floor of the administrator's compound. Hal was making some kind of speech below, and the half-drunk crowd roared at every other line. Carter stood silhouetted against the blushed night, dark and brooding. She searched her heart for some way that she could help him. There was so much to do to prepare for what was coming, but sometimes even the smallest gestures could mean the most.

She raised her chair to his shoulder, joining him at the window. Hal was just finishing his speech, and then he dropped his hand and five streaks shot into the sky. Flowers of gunpowder popped into existence above them, leaving sparkling trails as they drifted to the ground.

"You know Atlas, sometimes we can almost forget we're alive. I don't wanna forget anymore," she noted as she pressed her lips to his cheek.

Chapter 8

The Tranquility

Weapons Ensign Bryon Purcell's first thought upon waking had been to get the *Fate's Winds'* laser operational because the Bwainhome was bearing down on them. He tried to tap out the diagnostic sequence on his holostation, but a gray blur had replaced his holocontrols, and his hands didn't seem to want to respond. Shapes blended in front of him, blurring through his hazed vision. Something had happened to the ship, but he didn't have time to figure out what it was. He needed to inform Captain Carter that he was down, and that someone would have to take over his weapons station. They needed to know that the starboard missile batteries were fifty percent depleted, that the forward magna cannon was down.

"I think he's awake," a familiar voice sounded in his ears.

Gradually, his senses returned, and he realized that he was laying down with a soft pillow cradling his head. He tried to move his arms once more, and found them restrained only by a clean white blanket.

"What happened?" Bryon tried to say, but all that came out of his throat was a dry gasp. He felt a tube against his lips that pushed down into his throat. Gagging, he shook his head back and forth to try and clear the obstruction. Suddenly, the tube was pulled out, scraping against the back of his throat before separating from his lips.

"Bryon, can you hear me?" the familiar voice asked again.

"The laser," he croaked. He felt incredibly drained. It took all of his strength to turn his head and focus on the source of the voice. Beside him was a blonde-and-white blur that gradually resolved to another crewman that was wearing the light green jumpsuit of a convalescent. The woman shifted nervously before him. Her dry hair cascaded down over her shoulders, and brown hollows circled her eyes. She'd had her hand on his head, but she pulled it away as he awoke.

"Julie?" he whispered.

"Welcome back, Bryon," she said with a relieved smile.

"You look good," he managed to croak through his dry lips. On the *Fate's Winds*, Julie had been starving herself with diet pills that Danny Xiao had smuggled for her from Earth. Yet here...wherever here was...she had filled out somewhat. She was a far cry from the heavier woman whom he'd first trained with for their assignment, but she also wasn't a brittle skeleton that could barely function.

Julie's eyes flicked away for a moment, but then returned to him.

"I'm all healed up already, but you took a lot longer," Julie said as she stepped back away from his bed to allow the doctor to examine him.

"Ensign Purcell, look at this light, please," a man's voice instructed. The doctor was circling a small laser pointer above Bryon's head, and he followed the light with his eyes. It hurt to move them, and he realized with a start that he had no idea what was going on.

"What happened?" he asked Julie. It was the doctor who answered his question however.

"You sustained a severe head trauma in the Bwain attack. A piece of debris struck your helmet with explosive force and caused intracranial bleeding. Honestly...you're damn lucky to be alive right now."

The light clicked off, and Bryon rubbed his sore eyes. Julie and the doctor helped him sit up, and he saw he was in a large med bay with twenty some-odd beds. The two nearest him looked slept in, but the rest were empty. As he was sitting up and started to get his bearings a little, a nurse came over to join the doctor and Julie by his bedside.

"You're on the *Tranquility*. The Bwainhome attacked us, and then Aric and Pandith got us off the *Fate's Winds*," Julie explained.

"The Bwain are still out there! I need to get to my station!" Bryon exclaimed. He threw off his blanket and tried to swing around to get out of the bed, but six hands reached out and held him in place.

"It's all right Bryon. We're safe now," Julie's said. He looked up at her, and as soon as he processed what she'd said, he relaxed and stopped struggling. His head was aching, and a whining had filled his ears. It felt as if his mind was not quite catching everything, and it seemed as though everything in the med bay was just a little brighter than it should be.

"I always knew we'd beat those damn lizards. God, I'm so tired," Bryon said as he adjusted himself back into a comfortable position. The nurse adjusted his pillow and straightened his blanket for him once he was settled.

"The best thing you can do right now is to rest, Mr. Purcell. You take whatever time you need to heal," the doctor said, eyeing him sternly. Clearly he intended his remarks to be taken as orders, rather than a mere suggestion.

Bryon nodded lazily, let out a heavy sigh, and then his eyes slowly started to close as he felt the need to sleep asserting itself once again. Just as he was about to succumb to it, his eyes opened wide once again, and he reached out to seize Julie's wrist.

"Wait, where's everyone else? Where's Danielle? Where's Aric?" Bryon asked in a panicked voice. He was almost afraid to hear the answers to his questions, but he knew he wouldn't be able to rest until he knew what had happened to the rest of his crewmates.

* * *

The next day Julie stayed beside Bryon as they floated through the *Tranquility*'s corridors. They had both gone through zero-G movement training in the SSC academy, but Bryon was still recovering his balance and coordination. She found herself frequently having to correct him, or hold on to his waist as they made their way through the big ship, pushing themselves from handrail to handrail. Not that she minded. She'd been the third of the *Fate's Winds'* crew to recover, but Granger had already left the med bay's artificial gravity, while Julie had been under doctor's orders to remain for observation. Danielle had been moody and sullen ever since her prosthesis therapy had started. Always shy, Julie had tried to make a point of engaging in conversation with the last few *Tranquility* crew members that were still recovering in the med bay, and they'd shared their stories about the obelisk, and the attacks by the First Ones. The mood on the ship was tense, and she'd had nothing to do but worry until Bryon woke up.

She'd had her differences with the cocky weapons officer on the *Fate's Winds*, part of which had to do with Bryon's romantic interest in Danielle. Julie had been insecure and bitter, the youngest member of the crew and unsure of both herself, and her ability to do her job. She'd learned from Captain Carter that as long as a person was strong and helped those around them, that anything was possible.

She still hoped that Bryon would notice her when she bumped against him as they glided through the corridors, but the tense nervousness that had gripped her on the *Fate's Winds* was gone. She felt more mature now, more herself, and what mattered to her was keeping her old crew together in spirit, no matter how far apart they grew. Danielle was on the *Tranquility's* bridge doing her training, while Danny was on Gertie helping the colony prepare for what was coming. Pandith and Granger were on the Bwainhome with Captain Carter, and if by some miracle Aric was still alive, he'd be the one who'd need her the most. Her job as communications officer was to keep everyone connected, and she wouldn't let Captain Carter, or the rest of her crewmates down in that task.

"I think I'm startin' to feel a little better," Bryon said.

Swinging his body so that his feet were pointed forward, Bryon pulled himself to a stop on the handrail. He squeezed his eyes shut for a moment to fight the headache that he'd been experiencing since he first woke up. When he opened his eyes once again, he noticed that Julie was giving him a concerned look, and seemed to be at a loss for how to help him. He offered her a reassuring smile, which seemed to relax her a little.

"Hey, don't worry. I'll be ready to make the beast with two backs in no time. Know anyone who might be interested?" he said playfully.

Blushing, Julie couldn't help but smile. Instead of responding though, she pressed her boot against his thigh and pushed away from him toward the bridge. It was good to see his humor returning. She didn't realize how much she had missed it, especially with so much tension on the ship.

"All right, I'll try to be professional, but I am brain damaged, remember? I might just have a little slip here and there," he called from behind her.

Julie nodded to the marines on guard outside the bridge. Captain Mephista had been kind enough to allow the *Fate's Winds'* officers crew to be given the run of the ship, and Julie wanted to stop by the bridge to apprise herself of the latest tactical situation. The airlock's double doors hissed open, and she and Bryon floated onto a command deck much larger than that of the *Fate's Winds*. At its front was a ten-meter-square holoscreen, with a bank of five weapons officers floating before it in the first row. Science and data officers flanked each side of the communications, engineering, and navigation stations. The *Tranquility's* crew wore their EVO suits with helmets tethered behind them, and they were hard at work studying scenarios and data simulations on their holoscreens.

"Looks like they're really busy. Maybe we should come back later," Julie suggested. She started to pull Bryon back toward the airlock with her, but suddenly they came to a halt as he grabbed ahold of a strut.

"Hey, there's Danielle! Let's go say hello," he said as he pushed on ahead without waiting for her.

The *Fate's Winds'* former navigation officer, Lt. Danielle Hoff, floated beside another lieutenant at one of the helm stations, her single boot lifted a few inches off the ground, while the other leg of her EVO suit hung slack. Julie had seen the wound and heard Danielle scream in pain. She knew that Danielle had thrown herself into training on the bridge to avoid having to face the fact that she'd lost a piece of herself. Danielle had shiny brown hair, perfectly balanced shoulders, strong cheeks, and a perked nose. She was beautiful in so many ways that Julie wasn't; and while a part of Julie wished that Bryon had taken more of an interest in her, she knew that Danielle and Bryon were a good match. They had certainly dated against regulations on the *Fate's Winds* before Captain Carter showed up, and she could see the interest in Bryon's eyes rekindled.

"Wait…Bryon," Julie called after him. "There's something you need to know about Danielle before you go talk to her. Something happened…"

"I can see that," he replied. When he reached the helm station, he pulled himself to a smiling stop.

"There's a little less of you to love, but I still think you look beautiful," he said as he approached her. He waited expectantly, hoping she would be excited that he was finally awake and out of the med bay.

Startled, Danielle glanced at Bryon for a brief moment before returning to her holoscreen.

"This isn't a good time, Bryon," she answered distractedly.

"Why's everyone in their combat gear? What's goin' on?" Bryon asked.

Danielle's screen was filled with flight solutions for leaving the Swordbelt. Nearly every one of them was earmarked for maximum induction thrust; but there were no other systems even remotely close to the Swordbelt. Where were they planning on going?

"Ensign Ford, Lieutenant Purcell!" a voice called from behind them. It was Lieutenant Thomas, the duty officer in command of the bridge's second watch. Thomas was an older, no-nonsense career officer, and in the brief time she had known him, Julie had envied his confident, professional attitude.

"Sir!" Julie and Bryon echoed in unison as they snapped to attention.

"We are on high alert. Please return to the medical bay until you're ready to resume your duties.”

“I’m fit as a fiddle, Lieutenant. Why am I seeing combat scenarios for SSC ships? I thought you weren’t pirates anymore,” Bryon asked, not realizing his mistake until he saw the look on the lieutenant’s face.

Thomas’ eyes flared. The words that followed were stiff with the strained tension Julie had felt all over the ship ever since they had learned that the SSC navy was on its way from Earth and might be hostile. At least they still had nearly a week to prepare.

“Mr. Purcell, I understand that you’ve recently experienced a head injury, so I’m going to allow you some slack this one time. You may request a briefing when our doctors declare you fit to resume your duties. Until then, please exit my bridge.”

Julie could feel Bryon stiffen beside her. The weapons officer was a natural fit for his job, quick-tempered and always up for a fight.

“Bryon, I’ll visit you later. I promise. Now please go. We’re in a rough spot right now,” Danielle said over her shoulder.

“Of course...sirs. My apologies for my behavior. I must have been...,” Bryon started to say, but he clamped his mouth shut when he noticed one of the officers whirl rapidly to address the bridge’s officer in command.

“Lieutenant!” the navigation officer beside Danielle called. “I’m showing multiple Alcubierre signatures. Two...no...three ships coming into the system.”

“Where? What class?” Thomas demanded.

“Ten thousand kilometers behind us. Coordinates 46-dot-234-dot-90,” he reported. Another nav officer called out right after.

“Sir, the class of the ships is unknown. They appear to be heavily modified SSC cruisers.”

"What the hell? They shouldn't have been able to get here for at least another six days. Sound battle stations!" the lieutenant ordered, and the bridge suddenly exploded into a flurry of activity. Warning horns sounded, and the bridge's lights flashed red.

"Bryon, we should go," Julie urged, but once again he held firm to a railing.

"We can't do any good down in medical, Julie. Those are light cruisers, but they look like they've got a second Alcubierre drive in the back. That means they can probably take us home. They've probably got antimatter. Why are we at battle stations?" Bryon asked as he struggled to grasp what was going on around him.

"Seven signatures, sir!" a weapons officer called.

On the main holoscreen, a view of Gertie materialized, showing the cruisers appearing in a circle around the planet. The *Tranquility* was orbiting near the equator, and the vessels had arrived in perfect position in a ring behind it that was spread just wide enough to prevent Thomas from engaging the vessels simultaneously.

"Broadcast the Captain's message. Inform Gertie and the Bwainhome," Thomas barked out orders like the seasoned officer he was – calm, efficient, and no nonsense.

"Julie, I never thought I'd say this, but we're goin' home!" Bryon said. His grip tightened on her arm, and he was smiling as broadly as he had since he had awakened.

"No Bryon, we're not. I'm sorry, but things have changed," Julie answered as they edged away from the stations on the bridge to grasp the railing.

* * *

Gertie

Mephista woke to a battering on her door at the same time her cochlear implant buzzed with a flood of incoming messages. Gertie's dawn was just breaking through the window of the small room that Carter had found for her in the administrator's quarters, and for a moment she was disoriented. She wasn't used to gravity, or to pulling herself hand-over-hand out of bed. It took a few moments, but the words coming through her implant finally started to sink in.

"We're under attack. Somehow the SSC figured out a way to arrive earlier than expected. We're responding as appropriate, and will keep you informed," Lieutenant Thomas reported.

The pounding on her door shook the frame until she thought the door would give out. She had to find her blouse before answering, and she had to get herself back on her hoverchair. The priority now was to get out of there as soon as possible, so she could get back to the shuttle pad and return to her ship.

The door bleated as its override command engaged, and Carter suddenly burst through it with an intense look of concern on his face.

"Mephista, the SSC is here. They're attacking... Oh, sorry...," he said, suddenly rather embarrassed that he'd walked in on her in a state of partial nudity. She clutched the sheets to her chest as he spun around to face the hallway.

Her blouse was at the foot of the bed. She quickly grabbed it and slipped the garment over herself, sealed its seam, and then rolled toward where she had left her hoverchair at the side of the bed.

"Lieutenant Thomas just informed me. I need to get to my ship," she said as she was about to pass him in her hoverchair.

"You can't," he replied.

"Don't tell me what I can't do!"

"Mephista, there are seven ships up there going up against the *Tranquility*.

You'd be vaporized before you could get anywhere close."

Snarling, Mephista wrenched her hoverchair around and knocked into Carter's thighs.

"I'm not gonna be marooned down here while my people are up there dying!" she said with a combination of frustration and anger.

"Well, we are marooned, at least for the moment. We just have to trust that we've trained our people well. It's the only thing we can do," Carter reasoned. She gave him a dirty look and tried to turn her hover chair back toward the door, but he quickly stepped in front of her and put his hands on her shoulders as he leaned forward and looked deep into her eyes.

"Atlas, don't do this. I have to," she said, but he stopped her before she could finish.

"Look, I could let you go, and if those SSC ships vaporize the Tranquility, then you'll have died with your crew, but there's nothing noble or honorable about looking for your own death. Believe me, when I came to this system, I wanted nothing more than to die, but I found a reason to live. More than one reason actually, so I'm not gonna let you throw your life away over some romantic notion of going down with your ship. We have to trust our people now, and just hope for the best."

"But...," she started to say, but then she saw the look in his eyes and knew that he was right. A pointless death served no purpose, and as long as she was alive, at least she could spend the rest of her days finding a way to avenge them. Finally, she let out a heavy sigh and relented to his logic.

"Fine. We'll do what we can to direct things from down here," she said as she turned her hoverchair and eased it back over toward the bed.

"And that's why you're a good captain," he said. "You're able to see reason and make sound decisions, even when it goes against your instincts."

"If I was a good captain, I'd be up there on my ship right now," she said with a frown.

*   *   *

The Tranquility

"You have been declared in willful violation of your orders. You will surrender immediately or be engaged," the transmission from the lead SSC vessel barked.

"You don't understand. The situation is much more complicated than you've heard," Lieutenant Thomas responded.

"Then surrender and submit to boarding."

"What guarantee do I have that you'll listen and not just take us all prisoners?"

"None."

Danielle's heart sank. Thomas was a good officer, and she could see the conflicting emotions on his face. He didn't want hostilities, but the SSC captain was purposely giving him little choice.

"I need to put you in touch with my captain," Thomas transmitted in reply.

"You have 15 seconds to comply."

"They've gone weapons hot!" one of the weapons officers called.

"Captain Mephista, please advise," the lieutenant called over his implant. He cocked his head, and then nodded at the incoming response.

"Comms, put this on speaker."

"*Tranquility* crew, this is Captain Mephista. It's clear to me that the SSC does not want our surrender. They'd rather pursue a righteous crusade than listen to our side of the story, and that's what we're fighting against. We're fighting for truth and brotherhood, even with creatures that, frankly, I wouldn't have thought twice about spacing just a few days ago. Know that you've trained for this moment, that you will do the right thing, and that history will remember you."

"Now, Mr. Thomas, please put me through to the SSC."

"Yes, ma'am," the lieutenant acknowledged.

"This is Captain Mephista. Who am I speaking with?"

"Captain Agricourt of the SSC *Brittany*. Captain, I must tell you that we recognize the *Tranquility* as a pirate vessel, and…," he said, but Mephista interrupted him before he could continue.

"You see our lines, and you know what we are. We're human, just like you. We don't want hostilities here Captain. We just want to explain ourselves. If you won't allow that, then we cannot allow tyranny."

"My apologies then. Farewell Captain," Agricourt sneered.

"I have missiles inbound!" one of the weapons officers called.

"Evasive maneuvers!"

Danielle triggered her boot magnet to lock her to the deck as the *Tranquility* jerked and lurched. Officially, she had only been on the bridge to begin her training on the cruiser's navigation systems. She had no duties in the battle and could only watch as the engagement played out.

"Why are they shooting at us? They're not even listening," Danielle heard Byron say behind her.

"Countermeasures deployed!"

"Bring us up to the north pole," Thomas ordered.

Isai, the navigation officer who'd been training Danielle, computed signatures in a blur of flashing fingers with his implanted nav computer connection.

"Captain, we don't have a clear path. They've got us surrounded."

"Dammit! How could they have come in hostile like this, and how the hell could they have gotten here so fast?" Mephista said angrily, her voice tinged with exasperation as her mind raced through the possibilities.

Danielle didn't know the answer either. The ships must have been a new experimental model or something. As for the hostilities, that she knew well. She had met Phuri and Tannin enough times to understand exactly the type of lying scum they were. She had no doubt that they'd whipped up the SSC's natural fear of the Bwain to an absolute frenzy back on Earth.

"We've got missile and laser fire from all cruisers incoming," a weapons officer called.

On the holoscreen, red streaks crept toward the *Tranquility*. The ship was maneuvering crazily, trying to pull Danielle away from her anchored boot in every direction. At first she thought the accelerations were simply random, but then she saw that Isai had developed an inspired solution. He was trying to pull close enough to one of the attacking ships that the *Tranquility* could use that ship as a shield. It was a tactic she'd read about when dealing with superior numbers, and it might have even worked against the Bwain, but the SSC's crews had received the same training. Their firing solutions would calculate all possible course destinations and be prepared to adjust at a moment's notice. It was only a matter of time until the streaks on the holoimage connected with the *Tranquility's* hull. When they did, the results would be devastating.

The massive ship groaned and shuddered underneath her boot heel.

"Multiple impacts aft, sir."

"Dammit, return fire. Target Agricourt's cruiser and give him everything we've got. He'll have to listen to that," Thomas ordered.

"Firing," the weapons officers called.

"Captain, we've got damage in engineering. We've lost induction thruster banks four through six," called another officer.

On the holoscreen, the *Tranquility*'s lasers and missiles lanced out above Gertie's surface. The way the SSC vessels had entered the system allowed them to use the curvature of the planet as a defense, and Agricourt's ship needed only to make a small acceleration in order for the line-of-sight weapons to hurtle harmlessly into space. The *Tranquility*'s missiles blossomed a half-second later, shredded by the other ship's near-field defenses.

"Additional missiles incoming, sir. I count one-hundred and twenty-seven."

"It isn't gonna work," Danielle whispered.

Agricourt's tactics were foolproof. His ships could launch hundreds of missiles while staying far enough from the *Tranquility* to give the SSC ships plenty of time to launch their countermeasures and keep out of the line-of-sight field of fire for the lasers. One ship could never outlast seven. There was just no chance.

"Helm, get us away from the planet as fast as possible. Set a course for Judgment. Target all weapons behind," Thomas ordered.

"Countermeasures have been breached aft, sir! Prepare for impact!" a weapons officer called.

The ship lurched again as Isai tried desperately to twist it out of the way of the approaching missiles; but several had already broken through the sleet of chaff and projectiles that protected the ship, and all Danielle could do was watch as they struck the hull.

"Strike three-quarters aft, sir," an officer reported. "I've lost contact with engineering.”

“We’re down to forty-five percent thrusters, Lieutenant!”

“Damn it! Comms, open a channel to Agricourt,” Thomas barked.

“This is Lieutenant Thomas, acting captain in command of the *Tranquility*. You are firing on an SSC vessel, and we request you cease hostilities immediately. We are not...”

“You had your chance to surrender, Lieutenant. Traitors don’t get to dictate the terms,” a voice responded harshly.

“Wait...what’s that?” the same voice exclaimed, now colored with alarm.

“Multiple unknown signatures entering orbit, sir!” Isai cried.

“What are those?” Spar asked.

Danielle’s fingers flashed, matching the data from the flickering black shapes that suddenly appeared to swoop in and out of range of the SSC fleet.

“I’ve seen them before. The Bwain are coming to our rescue!” Danielle said, barely believing the images that were flashing across her screen.

*   *   *

The Bwainhome

Pandith’s primary duty on board the *Fate’s Winds* had been to help and preserve life. He had never led a ship into battle before. He would have preferred to have Granger doing this, but the science officer was somewhere within the bowels of the ship, and the Bwain couldn’t seem to locate him, so when the SSC navy showed up days earlier than expected, he had no choice but to convince the Bwain to attack.

“You’re doin’ well, Pandith,” one of the aliens on the bridge squawked out, echoing Captain Carter's words of encouragement from Gertie.

"Kill all!" one of the other creatures cried.

"No! No, we're trying to make them run away," Pandith thought to them all through the Bwainsong.

"Kill all! Take ships!"

"I'll work on that Pandith. You just feed me anything else I need to know," Carter instructed.

"Yes, Captain," Pandith acknowledged.

In reality, there was little he could do. Pandith had fashioned a rudimentary holoscreen on the bridge, but without a network of instruments to feed into it, it was more or less useless. Where Captain Carter was able to tap into whatever mental inputs the Bwain used to control their ship, Pandith was effectively blind. He could only stare into the distance as brief flashes and razor strikes marked the progress of the battle.

"What's happening?" he asked.

The creatures had little knowledge of the human command or reporting structure. It was irrelevant when they could tap into each other's thoughts, so they seemed to forget this fact more often than they remembered. Perhaps at a nudge from Carter, one of the aliens turned to Pandith and stilled.

"Bwain attack bad ships. Bad ships cannot see Bwain. Bwain good fighters. Bwain win."

"We're winning? The human ships are leaving?" Pandith asked.

The alien cocked its head.

"No. Bwain win."

Pandith shook his head, frustrated. Subtleties of meaning were lost on the creatures as well, which reinforced Captain Carter's belief that their intelligence had been artificially forced by the Endless Knot, rather than evolving as humanity's had.

"What about the *Tranquility*? Is it all right?" Pandith asked, trying to keep the frustration out of his voice.

"Other ship hurt. Fire. Slow down. Other ship weak, but Bwain strong!"

"I know you're strong. I know you're fighting. But what is *happening*, for the love of Vishnu? One of you please tell me!" Pandith pleaded.

* * *

Gertie

Captain Carter felt his mind fracture into hundreds of pieces as he tried to keep track of each of the individual Bwain in their intradimensional fighters as they battered the SSC ships. The fighters were so small that the big vessels couldn't track them. Even though Agricourt employed his missile countermeasures, the fighters could slip into their cloaked status and avoid any physical projectiles that they encountered.

The Bwain's battle lust swelled within him. He felt their anger and frustration pouring through him as their pilots mashed the controls to send their lasers, projectiles, and plasma weapons out like screams in the darkness. These ships shouldn't be here. These ships should be theirs. They weren't slaves, they were fighters, warriors. They had beaten the First Ones. They could own the universe!

"No, we do not want to kill. We want to scare," Carter willed with his mind.

"Kill! All must die. We are Bwain."

"You are more than that. You must understand the bigger picture. If these ships die, I will have killed my own kind."

"Not our kind."

"We're the same. We're helping you," Carter focused his thoughts through the Bwainsong.

"Not the same."

He was trying to hold together too much. Pandith's questions needed answers, while at the same time he was trying to update Mephista, help Granger get to the Bwainhome's bridge, and keep track of the fighters.

For a moment, the Bwainsong swept him up and he felt his own identity fading. That moment was all that the Bwain needed.

Their fighters swarmed over one SSC ship after another, battering the vessels and cutting them apart. There were thousands of fighters, and though some listened to Carter, most had slipped from his control. He felt their elation as ship after ship broke apart, engulfed in spark and flame.

Then suddenly the human ships were gone, leaving only the *Tranquility*. The navy had retreated back to Earth using their Alcubierre drives. Carter had won.

"We kill!" the Bwain echoed in victory as their fighters turned toward the *Tranquility*.

"NO!" Carter screamed into the Bwainsong. *"ONLY I KILL!"*

He reached deep within himself, leaving the fighter pilots' minds and harnessing the Knot itself, gathering every consciousness to him and repeating one word over and over again. *"Save."*

The fighters slowed, and then turned. They shut off power to their weapons and glided back toward the Bwainhome. The effort it took to pull of that level of control was almost too much for him, and Carter suddenly collapsed into Mephista's arms.

"Atlas, what is it? What happened? Did the *Tranquility* survive?" Mephista asked. She was concerned about his exhaustion from the stress he had endured while communicating through the Bwainsong, but her first thought was of her ship and its crew.

Carter took a deep breath, remembering the massive damage the SSC had sustained.

"The *Tranquility's* damaged, but it's ok. As for the SSC ships, what the Bwain didn't destroy, they drove off. Thing is, the navy's gonna come back here looking for blood, and they're not gonna be in any mood to listen to reason."

"Then somehow we're gonna have to be ready for 'em when they do," she said as she placed her hand on his cheek and looked into his eyes.

"We'll figure something out. We have to. We have no choice," Carter said.

Chapter 9

Gertie

"It doesn't change anything," Carter said. Even as he uttered the words, he could see in the faces of the others the same doubt he had felt ever since letting the Bwain slip from his control. Gertie's wind was cold this day, but they had chosen to meet outside near the shuttle pads, away from any of the other administrative staff who would hear their concerns.

"Captain, the navy's coming back. The only questions are when, and how many of them," Danny added.

Hal frowned as he mentally reviewed production levels. "We're not ready "I'm pushing the factories as hard as I can, but it still takes time."

"The trainees have a few flights under their belt. Some of them will have a chance," Danny noted.

A Bwain shuffled next to Carter and scratched at his sleeve. The creatures seemed apologetic after he had forced them back to protect the *Tranquility*. It was a comforting gesture, but Carter had still seen what they were truly capable of.

"Go ahead," Carter acknowledged the Bwain's presence as an indication of an incoming message to be relayed from one of his crew.

"This is Pandith, Captain. Granger's not having much luck on the Bwainhome. I'd say more, but it's hard to communicate this way. It can wait until you're back aboard."

"Thank you, Mr. Pandith," Carter acknowledged, and then he nodded to the Bwain, and it scuttled off toward one of its race's landing craft. Dozens of them soared above Gertie's rolling plains, but no aliens were disembarking just yet. They thought Carter was punishing them, and in a way he was, but there was a much larger question in his mind about where any of them would end up if the First Ones couldn't be stopped. There was one member of the group he was particularly concerned about though.

Mephista had let her hoverchair drift to the edge of the tarmac, still within earshot, but from where she was she could at the grass covered hills.

"What's the status of the *Tranquility*?" Carter asked.

"Forty more crewmen dead. Out of an original compliment of two-hundred and fifty, we've got less than half of that left. Main engine room is destroyed, but she has a backup. The ship can still fight, but her countermeasures are mostly depleted, and she'll be slow as hell until we can get the repairs taken care of," Lieutenant Thomas reported from the Tranquility's bridge.

"At least they're still alive," Carter said, turning his attention to Mephista. He was trying to find something positive for them both to hold onto in a situation where very little was very little to be positive about.

"Does it even matter? The next time the SSC comes, are they gonna do anything different?" she asked, her voice betraying her deep sorrow at the loss of more of the lives of her crew members.

"They might. We just have to find some way to get Sol to listen to us," Carter said as he reached out to touch her arm, hoping it would let her know he felt her anguish. Suddenly he thought better of it, and clenched his fists in frustration.

"Atlas, I came here because Sol didn't listen, and my crew followed because they believed in me. Now half of them are dust for nebula, and the others are all expecting to join 'em at some point soon. So what am I supposed to tell 'em? Am I supposed to tell 'em that the aliens are gonna fix everything? That the navy will turn around and forget about us? Tell me what I'm supposed to say, because for once I'm at a total loss here."

Her chest was heaving in rage, and her hoverchair bobbed back and forth under the force of her gestures. Carter let her go until she got it all out.

He'd long ago learned that a berserk puncher in the ring could only sustain his high level of effort for a few minutes. It was always best to maneuver his opponents around, and let them wind themselves down before engaging with them.

"Well...I supposed you could tell 'em that we aren't all a bunch of screw-ups and misfits out here. That we could build something incredible if we had the chance," Hal chimed in.

"You can also tell 'em that it's our job to make each loss mean something," Danny added sincerely.

The wind pulled Mephista's hair back from her neck, revealing scars on her back from the surgeries that had been performed in an attempt to restore her spine.

"I came to this system looking for a fight, and I found one in you. I thought I wanted to die when I got aboard the Bwainhome, and now...," Carter said, but then he fell silent. He knew Mephista understood where he was headed with this line of conversation, and he was almost relieved when she cut him off midsentence. He didn't really want to get into it again with all the others listening to his every word.

"Now you think we can reason with a government that already abandoned me once, and that's now trying to exterminate us? You're insane!"

"That's not what I think at all. I think that the only chance we have of fighting the First Ones is to get a whole lot more people on our side. Bwain, human, or some three-legged spider with twelve eyeballs from Alpha Centauri. I'll take anything I can get. In order to do that though, we have to show Sol that they're wrong about us out here. We have to make them understand that they're facing something far worse than the Bwain ever thought of being. You were a pirate when I first met you, but now you've changed. We've all changed, and no one more so than me. Would you rather die without setting the truth straight, or die having done your best to at least try?"

Her hair curled around her head like funeral streamers, and tears glistened in her eyes.

"I'm tired of this, Atlas. It's too hard. There are times when...," she said, but then she paused for a moment, trying to reign in her emotions.

"When what?" he asked.

"When I just want it to end," she finished. Carter took her in her arms and held her in silence for a few moments.

"Remember how Kaylee fought?" he asked. "She refused to give up, and she found a way."

"That's what we do out here. We find a way," Hal commented.

The four of them stood silently in a cluster on the tarmac, each trying to find some way they could manage to survive the impossible odds against them. Mephista wiped the back of her hand across her eyes, as if to erase any suggestion she might have been tempted to give in to despair. A sudden sense of resolve filled her, and as she met the eyes of the others, she nodded at them all solemnly.

"Well, gentlemen, it appears we've got work to do. We'd better get to it before it's too late," she said. Carter smiled at her, but she didn't return his smile. She just didn't have it in her at the moment.

*   *   *

Earth

Capra Falconi shifted uneasily. Ever since he had returned to Earth with Phuri, he'd been placed on special assignment, which meant he had remained in his small Cape Canaveral apartment just off the SSC spaceport waiting for orders, until the inactivity grew unbearable. Usually when he was back on Earth, he spent his days on the beach letting the ocean lap his feet while he stared up into the beautiful blue sky overhead, but this time he couldn't escape the feeling that something seemed different, or even wrong somehow, and this feeling was causing him an increasing level of concern.

On the *Mosquito*, Phuri had been mostly silent and brooding. Where before Tannin's assistant had been happy to discuss all the latest news, he had barely spoken on the trip back to Earth. The only thing he seemed to want to talk about was politics. Things like what President Kidewange was doing about the economic prosperity of the outer planets, and who had run against him in the last election. They were topics that Capra found odd, especially given what had just happened on Gertie, and yet when Capra had tried to press Phuri for more information, the man just shut down completely.

He hadn't thought anything of it at the time. After all, he had survived a trip with the taciturn Captain Carter, but then less than a day after he had landed, he'd received word that his messenger's rating had been suspended. There was no word of explanation from the dispatch office, or from his superior, and Phuri hadn't returned his messages. He had simply been filed away, as if he'd done something wrong by rescuing Phuri. He just couldn't understand what had happened, which made it all the harder to swallow.

Capra had always been a trusting sort, and a part of him wanted to believe that there was a good explanation for it, but now that he was standing at attention in Admiral Nico's office with nervous sweat dampening his armpits, he was downright scared of what he was hearing.

"Captain Agricourt to see you, sir," the intercom chimed.

Nico's heavy fist dropped on the response button. The man had said little in the two minutes since Capra had entered and found Phuri present in the room as well. Rather than let the questions that had been building in him spill out, Capra snapped to attention in an attempt to show his disciplined precision to a man so many levels his superior. Nico had been glaring at Phuri the whole time without even acknowledging Capra's existence, leaving the messenger in a perplexed limbo. Some silent battle of wills hung in the air between the two men, while he could only stand there as a spectator in the whole thing.

"Bring him in," Nico growled.

The door opened, and a man about Capra's height with a tight bandage wrapped around the side of his face and covering his left eye entered. Agricourt grimaced as he snapped to attention, clearly in pain, and the blade of his palm fluttered against his forehead. In a way, Agricourt's failure at Gertie would take the pressure off Capra. Capra just needed to get through this meeting, and then he could ask Phuri his questions about his assignment afterward.

As with Capra, Nico kept Agricourt at attention. Instead of remaining behind his heavy wooden desk however, he rose and stomped toward Agricourt as if he would punch the wounded captain in the nose. Nico halted just inches from Agricourt's shaking hand, a sly smile spreading over his face.

"You were wounded?" Nico asked.

"Yes, sir."

"I've asked that you receive the solar flare in recognition of your sacrifice. It is my pleasure to personally pin it to your uniform," Admiral Nico said, though he seemed anything but pleased.

Nico unveiled the small starburst pin that marked a member of the SSC who had been wounded in battle. He unsnapped the clasp, then drove his palm forward and pierced Agricourt's chest. The captain gasped but remained at attention as a drop of blood spilled down the vest of his uniform blues.

"How many of our classified, fast ships did you lose?" Nico snarled.

"Four, sir."

"Against how many?"

"As I indicated in my report, our intelligence was inaccurate. I cannot report with confidence how many Bwain ships are active in the Swordbelt.

The only ship we could positively identify was the *Tranquility*."

"And you withdrew without destroying it."

"I thought it prudent to save lives and return with my report, sir."

"You knew Carter was allied with the Bwain. You knew you'd be facing a potentially mutinous cruiser, and an alien force of unknown strength."

"The Bwain appear to have some sort of stealth technology, Admiral. Our weapons systems were ineffective against them. You'll find details in my science team's report."

"I won't be reading your report, Captain."

Nico dropped his hand, revealing that the bloody streak now extended halfway down Agricourt's chest.

Capra held his breath, locking his eyes on the picture of a Britain-class megacruiser silhouetted against Saturn that Nico had mounted on his office's far wall. This was Nico's flagship, *Gravity's Hammer*, and the man who had been granted command of a ship like that was not one to be trifled with. While he somewhat sympathized with Captain Agricourt's predicament, he was relieved that, at least for now, he was not the object of the admiral's wrath.

"I DID NOT GIVE YOU PERMISSION TO REMOVE THAT INSIGINIA, CAPTAIN!" Nico screamed as Agricourt began to remove the medal. "YOUR MISSION WAS A COMPLETE FAILURE, AND I HAVE LEARNED NEXT TO NOTHING FROM READING YOUR REPORT!"

"My apologies, sir," Agricourt said as he dropped his hand and returned to an expressionless attention.

"Captain Agricourt, you are relieved of your command effective immediately. You will be scheduled for reassignment when I figure out what to do with you. Now *get out of my sight*."

Unbelievably, Agricourt remained in place. Capra longed to wipe the sweat from his forehead as he stood there fighting against the gathering fatigue in his knees and his crawling empathy for what Agricourt was going through. Nico was being completely unreasonable. He was destroying a man's career because he had been faced with a superior enemy. In his brief time with the admiral, it had already become abundantly clear that there was no use in facing off against him.

"Replacing me won't work, Admiral," Agricourt said dully. He was still at attention, and the blood had started to congeal on his uniform.

Instead of screaming as Capra expected, Nico stilled. He seemed to condense into a hard piece of motionless coal.

"Are you questioning my orders, Captain?"

"No sir. I simply would like to outline the circumstances. An SSC officer, possibly two, is in league with aliens who possess superior technology. We have no way of understanding their force dispositions, their intentions, or their tactics. They didn't fight like the Bwain. Even though we surprised them, they responded with well-coordinated tactics. Regardless of how you feel about Carter's politics, he's a damn good military commander."

Nico's nostrils flared, and a muscle above his thick eyebrow quivered involuntarily.

"Atlas Carter was a traitor to the human race before he ever left Earth. I'll never give a man like that the benefit of respect. And as for you, he reduced you to an absolute failure. Now get the hell out of my office!"

Agricourt saluted a final time, spun on his heel, and left Nico's chambers.

"You see the danger," Phuri noted craftily when the door had closed.

"I see incompetence."

"It's not that," Phuri replied. "Carter cannot be discounted. Tannin tried the same thing, and look what happened."

Nico's glare pivoted to Phuri. Again, Capra felt something pass between the two men. What was the point of bringing up Tannin?

"I'm not your disgraced, bush-planet senator. You'd do well to remember that," Nico growled.

Phuri's face blanked in calculation. His body still painfully tensed, Capra wondered if there hadn't been more to Phuri than had met the eye. He seemed in some way to be a power broker. What exactly was going on around him?

"So what do you recommend, Admiral?" Phuri asked.

Instead of answering, Nico turned his broad back on Phuri, and headed toward the door that led to his inner office.

"This isn't the end of things," Phuri called after him.

"No, it's not. Lucky for you, I plan for failure as well as success," Nico retorted as he held open the door.

Another officer entered from Nico's office. This man was lean to the point of ill health, his eyes intelligent and probing, and his hair cut severely short.

"You heard your predecessor's excuses, Captain Decival?" Nico asked.

"Every word, Admiral."

"Mr. Vongsa here would like to know your plan. He's afraid of this Carter, simply because his former boss got outsmarted."

"I suggest massive force, Admiral. We have no way of knowing if Carter still has faster-than-light capability, or how many ships he has at his disposal. We've also lost the element of surprise. I suggest we strike as hard as possible with as many ships as possible," Decival answered without hesitation.

"When can you launch?" Phuri asked.

Decival's long neck twisted toward where Phuri sat. His eyes flicked to Nico, asking another silent question.

"He is aware. In fact, you might say that what's happening is because of Phuri here," Nico acknowledged. Decival nodded.

"The battle group is awaiting orders. We can launch whenever it proves…politically expedient."

Nico's smile was like a bear leering with a full stomach.

"You see, Phuri, why I believe Captain Decival will be our ideal instrument?"

"I do," Phuri replied. The small upturn at the corners of his lips seemed to indicate an attempt at forcing a smile, but there was no mirth in his eyes, only sly contemplation.

"But, Captain, I have just one question. What Agricourt reported has merit. We have a severe intelligence gap on our hands. How would you recommend dealing with the situation?"

For the first time, Nico's eyes pivoted toward where Capra stood in a sweaty mess of tension.

"Oh, I think I can come up with a way to tilt the balance in our favor," the admiral said, smiling disconcertingly.

*　*　*

Nico was ordering Capra to commit suicide. Of course, the admiral had tried to paper over that fact by telling him he needed only to stay in the Swordbelt long enough to conduct a deep scan of the system. A deep scan would take hours, and while it was active his ship would be very easy to find in the vastness of the Swordbelt. From what he had seen in Nico's office, Capra knew that if he made the jump back to Earth without performing the full scan, it would be the last time he ever set foot on an SSC craft.

He strolled along the shoreline while the salt breeze pulled at his hair, letting his heels sink into the sand while he tried to process everything he'd learned.

The Captain Carter whom he'd taken to the Swordbelt had been closed off, and hurt in some way he hadn't wanted to discuss, but he hadn't seemed like a traitor. If anything, he'd seemed far more dedicated to protecting the colony than Tannin ever had, or Phuri for that matter. Tannin's former aide had sworn Capra to secrecy about his upcoming mission, which was redundant, given the oath that all messengers take to preserve the sanctity of the SSC's communications. Wouldn't the SSC want to know as much as possible about his mission? Shouldn't there be warnings spreading through all of human-occupied space?

Capra stopped where a hermit crab had washed up on shore. The creature lay half-buried in the sand, a relic of a former age slowly eroding into nothingness. It gave off the faint odor of rot, and Capra wrinkled his nose.

Something was wrong with the whole operation, but he just couldn't quite put his finger on what it was. Tomorrow, when he lifted off in the *Mosquito*, it might bring him a bit closer to the truth, but it might also be for the last time.

*   *   *

Later, when Capra returned to his apartment, he was slightly drunk. At first he didn't see the two shapes waiting in the shadow of a copse of palm trees. The hands that reached out to guide him away from the building's entrance seemed disembodied, and he concerned himself mostly with not stumbling on the breakwater's rocks, until the two figures stopped him.

He squinted, swaying. He could have tried to get away, but a part of him almost wanted to be hospitalized to avoid tomorrow's flight. He resolved to fight whoever had come for him. He was going to put up such a fight that they'd have to bludgeon him to put him down. When he started swinging however, one of the figures slipped behind him and froze him with a headlock he couldn't escape.

"Who are you?" he slurred.

In the sliver of light that cut through the trees, he saw a green eye and a dash of raven hair.

"My name's Lana. We spoke on the phone," the woman said.

"And we met earlier today. If I let you go, will you promise to hear us out?" added the man who held Capra in his grip.

"Yeah, ok," he choked out.

The pressure against his shoulders and neck relaxed. Capra stepped forward and turned, stumbling as he tried to snap to attention.

"Ensign Capra Falconi reporting for duty, Captain," he slurred to Agricourt, with a limp salute.

"You may change your mind about that once you hear what we need to tell you," Agricourt replied. Capra looked at him nervously, swaying in time to the palm trees while he tried to decide if he wanted to run or not.

*   *   *

Gertie

The dark, human-shaped object was still steaming when Hal lifted it with his thermo gloves and pulled it onto the hovercart he had brought with him to printing factory number 12. The factory's interior smelled of a caustic mix of high temperatures, metal, plastics, and carbon. Once he was back out in the cool, fresh air of the outside, he slipped off his respirator and took a deep breath. It was getting toward sunset, and the assistants he had rounded up were tromping through his factories checking on production.

Captain Carter himself stood in a ring that included Danny Xiao, Mephista, the Bwain they referred to as The Voice, Threed, and a few other farmers. The shape on the hovercart before them spilled vapor into the evening as Hal checked the seals and fittings.

"It's not top of the line, but it'll work," Hal noted.

Threed bent close to examine the EVO suit before him. The hardscrabble mayor of a former penal colony seemed downright nervous.

"It doesn't look like the ones we've been training in," Threed commented nervously.

"Don't worry, they'll fly exactly the same. I can't give you any nanos, but you've got nearly everything else you need."

"Nearly?" Threed asked.

"Well I can't give you luck, and you're gonna be needin' a hell of a lot of it," Hal answered.

Threed smiled as he lifted the suit's pants and stepped inside.

"I still think it would be easier to just build ourselves more ships," he said.

"It's a matter of available materials. The nanobots and my terminal can build anything mankind has ever created. We've got every template in our databanks. The issue is building the smaller components that make bigger things, and finding the components necessary. For example, I can't make plasma for you. I can't make antimatter, or anything nuclear. Gertie doesn't have those elements."

"But you *can* repair a cruiser?" Carter asked.

"We're doin' everything we can for the *Tranquility*. Some of Threed's boys have even been doin' the piloting runs for your spare parts."

"Hal, we can't thank you enough. Everything you've done here for us is giving us a chance we wouldn't have had otherwise," Mephista said with sincerity.

Instead of answering, Hal looked at Threed as he stepped into the prototype EVO suit. The man winced where the hot components brushed against his skin, but when he sealed its chest and brought the helmet down over his head, the suit's indicators flashed green.

Threed's lips moved, but no one could hear him outside of the suit. Hal smiled in relief. A part of him talked a good game, but he had never been sure if his nanos could manufacture an entire complex, finished product in one run. When Hal motioned that Threed needed to pull off the helmet to be heard, the former prisoner was grinning as well.

"I said to bring on the SSC. The good people of Judgment have a score to settle with their jailors."

* * *

Night had fallen by the time Carter finished the last of his planet-side preparations. A crowd gathered once more in the plaza surrounding the administrative compound, but this one was much less festive than the last gathering he had seen. Most of them eyed the Bwain with a mixture of disgust and curiosity as Carter laid out the plan to defend the colony.

"With a little luck and perseverance, we might just live through this whole thing. Does anyone have any questions?" he asked as he concluded his remarks.

The assembled colonists murmured among themselves. Three days ago they had been celebrating reunification. Today, they were contemplating their own desperate place in the coming struggle, and survival was a sobering prospect.

"Where are you going to be?" a voice called.

"I'll be with the Bwain and a few of my crew on the Bwainhome."

"Is that thing going with you?"

One of the Bwain, The Voice, was plucking at the stone beside Carter.

"It's not a *thing*. It's a living being just like any one of us. Although, I'll grant you that they aren't the most handsome," Carter added. The crowd chuckled in response as the Bwain beside him fanned streaks of red through its feathers.

"Question," a dim thought reached him from the Bwainsong, *"What is handsome?"*

"A number of the Bwain will stay here. I can communicate to you through them in a way that can't be traced or intercepted, and that will be a valuable tactical advantage."

"What if they come here?" someone asked.

"You're leaving us wide open!" another colonist exclaimed.

"Now, that's not entirely true. You've got me and my men," Threed replied. The prisoner had bathed, shaved his face, and was dressed in a relatively new set of civilian clothes. He looked more like the former barrister he had been back on Earth rather than the cruel mayor Judgment had transformed him into.

"But you're not marines!"

"I think you're missing the point," Mephista commented. In spite of her small stature, her voice carried to the edges of the crowd.

"To Sol, we're all criminals. We're trying to do what's right for everyone involved out here, but in the Planetary Parliament's eyes, cooperation like this is high treason. Now, each one of us knows we made the right choice, but the SSC doesn't care," Mephista said, meeting the stares of the crowd without flinching.

"Which is why we have to show them, with as little loss of life as possible," Carter finished.

"What happens if they find out what we're gonna do?" another farmer asked.

"I can promise you that they'll never know what hit 'em. Remember, believe in yourselves, stick to the plan, and above all else have hope. There's nothing in this universe as strong as hope, not even the First Ones," he said. The farmers didn't look convinced, but some hope was better than no hope at all, but at least it was something for them to latch on to.

*   *   *

Carter had to shout to make himself understood over the roar of the orbiter's engines. The Bwain craft crouched on the shuttle pad at the rear of the administrative compound, shuddering on pillars of flame, while Hal, Danny, Threed, Mephista, and a few dozen other Bwain surrounded him.

"This might be the last time we see each other for a while. I wanted to take this moment to say that I'm proud of each one of you. Wherever we go, however this turns out, we're all in it together, and that's a bond that won't ever be broken. This won't be the end. This is just the beginning of something much bigger," Carter said, addressing the group. His confidence and earnest expression masking the self-doubt that he had been feeling earlier.

There had been a time when he'd let his own fear overcome him, but now he knew that fear was just a shackle. It was an illusion created by the desire for a better outcome; a wish in hindsight for things that were not to be. He had already seen his worst fear realized when Aida disappeared in a cloud of fire on their home on *Calle Boxer*. With nothing left to lose, he'd managed to find a sense of calm similar to what he'd experienced during his best fights.

There was certainty in commitment. In the same way as he had thrown his entire being into the Bwainsong, he was doing the same here for the people that were gathered here with him, and everyone they cared about.

One by one, Carter gripped his friends' hands.

"Thanks Hal," he said to the engineer. The man nodded, firmed himself up, and offered his best salute.

"We'll be ready down here," he replied huskily.

"I know you will," Carter answered.

Next came Danny. As Carter returned the young lieutenant's salute, he saw tears welling in Danny's eyes.

"I owe you everything," he managed through a tight throat, as he reached out to shake Carter's hand.

Carter pulled the boy into an embrace, leaning close to his former supply officer's ear.

"Take care of 'em for me Danny. Do the job I know you can do," Carter said firmly. When he let go of Danny and stepped back, the young officer nodded at him tightly.

"Captain, we're gonna be on our own up there. How do I know if I'm making the right call?" Danny asked.

"You'll always make the right decision, Danny. I have faith in you, and if you do need me, I'm just a Bwaincall away," Carter said, flashing a barely noticeable grin at his own humor.

Danny chuckled in spite of himself, nodding as he stepped back in line with the others.

Threed stepped forward for his turn in line. Him standing next to Danny would have been an awkward sight even a few days ago, but if anything, the two men seemed to have even more respect for each other after their training flights. As a group of Threed's former subjects trotted up the gangway of the *Tranquility's* orbiter, the mayor's smile revealed a missing canine tooth.

"Well, Captain, I sure appreciate you letting us live to stick it to the people who tried to kill us. Even if we bite the desert up there, it sure beats jumpin' off a ledge on Judgment," Threed said.

"It's better to die having had a fighting chance, than no chance at all. Let's just hope it doesn't come to that," Carter said. He smiled at Threed reassuringly, and then stepped over to Mephista, who was floating there in her hoverchair. Her face a mass of emotion.

"You should be safe. If everything goes according to plan, you won't need to lift a finger." Carter assured her.

"You really think we can beat an SSC armada with one crippled ship and an alien garbage scow?" she asked with a nervous grin.

"Don't forget about the First Ones," Carter said as he pulled her into an embrace.

"Don't forget about me out there," she whispered.

"Never," he whispered back to her as he pulled back and looked at them all once again and snapped them all a salute. "Well, this is it. Best of luck to all of us."

They returned his salute, and then he turned and started walking up the undulating ramp that led into the Bwain's landing craft.

Chapter 10

The Bwainhome

Granger had seen something in the engine room during Pandith's fight with the SSC. It was a small thing he couldn't be sure of, but as he passed through the Bwainhome's strangely swollen decks to meet Captain Carter, he thought he might be onto the secret of the great ship that the captain had tapped into when he fought off the First Ones.

"Is the shuttle bay much farther?" he asked the Bwain who was guiding him. The creature scurried from side to side as if scenting along the deck. At his question, it twisted its head back over its shoulder and swung its head back and forth. He couldn't tell if it was telling him no or simply acting in whatever native fashion the Bwain did. It would be fascinating to do a study on them when he had more time. *The first scientist to undertake a xenoanthropological study.* It had an incredible ring to it.

For now though, Granger needed to verify that what he had seen had been true. To do that, he needed to understand what Carter had felt, but he could barely find his way around the massive ship. In many ways, the Bwainhome was similar to human engineering, but in so many other ways it was completely different. The Bwain had not built it, so they were unable to answer very many of his questions about the biomachinery he had uncovered while cleaning off the filth of centuries from the decks.

At times while he had been working, he would feel as if he was losing his balance, and like he was falling toward the silver torpedo-like object in the center of the room. It had happened so often that it made him think it couldn't be a coincidence, but it never seemed to happen to the Bwain. He was still recovering from a recent head injury, after all. He was almost certain he had removed his observer bias. What he wasn't sure about was what his hypothesis would mean if it was true.

The gangway opened onto an electroglass wall that looked out over a massive cargo bay. Spare parts and cannibalized orbiters littered the deck, but those that still flew were returning from their preparation efforts. As they entered from the black of space, they seemed to jitter and bounce in his vision before settling into the cradles that had launched them. It could have been a subtle dimensional shift, but Granger wondered if there was something much more going on that he would have to add to his ever-growing list of Bwain technology he needed to study and understand. If only he had more time.

Below him a cluster of Bwain struggled to pass down the orbiter's ramp together, acting as a sort of body guard for Captain Carter. Granger followed his lackadaisical guide down a fluted spiral staircase that led to the bay.

"Captain!" he called.

Carter had paused in the middle of the deck, his eyes half-closed and a trance-like look on his face. The Bwain around him stilled with their eyes wide open, but dull. They were communing with the Bwainsong, asking whatever telepathic questions the bird-lizard aliens needed of the captain. It was fascinating, really, and yet another aspect of the Bwain that was worthy of future study. That would have to be Pandith's department though, because he'd be too busy learning about their technology.

"Captain," he repeated as he tapped Carter on the shoulder.

Carter's eyes fluttered open. For a moment, they were focused on an infinite space over his shoulder, until he finally managed to refocus himself on Granger.

"Mr. Granger, I'm sorry. What can I do for you?"

"Captain, I need to know how you beat the First Ones, and what happened when the Bwain fought the SSC ships," Granger replied, getting straight to the point.

Concern flickered across Carter's face for a moment, and Granger frowned at the captain's reluctance.

"Is it urgent that I give you those answers right at this particular moment?" he asked.

"No, I guess not, but I think I may have a hypothesis about the First Ones that you'll want to hear."

Carter's eyes flicked to the Bwain on either side of him.

"Do you think you could fashion two more cowls, and find us a private place to talk?" Carter asked.

"Of course, Captain," Granger's first impression had been correct. Captain Carter had something of importance to discuss, but he clearly didn't want his thoughts spread through the Bwainsong. His curiosity piqued, he nodded to indicate his understanding to Carter.

"Good. Let me know when you're ready. I have quite a bit to tell you."

*　*　*

Gertie

"Three ninety-nine," one of Hal's apprentices called as he hefted the heavy carbyne steel tube onto a hovercart that was barely able to stay above the grass thanks to the heavy burden of the load that had been placed on it.

"Four hundred now," Kilver said. He'd only been eleven years old when his family had shipped out for Gertie, and he had grown into a strong teenager who'd been more than helpful with whatever labor projects that Landfall had scared up for him. Now, he was quickly becoming one of Hal's most competent assistants. This much-needed help was critically important, because if Hal couldn't finish these final details, there would be no protecting the colony from the SSC, much less the First Ones.

Kilver wiped the sweat from his forehead, and then patted the still-warm laser satellite underneath him. The little craft had a ring of inducers, and a series of internal mirrors that could focus its beam across a distance of thousands of kilometers, but it was powered by an archaic, photovoltaic power source. The satellite would work well enough for defense, but it would have nothing like the punch of a modern fusion laser.

"Think it'll be enough, Mr. Yellowknife?" Kilver asked.

Hal scanned his factories. All around him apprentices were taking the latest loads towards the shuttle pad next to the administrator's compound. They had made so many trips they had finally worn a road through Gertie's thick grass. *"The next thing you know, we'll have skyscrapers and space elevators. If we live long enough, that is,"* Hal thought distractedly.

"It doesn't matter if I think it's enough, Kilver. The only thing that matters is that we keep making 'em," Hal answered.

"You know, I've been thinkin' about that too. Have you uploaded any plans for the new factories that are coming online tomorrow?" Kilver asked. He'd been quite eager to be a part of the emergency preparations.

Hal squinted into the sun in the direction of where his nanobots were invisibly assembling a thirtieth and thirty-first factory, both to be much larger than the other printing facilities.

"I've been so busy, I haven't gotten to it. Why do you ask?"

"Well, I was thinking. I did some CAD/CAM programming in school, and I could brush up on it to see if there's something else maybe we could put out there that would help. I know we've only got a few days. I just figured you could use all the help you could get."

Despite his weariness, Hal smiled.

"So, what are you thinkin' about? Tell this old engineer what you've got up your sleeve."

"Well, the new factories are a whole lot bigger than the old ones, and we've been doin' a *lot* of excavating. With a ten-yard printing area, we could do something with a big enough bucket."

"You talkin' about earth movers?"

"That's right. Even if we only finish one or two, that'll really help out with what Threed and Danny are doing."

Hal scratched at the three-day stubble along his jaw. The more he thought about the boy's suggestion, the more it made sense.

"Son, if you keep this up, I'll finally be able to retire. Why don't we start with...," Hal started, but then he heard someone calling his name.

"Hal!" a voice cried from three factories over.

Turning, Hal saw another of his assistants waving in a panic. Hal's first thought was an accident. He'd had little time to train everyone, and several of them had already burned themselves badly by following poor entrance and exit procedures in the factories. He set off at a run, reaching the factory as a small crowd gathered around the open entrance.

"What happened? Is everyone all right?" Hall demanded as he caught his breath.

"We're all right, but I don't know about the factory," an apprentice offered.

Pushing through the crowd of workers, Hal stopped just inside the narrow confines of the printing station. Factory seven was supposed to be producing simple chaff to restock the *Tranquility*, but what rested on its finishing conveyors was something much different.

Squatting down, Hal studied the strange, iridescent white filaments that stretched between the carbyne steel fragments. They looked almost like cotton candy, and when he reached out and touched one, it felt slick and cool in his hand.

"What the hell's that?" Kilver asked.

"I have no idea kid, but I think we've got a problem here," Hal murmured.

* * *

"This is over my head, Hal," Danny Xiao said. Bags swelled under the lieutenant's eyes. He'd gone days without sleeping as he supervised the last-minute excavations and preparations, and the strain was clearly catching up with him.

Hal lifted a section of the strange webbed substance to show Danny. The material had wilted somewhat after he had removed it from the factory, and it could have been mistaken for melted wire if one didn't look too closely. On closer examination, they could see the irregular formation of the cord, and the bright blues and purples glinting where a second before no color had existed. There was something about it that was unmistakably alien, and Hal's only concern right now was where it was coming from.

Slipping his nanogoggles over his eyes, Hal tapped a control that sent his view to the holoscreen in front of Danny. Where before the hills surrounding the printing stations had been empty, now a river of microscopic machines poured toward the factories. The nanobots shimmered in the golden photonic-powered swarm, bringing molecules of iron, carbon, protein, silica, hydrocarbons, and everything else the colony needed to be assembled in Hal's factories.

"These are the nanos. Each one of them gives off a tiny electromagnetic field that links with the others to keep them together. I control them through that field, linking it to an elemental composition, and then a swarm of them goes off and finds that element and brings it back. I've looked everywhere, and there aren't any nanos off the grid in any significant quantity," Hal explained as he reached up to adjust the nanogoggles.

"I'm not sure I'm following you," Danny said through a yawn.

"Basically, it means that there's no chance that the nanos harvested some new element by accident that would gum up the works. So the next stop in troubleshooting this is the printing station itself."

Hal zoomed in on station seven, splitting the display window into three panes.

"On the left here is a video recording of seven's batch just before the bad one," he explained. The mirrored caltrops began as nearly invisible lines, and then built up as they moved along the conveyors until they were complete productions of ultra-polished, foil mirrors that would turn away all but the most powerful fusion lasers.

"Now, here's where things get interesting," Hal noted as he brought up more images.

In the next video, the printers sputtered and flickered in and out of view as the lights in the factory dropped away. White sparks glowed, and the strange coils of wire were suddenly just there.

"What's that interference with the camera?" Danny asked.

"I don't know, but I can tell you exactly when it happened." On the third panel, he showed the overhead view once more. At precisely 3:45 p.m., the nanobots surrounding factory seven pulsed. The effect on the flow of the tiny machines was as if someone had tossed a rock into their river, and they rippled with the after-effects.

"What was that?" Danny asked.

"I don't know. I can show you what happened, but that's about as far as I go. I need to talk to Granger on the Bwainhome about this, and see if he's got any theories about what happened. The only thing I can think of is...," Hal said, but then his eyes widened with alarm.

"Mr. Yellowknife, get out of there!" Kilver cried.

Hal tore the goggles off his face just as the wires on the table before him sprung to an undulating life. They expanded into white ribbons of cold plasma, sputtering and hissing as Danny pulled Hal back through the trailer and out into Gertie's daylight.

White light arced through the trailer's walls, but it wasn't laser plasma. Strangely, there was no damage to the trailer walls at all. It seemed as if the coil was trying to make a pattern, like some kind of signal, or a beacon to whoever or whatever had created it.

"Are you all right?" Kilver asked.

"Yeah, I'm all right. Thanks kid," Hal replied. The apprentices were all gathered a short distance from Hal's trailer, watching the strange aurora writhe into the sky. The strands pulsed erratically, growing thicker and then fading, until with a last final swell they faded. Just as quickly as it started, the phenomenon ended. Tentatively, Hal walked to the side of his trailer and pressed his hand against the metal. It was as solid as ever, but he could swear he had seen something else. Something much different.

"What the hell was that?" Danny asked.

Hal craned his neck up to look at the pinkish-blue of Gertie's sky. Though he hadn't seen it with his own eyes, he could think of only one thing that would have similar properties, and the thought that the obelisk could reach out and touch them from that far away terrified him.

"Danny we've got a problem. We need to get in touch with Carter immediately," Hal said as he wiped sweat from his forehead.

*   *   *

The Tranquility

"Does it hurt?" Kaylee asked.

Danielle grimaced as the ship's doctor injected another round of accelerated stem cells into the mass of tissue and bone that ended halfway down her shin. The injections served a dual purpose: triggering her body to keep the wound open, while also taking cultures of her DNA to grow a new foot. It would be months until the limb could be restored. Morbidly, she wondered if part of her foot was still out there on the *Fate's Winds,* freeze-dried and waiting for whatever would come through the obelisk to find it.

"It's just staying there so it can kick some ass later," Bryon had told her when he'd found her floating in a corridor, staring out at the dim glimmer of the obelisk as the *Tranquility* circled Gertie one last time.

She hadn't been thinking about her foot at all. She'd been thinking about what would happen next in the Swordbelt and what had brought her to this place. She'd become a much different person from the inexperienced navigation officer who hadn't cared much about training and protocol on the *Fate's Winds*. In a way, she welcomed the pain of the injections and the tenderness of new-grown bone and tissue exposed to the open air. The pain distracted her from feeling that she could have done more, that if she had been better at her job Aric would still be with them, and they could have left the Swordbelt behind.

"It hurts Kaylee, but it's okay. Nothing good is easy."

"You're handling the therapy very well. The stem cells will take a week or so to sort into the appropriate categories: bone, muscle, nerves, cartilage, and skin. Once we confirm the ratios are correct, we'll begin the growth cultures," the doctor commented as he withdrew the needle.

Kaylee squatted down to study Danielle's amputation. For all the girl's shyness and polite mannerisms, she was surprisingly unsqueamish in the med bay. Whenever her wound was exposed Danielle herself had trouble looking at the gray-white bone, the ground meat of her muscle, and the yellow streaks of fat and tendon dangling uselessly. She could have had the doctors clean up the wound, but it just would have extended the healing time and she hadn't seen the point. All she really wanted was to get it all over with, so she could finally leave her mistakes behind and move on with her life.

"Does it remind you of before?" Kaylee asked.

"Yes, and about how I can do things differently next time," she replied after thinking about it for a moment. It was surprising how perceptive the girl could be.

"I think about that too," Kaylee said.

The doctor exchanged a glance with Danielle, and then leaned forward to whisper in her ear.

"The psychologist was concerned about Kaylee. Dr. Parson didn't make it through the last attack, so I've been trying to get her to talk, but she won't open up to me."

Danielle watched the former comfort girl pick at her nails. When she had first arrived on the *Fate's Winds*, the girl had been fastidious about her appearance, but now her hair had clearly not been brushed, and there was a grime to the poor girl. She seemed even more distracted after her latest episode.

"She won't sleep without sedatives, but it's not healthy to give them to a girl her age for extended periods of time."

"Why don't you let me talk to her?" Danielle offered. The doctor smiled, sweeping back his hair in relief.

"I'd appreciate that. There are so few of us left, and we're really doin' all we can to keep up, but we're stretched pretty thin at the moment," he said. Just then, Danielle's implant buzzed with an incoming message.

"Attention training crews. Round three of your training will begin in ten minutes. Please report to your stations."

"Kaylee, do you wanna learn how to repair the ship?" Danielle asked.

The girl looked at her with a strange blankness in her face for a moment before a smile replaced it. She nodded, and then drifted to Danielle's side just as the doctor the doctor replaced the bandage cap that would keep her wound protected. The pain was unbearable, and she realized too late that she had been squeezing the girl's shoulder in an effort to bear the agony.

"Oh god Kaylee, I'm so sorry!" she gasped.

"It's all right. I like to help my friends," the girl replied with a smile that didn't seem forced at all. Danielle took a deep breath and let it out slowly as the doctor finished his work.

"There now, that should do it. Off with you now," he said, smiling at them both pleasantly.

"Thanks doc," Danielle said as she eased herself off the bed and took Kaylee's hand. "Come on Kaylee, let's get to it."

* * *

Bryon greeted the newest members of the *Tranquility*'s crew gathered in a huddle on the bridge. With the ship being so short-handed, the responsibility for training the prisoners from Judgment on how to be competent sailors had fallen to Bryon, and the rest of his friends from the *Fate's Winds*. Most of the prisoners had been fairly well educated back on Earth. Many had simply been members of an opposition government, or lawyers who asked too many questions; but they didn't have Bryon's two years of simulation at the SSC academy to fall back on. More often than not, he was speaking to a group that wore a perpetual look of confusion on their faces.

Bryon pointed to the holosim in front of the station he was borrowing, and began his presentation.

"Now, so far we've calculated the probabilities of our target's course corrections and input our ideal sub-targets, which are the individual areas you want to strike on the opposing ship. Does anyone remember target priority?"

Furrowed brows met him. A tentative hand rose in the back from a stocky man missing two teeth.

"Engines, bridge, life support."

"Close. You always target the hostile's weapons systems first. They can't hurt you if they can't fight back. Anyway, the computer will remember those locations, then wait for you to select your weapon type and give the command to fire. Once you do, the computer will automatically select the target from your rank order, based on the likelihood of scoring a critical hit. Critical means a hit that will cripple the enemy, like taking out an entire missile bay, or blowing a reactor. That catastrophic chain reaction is what you live for in this job. You want the fight to be over as quickly as possible, so you can all go home in one piece."

"You said earlier that the computer was cycling through the available weapons?" one of the prisoners asked.

"That's right."

"But why's it doing that if you're just gonna tell it what to do anyway?"

"Because there might be damage. You have to understand you're quite possibly gonna get hit and take damage in a fight, and you might not have all of your offensive options available at any given time. You can even set the defense computer to automatic mode if you think you'll be incapacitated, but that's a last resort. The targeting will be more methodical in nature, so it's a lot easier for your hostile to predict."

"We know all about gettin' hit," the prisoner with the missing teeth said with a grin.

The airlock behind the group opened, and Kaylee and Danielle entered the bridge. Kaylee floated toward Bryon, her eyes on the man who was speaking.

"In the med bay, the doctors can regrow those for you," Kaylee commented to him as she joined the group.

The man frowned, covering his mouth with his hand.

"I didn't know there were families on this ship?" another of the trainees said.

"Kaylee is a survivor. The *Fate's Winds* rescued her," Danielle answered.

Bryon nodded his thanks to her. There had been a time before Captain Carter's arrival on their old ship when the two of them had been an item. A part of Bryon wished they still were, but something had changed in his crewmate. Danielle was much more serious now, and she'd been spending as much time as possible training on the simulators. The woman he had known would have much rather have spent her time in bed with him, but he was happy that she seemed to have found her purpose in life.

"Aren't we all," another of the rescued prisoners from Judgment added.

"Mr. Purcell, I'm afraid your lessons for today are over. Our time is up. It's time to begin the first phase of the plan," a voice called from behind Bryon.

"So soon, ma'am?" Bryon asked with a surprised look. "We sure could use at least one more day of simulations."

"I understand, Lieutenant. We could use a lot of things. But we're on the SSC's timetable, and there are other forces out here that we can't control. Helm, plot our course," Mephista responded as she moved forward to assume command of the bridge.

*　*　*

The Fate's Winds

In a way, the First Ones were more or less perfect, and thus their rise to power was inevitable. Their obelisk grew in fractal patterns that extended deep beyond the dimensional limits of space. The constructions were ingenious, designed to draw power and sustenance from the physical fabric of the universe in its 12 different planes, and the engineer in Aric was awed by it all.

He had somehow gained the skill to see the clockwork that the First Ones were assembling, though he did not how this, or any of the other additions to what he still thought of as himself had been made.

He found that he understood the creatures more and more as their reality blended with his own. Creatures was a misnomer really. It would be more appropriate to call them beings, or even elements. The First Ones were a form of life that had been reduced down to its simplest component. They were creatures of will, but the will that made them so powerful, also made them weak.

In the early days of creation, the First Ones had been physical beings. They now existed between dimensions, incapable of fully entering any of the 12 that made up all of the universe. They could project themselves into any plane of existence they chose; but when doing so, they could only project their will, and whatever materials they could manipulate from their previous dimension. To take physical form, to interact with the matter that constituted a particular dimension, they required a bridge. These structures could only be constructed by beings already in the plane they chose to enter. Will alone was not enough. They needed slaves to do their bidding.

Aric's body worked with a strange new combination of crystalline, biological, and mechanical machinery that grew on the *Fate's Winds*. He was synthesizing parts and components that existed, both in his hands and outside of them. They were objects that either vanished into thin air, or floated toward the obelisk as if they were possessed of their own intelligence. Gradually, the First Ones had grown stronger, and more stable.

For a long time, he didn't realize that a voice from his former life had been calling. It was simply a scratching in his ear, and he had been stripped of his physical sensations. His body no longer needed food or rest. Its machinery was immortal, but the long spaces of repetitive assembly gave his mind ample time to wander, and eventually he returned to that nagging little scratching in his ear.

Compared to the First Ones' orders, the voice sounded like an insect's whispering in his ear; but a part of him remembered how to understand these sounds. A part of him made sense of the words, and knew their speaker.

"Aric, this is Danny Xiao. I don't know if you'll get this. I don't know if you're still alive, or what's happening, but if you are alive out there somewhere, hold on. We're gonna be goin' away for a while, but we won't forget you. I promise."

Danny Xiao. Aric felt a remnant of emotion cross his heart. It was a vague feeling of hatred, but there was a deeper understanding as well. It was something that moved him more than any vision the First Ones had given him of the mechanical interaction between quarks and geometries.

Aric lurched to the rear of the ship, compelled by the First Ones' invisible hand to increase the radiation levels emitting from the *Fate's Winds* reactor.

He considered the whisper in his ear as he made his way through the ruined ship. The broadcast repeated itself over and over, and the words drew Aric forth like a line drawing a fish from water.

It took every ounce of strength within Aric to force his mechanical legs to still before he reached the reactor controls. His cold hand touched a flickering holocontrol. His lips moved, but no sound emerged. There was no atmosphere in engineering. The hull had been ripped open in what felt like a lifetime ago. The muscles that remained in his throat still worked, vibrating against his skull and jawbone where surgeons on Sol had once inserted an implant that was always on, listening and transmitting, always waiting for a signal to be sent.

Then Aric spoke.

*   *   *

The Bwainhome

"One more time, please," Carter said to the Bwain that was struggling to communicate Hal and Danny's point. Speaking through the creatures was like playing a game of telephone with a child in the middle, but at least he would have the tactical advantage of instantaneous communication when the SSC arrived.

"Could the obelisk's range be expanding? Could it be affecting the factories on Gertie?" the Bwain croaked.

Carter turned to where Granger stood squeezing his beard in thought.

"If what you told me about the First Ones is true, then it's certainly possible. They're obviously coming here with a purpose. The Bwain are terrified that they'll return and try to reclaim the universe. This could very well be how they're doing it."

Tell Hal on Gertie," Carter relayed his thoughts to the Bwain. The creature's full attention settled on him, and Carter spoke.

"It's a good bet, Hal."

"So what should we do?" Hal asked.

"Do the best you can, Hal. I can't really explain this to you in a way that will make a whole lot of sense, but I know the First Ones can be blocked if you want to bad enough. That's the best I can tell you for now. We've gotta focus on the SSC first. That's our most immediate threat."

"Understood. We're gonna go underground here in a few hours. Hopefully we'll…"

"Hal?"

"Sorry, Danny just got here. He's got someone he wants you to speak with."

"Danny, I don't have a lot of time right now," Carter replied.

"Captain, it's Aric," the Bwain relayed.

* * *

Gertie

The voice that filled the communications room sounded dull and distant, a monotone passed down a long hallway.

"They're coming," it said in the strangled tones that once could have been Aric's.

"Aric, who's coming? The First Ones?" Danny asked.

"The obelisk will draw them. They will return…"

"Aric, what are you telling us?" Danny asked, but the droning voice trailed off.

"Can we get him back?" Hal asked. The lieutenant checked his holocontrols for a moment, and then frowned.

"The signal's still there, he's just not…"

"I'm not there," Aric said. This time Danny heard a hint of the fire that had caused Aric to throw him off of the Fate's Winds. A hint of humanity.

"Then where the hell are ya?" Hal asked.

"I'm there," Aric's distant voice responded.

"We don't understand, Eric. We tried to get to you. The obelisk blocked us. It's got some kind of force field," Danny said as he strained to glean some understanding of what Aric was saying.

"The obelisk is the ark. The obelisk is life. The obelisk draws all."

"Is it a black hole?" Mephista asked.

"Or maybe a singularity?" Danny added, but Captain Carter broke in then and cut through to what really mattered.

"Mr. Keith, why is it there?" he asked through the Bwain.

Another silence fell in the room. Danny should have heard breathing, some sound of life, but it was as if a mechanical switch had been flipped, and the line had deadened. Then from an even farther distance, as if speaking through parallax, came Aric's last words.

"It's here for all of you, and there's nothing you can do to stop it."

"Aric! Aric!" Danny called, but the console's signal indicator failed.

"The First Ones are coming for us, so just what the hell are we gonna do now?" Hal demanded as he turned to the Bwain angrily. "Captain your plan for the SSC is one thing, but how in the hell are we gonna fight the First Ones? I don't have anything in my printing schematics that can stand up to some creature that can fight us in 12 dimensions. We're just gonna be sitting ducks for 'em, no matter where we go."

He fell silent then, waiting for Carter to answer. Danny stared at the bedraggled Bwain, trying to see the man who had saved so many lives through the alien's dull eyes.

What would they do? With two ships and a few thousand colonists, how would they hold off beings that had at one time enslaved the galaxy?

"We're gonna do the only thing we can do. We're gonna fight. Right now I've got Granger working on how to deal with the First Ones. Hal, if you can learn anything from your factories, that would be a big help. For right now though, let's just focus on the SSC. This might just give us the leverage with them that we need."

"Captain...can we really do this?" Danny asked.

The Bwain cocked its head, rippling its feathers into a plume of red and purple.

"Well, we haven't let anything stop us before, now have we?" Carter replied.

Chapter 11

The Mosquito
Entering the Swordbelt

Capra came out of his Alcubierre jump with a combination of both dread and hope warring within him. He had spent the days of the jump drafting his will, leaving last messages for friends, and pacing around the messenger vessel's small, two-person cabin. He had no idea what he was about to find, or what he was walking into. He just hoped he would live long enough to get a message back. For much of his naval career, Capra had only cared about showing up on time and doing his job, but the visit from that girl Lana, and Captain Agricourt had changed his perspective.

The thing was, he didn't know which way he had been pushed. There were too many people trying to manipulate him, and he was terrified of choosing the wrong side when the stakes were so high. It was almost enough to make him forget that the Bwain, or either of the rogue captains could have a laser targeted at his head the second he re-entered standard space. When the Alcubierre bubble faded however, and the Swordbelt's star field and planets appeared before him, nothing happened. He had set his arrival point for the orbit of one of the gas giants at the outer edge of the system in an attempt to give himself the best chance of arriving in one piece, and it looked like his decision had worked. The most dangerous part however, was what Capra was about to do next.

Reaching out to tap the holocontrols on his console, he triggered a full scan, causing his ship to send out a steady wave in every frequency along the electromagnetic spectrum throughout the Swordbelt. Then he set his course at maximum thrust away from the gas giant that had shielded his entry signature. When the scan finished in approximately fourteen hours, he would have painted the entire system, and given the computer enough data to extrapolate out any dead spots that were caused by interference from planets or asteroids.

That's how it should work anyway, if he wasn't located and blown apart before it had a chance to finish. A full spectrum scan would light up the instruments of every ship and sensing device in the entire system. It would be easy to trace the signal's source back to Capra's tiny, unarmed messenger vessel, if one were so inclined.

There were also Bwain here, and pirates, and a revolution against Sol that may or may not have been invented by Phuri in order to curry favor for himself with those in power back on Earth.

It was all enough to turn him into a nervous wreck. He stood once more, pacing back and forth in the cramped living area while he rehearsed what he would say if Carter, or anyone else for that matter, gave him the pleasure of muttering a few last words before his execution.

*   *   *

The Dauntless, Flagship of Battle Group Lambda
Earth Orbit

To those who didn't know him, Captain - now Commander Decival's mannerisms always seemed odd. So many SSC officers were really nothing more than cowboys; children with ships that had never gotten over their fascination with using all of the bells and whistles that they had been assigned to command. Decival found little purpose in shows of force, parades, or honorary awards. He preferred the constant grind of training, the investigation of all problems, and most of all, the rational discussion of strategic and scientific discoveries. Through these tools, he was always prepared for any eventuality. It was because of these disciplines, that when Nico had approached him with a mission to eliminate a profound Bwain threat, Decival had not hesitated before committing to this new assignment. Still, he could not imagine serving a more disparate superior.

"Falconi's not coming back. You should be sending your first wave now," Nico's swollen face barked through Decival's holomonitor.

"Admiral, with due respect, the ensign is only five hours late. Alcubierre jumps have been known to be unreliable, and he was gathering quite a bit of data," Decival responded.

"Carter probably hulled his ship by now," Nico growled.

"That's certainly a possibility sir, but I suggest we wait at least another forty-eight hours."

"And if they have faster-than-light capability, Decival? If Carter and his alien pawns are on their way here right now?"

"Then they will run into one of the largest battle groups assembled in the last two centuries, and I assure you that my ships will perform in much better fashion than my predecessor's."

It was no idle boast. Decival's first act upon taking command of the battle group had been to run his ship commanders through scenario after scenario, developing plans for all eventualities, and testing those plans against simulations. If they arrived and faced superior numbers on the far side of Gertie's orbit, they would be prepared. If they faced ships hidden in the clouds of the Greater Orion Nebula, they would be prepared. What worried Decival the most were the strange fighters Agricourt had reported, but even if those weapons and other unknowns entered the fight, Decival and his captains had a plan. They would simply retreat wave by wave until they understood the pattern of their attackers and develop a counter plan. It was slow, methodological progress that would win the day for Battle Group Lambda.

Nico squinted, his heavy face scrunched like a fist as thoughts worked their way through his mind.

"You've got one day, Decival. If we hear nothing from Falconi by then, I'm expecting you to begin your jump."

"Of course, Admiral. Your orders will be followed to the letter."

Again Nico's face twisted, this time with a touch of anger. Decival had pressed too far with the last comment. In the past few weeks he had sensed that Nico was playing a different game. The man was unsubtle enough to let hints fall about how Decival would be perceived in the Senate upon his return. Yet Decival was his own man; he made decisions based on facts and evidence to understand the best course of action. He only hoped that he hadn't overplayed his decision to show utter loyalty to Nico. The suspicious mind could never be changed.

"It better be, Decival. If I receive one report to the contrary…"

"I can assure you that you won't, Admiral. In fact, I plan to…," Decival was saying just as a transmission cut through his response.

"Commander!" his navigation officer called.

"Go ahead, nav," Decival answered.

"Alcubierre signature dead ahead. It's the *Mosquito!*"

"Comms…," Decival began.

"Already on it, sir," his communications officer answered. This was the reward of a prepared crew. They'd drilled for this very moment, anticipating his orders before he could give them. A quick glance at the *Dauntless'* holostatus showed antimatter at full charge, and the Alcubierre drive ready for jump in a few seconds, depending on Falconi's report.

"Mr. Falconi, welcome home. Your report, please," Decival instructed.

For a moment, there was no response. The glowing specter of Nico's face frowned.

"If this is a trap…," the admiral began.

"No sirs, it's not a trap," Capra's voice came through their cochlear implants. The messenger sounded relieved, and a bit puzzled.

"What did you find, son?" Decival asked.

"Sirs, I'm uploading the data now. There's there's nothing there."

"What do you mean?" Nico barked.

"The colony, the *Tranquility*, the *Fate's Winds*, everything that Phuri reported, it just isn't there."

Decival pinched his brow, running the different scenarios in his head. If it was a trap, it was an elaborate one. How could Carter have hidden a whole colony? And if something else had happened, if the Bwain had truly come, their fury would have left behind some trace.

"Admiral, I suggest we…," Decival started, but Nico interrupted him once more.

"Get to that system, Commander. Search every inch of it. Find out where Carter has gone," he ordered.

Decival scanned the preliminary data Capra had presented. "Sir, I don't believe that to be prudent. If they've truly left the system, they could be headed to Sol, and…"

"And I have other commanders, Lucius," the admiral snapped. "Should I give your orders to one of them?"

"Of course not, sir. We'll begin preparations immediately."

"I'm returning to the Cape. Good luck, Commander," Falconi called.

"Not so fast, Falconi . You refuel and head back out there with the battle group. I'll expect you to return immediately with news. And if you're lying about what you found out there…," Nico said. He didn't need to finish the threat. The tone of voice left no doubt there would be serious consequences.

"Yes, Admiral," the messenger acknowledged. This time the messenger sounded more calm. Perhaps he was telling the truth. All the same, Decival would be well prepared for whatever they found when they got there.

*   *   *

Cape Canaveral

Lana replayed the message four times, struggling to understand what Capra had been trying to tell her in the brief encrypted burst he had been able to send upon his re-entry to Earth orbit.

"They're all gone. I don't know if you're barking up the wrong tree or not. I'm headed back out and may have more for you soon. Don't hold your breath," it said, and that was the end of his message.

"How could they all be gone?" she muttered to herself.

The message was intentionally general to avoid suspicion, but maddeningly so. Capra was the only tool she had to verify if anything that Agricourt had told her was true, but why would Agricourt lie? And what had changed in Capra just a week after he had spilled his drunken suspicions to her?

Lana walked to the door of her hotel, letting the warm breeze flow down her neck and chest. Today she had a day of sunbathing planned in order to keep up the appearances of her vacation. Florida wasn't Madrid, but it was pleasant enough. She'd brought a tablet to read and a tube of sunscreen, so at least she could enjoy herself while she waited for things to play out.

*   *   *

The Swordbelt

Commander Decival's entry into the Swordbelt was textbook perfect. His navigation and science team had verified that Falconi's data was accurate, save for anomalous readings a few hundred thousand kilometers from the system's home planet. Nevertheless, Decival had arrived prepared to join battle. His ships aligned in a series of arcs pivoting around a central axis that would be able to adjust to a threat from any location in the system.

Decival expected to meet any number of surprises that Carter might have in store, but when the gray of the Alcubierre bubble faded into the green of the planet Gertie, no threat came.

"Sir, we're receiving a transmission," his comms officer called.

"Put it through. Capra, you didn't say anything about transmissions."

"There weren't any," Falconi answered from his ship.

"Which means they're still here...somewhere," Decival said as he narrowed his eyes suspiciously.

A voice resonated through the communications system, "Attention SSC naval officers. This is Captain Atlas Carter. Our intentions are peaceful. We want to avoid any loss of life, but you are in grave danger. I understand that Phuri has told you that we've joined the Bwain. That's not exactly accurate. We've figured out a way to communicate with them, and hostilities have ceased, but there is another alien species in this system that is far more dangerous. If you signal that you can be open minded, I'll meet with you and explain our side of the situation. No tricks, no bloodshed. Broadcast to the surface to reply. And avoid sector G-18946 at all costs."

"It's a repeat loop, broadcast from what looks to be the colonial administrative compound," the communications officer reported.

"What are we showing on the planetary telescopes?"

"Nothing, Captain. The town looks deserted."

"And the sector Carter mentioned?"

"That's the heart of the anomaly seen in Falconi's data, sir."

Decival smiled.

"Ensign Falconi, Carter might have been able to fool you with whatever camouflage he's put on, but he won't get away from us so easily. Wing A, proceed to the anomaly and investigate. Wing B, tight orbit around Gertie. Scan every inch of that planet. There were 8,000 people down there. I want to know where they went."

"Commander, what is our threat response?" the lead captain in Wing A asked.

Decival considered for a moment. It was possible that Carter had been telling the truth. His voice stress inflections had sounded genuine, and he'd clearly made an effort to avoid any unnecessary confrontations. Then, again, he could also be baiting a trap for them.

"We'll proceed at battle stations but will negotiate with any ship hailed. I'll hear out Captain Carter, at the very least."

"Very good, sir."

Decival sat back and watched the holoscreen as his fleet separated. Unlike Nico, Decival favored a more measured approach in unknown situations, but if Carter betrayed him, he would strike with just as much fury.

* * *

Gertie

"Damn it Hal, how long are we gonna be down here with that thing?" Dax complained beside him in the underground storage cave that had been first dug by Mephista's marines and then expanded by the colonists.

Hal glanced at where the Bwain squatted above a puddle of reeking white guano in a corner of the cave. The creature ruffled its feathers, then returned to its usual activity of scratching for the worms that tunneled from the shelter's walls.

"I know it stinks. Just breathe through your mouth for now. We're down here for as long as it takes, so you better get used to it." Hal replied.

Yawning, Hal returned his attention to the radio uplink that connected the cave to the administrative compound's communications system. He had to hand it to Carter. The plan to lure the SSC was ingenious, and it just might buy them enough time to convince whatever space jockey Sol had sent this time that Phuri had been lying.

For a moment Hal listened to Carter's message repeat over and over. They had been in the caves for a day or so just listening, and had no way of knowing if the navy ships had entered orbit, or if there was already a battle being fought high above them. He was blind, waiting for a reply, and Carter's plan depended on a hell of a lot going right in a system where, so far at least, very little had.

"What if the SSC is already on the surface? We can hide from orbit, but the minute they get close enough to use ground-penetrating scans, we're toast!" Dax grumbled.

"The worst they'd do would be to take us prisoner," Danny answered.

"Is that right? The way you took all those prisoners to Judgment?" another farmer asked.

"Hey! Keep it civil in here," Hal demanded angrily. "That's an order."

The farmer turned his head, gripping the support pole that he was leaning against as he grumbled to himself under his breath.

"You all know your jobs. When the time comes, we'll do them. Right now however, our job is to wait and listen, so that's what we're gonna do," Hal reminded them. His voice remained steady, and allowed no room for further argument.

"How do we know we're gonna hear anything?" someone asked.

"Because Captain Carter knows what he's doin'. You'll see," Danny said with confidence.

The farmers finally relented and returned to their usual grumbling.

"Hey kid, you really believe that?" Hal whispered to Danny, while over in the corner, the Bwain twisted its head underneath a wing, folding itself so it could sleep.

"Yeah, I do," he said sincerely.

"Then I do too, but I'll tell you somethin'. If crazy plan of his somehow happens to work, then I'm gonna I'm gonna go up on that crazy ship myself and give him a kiss, right on the lips."

"Really?" Danny asked with an amused look.

"No, not really, but I'm sure as hell gonna buy that man a drink," Hal said returning Danny's grin.

*   *   *

The Bwainhome

Using what the Bwainsong remembered of the distances at which their former masters could be heard, and Granger's calculations of the gravitational anomalies based on the ripples that he'd seen in the Bwainhome's engine, Carter carefully probed the extent of the obelisk's reach, and then brought the Bwainhome just behind the gateway to hide the ship from the SSC fleet. With Hal and Danny managing the communication from Gertie, and the Bwain serving as relay, he could hide here and then emerge in a wide arc that kept the Bwainhome safe from the obelisk...at least for the moment. Any naval commander worth his or her salt would approach the anomaly extremely slowly, if at all, and Carter hoped the delay would buy him time to open a dialogue, and convince the SSC of what the true threat in the Swordbelt really was.

Granger's best estimates had the obelisk growing about ten percent larger each day. Carter had no idea how large it needed to be before the First Ones emerged, or even what they would look like or be capable of once they did.

Aric had fallen silent after his lone message, and the Bwain stubbornly refused to return to their memories of their former masters.

In his mind's eye, Carter studied the throbbing bar of white that now looked more like an expanding orchid than a pillar. The sight made him queasy. Its edges blurred into the blackness, like something seen under a few feet of murky water. He felt vulnerable, just sitting there waiting, and the Bwain grew more and more restless by the hour. At least he knew that the Bwainhome could resist the First Ones. It had a flicker of consciousness of its own, and if Granger was right, he would have at least one way to fight them.

"Ships come. Bwain attack?" the question came through the Bwainsong.

"No, only when I tell you," Carter answered.

"But they threaten."

"I have to speak with them first," Carter stated.

"Why?"

"Because that's how human interactions work."

"Stunted," the Bwainsong chorused. *"Weak."*

"I think we did pretty well against you, wouldn't you say?"

At this there was silence. The Bwain were learning about human emotions from Carter. Emotions like the competitive response to a challenge that humans employed, as opposed to the aliens' natural obsequiousness. Their escape of the First Ones had given them some confidence, but their impulsive bloodlust during the battle to save the *Tranquility* worried him. Perhaps they were not as weak and destitute as they had shown themselves to be on the rooftop of the alternative Belize City they'd shown him a vision of.

"You will teach. You will make us strong," the Bwainsong hummed. It was more of an expectation than a request.

"Yes, I will," Carter answered.

Abruptly, the tone of the Bwainsong shifted to one of concern.

"Bwainslayer," the creatures spoke, but he felt the one of their number on Gertie speaking as an individual, giving its experience to the collective.

"What is it?" Carter asked.

"Human ships not respond. Some go to obelisk."

"They're coming here already? Why?"

"Hal and Danny not know. Think other humans not trust you."

"No! Damn it!" Carter cried. The one thing he hadn't planned for could ruin his plan completely. If the obelisk attacked the SSC, there would be no way to resolve anything peacefully. The fleet's commander would never believe that Carter hadn't been involved.

"What we do, Bwainslayer?" the aliens asked.

"Get us into the open," Carter ordered. *"We need to stop them before the First Ones do."*

* * *

The Novosibirsk
En route to the Swordbelt's anomaly

Captain Drake had been chewing the same piece of gum ever since he had taken Battle Wing B toward the anomaly. He felt proud that Decival had chosen him to fly point, but at the same time the strange readings he was receiving from whatever lay ahead were concerning him. He'd had ulcers for years, and his guts burned with a queasy fire. When this mission was over, he planned to head down to the med bay and see what could be done about growing him a new stomach lining. In the meantime, he had to root out a traitor who could have an entire alien fleet at his command.

"Repeat that last part, Captain. We're getting interference on your signal," Decival's hologram requested.

"Copy, Commander. Comms, boost signal gain to max. Commander Decival, I'm not sure what it is that we're seeing out here. It appears to be some kind of an object, but our telescopes and other instruments are all giving us different readings."

"An object? Bwain technology?" Decival asked.

"I've got the science team looking into it right now, but there's no way to tell for sure until we get closer. Whatever it is, it's not something that the computer knows how to process. The best data we can get is from the telescopes, and even then, sometimes it just isn't even there."

"Your first priority is to identify that threat and tell me what Carter is up to. Are we clear, Captain? Transmit all your data to the *Dauntless* from this point forward."

"Of course, sir. Helm, ahead full. Comms, begin data synch."

"Copy, Captain."

Drake stood from his chair and joined his navigation officers one tier down on the bridge.

"Any idea what we're looking at?" he asked them.

Frustrated, the lieutenant in charge shook her head.

"No sir, and I don't even know how to get a reading. The only thing I can think of is...wait a second."

On the holoscreen, the object pulsed. For a moment it could have been an anemone waving tentacles in an unseen current.

"Did you see that?" the lieutenant asked.

"I don't know what I saw, Lieutenant," Drake said as he stared at the screen. "Science, I need a report. This thing is making me uncomfortable."

"Sir!" the lieutenant cried.

The main holoscreen lit with a threat assessment as the ship's computer algorithm recognized a Bwain ship's signature alloys.

"Jesus, I've never seen one that big! Where did it come from?" Drake asked.

"As far as I can tell, it was somewhere behind the anomaly."

"So they were using that thing for cover? Weapons hot!" Drake ordered.

His comms officer called, "I've got a transmission, but it's coming from the planet."

"Put it through."

"This is Captain Atlas Carter to the SSC ships approaching the obelisk. I am on the Bwain ship and in command. You need to turn back now. You're in terrible danger!"

"Carter, are you threatening my ships?" Drake shot back.

"The anomaly is an alien weapon. It's not me. You have to understand what's happening out here. Turn back immediately, or…"

"Captain," his navigation officer cried. "The object is…oh my god!"

The Bwain ship disappeared from the holoscreen. The screen itself disappeared, and then the lieutenant beside him. For a moment, Drake felt as if he understood the very fabric of space, how every molecule thrumming within him came together, and how the geometry of the universe built itself into something that could contemplate its own existence.

Suddenly that construction was torn apart, and in his last seconds of life, Captain Drake had time to wonder how Atlas Carter had outsmarted him so thoroughly.

*   *   *

The Dauntless

"Drake, what's happening out there!" Decival demanded, but the holochannel had been reduced to audio, and soon even the screams faded.

"What just happened?" Decival shouted.

"Sir, four of B Wing's ships are gone."

"Was it the Bwain, or was it that son of a bitch Carter?"

"Unknown, sir. The data from Captain Drake is garbled."

"Damn it, get the science officers on analysis. I wanna know what happened, and I wanna know now!"

"Sir, message from Carter," his comms officer called.

"Open the channel," Decival ordered. "Carter, you have just attacked the SSC. We came here prepared to discuss terms with you, but you've delivered your response."

"Whoever you are, you need to leave this system. There are aliens much worse than the Bwain here. Your weapons will be useless against them," Carter urged.

Decival cut the connection. He needed time to think. Four ships gone in the blink of an eye – without any weapon firing that his ship could identify was impressive. It *could* have been done by an alien weapon, and yet it could also make a convenient cover story for the coincidence that a massive Bwain ship had appeared just before the B Wing group had been hit.

"Where are the transmissions coming from?" Decival asked.

"From the planet sir, not the Bwain ship."

"He's lying to us. This was his plan all along. Comms, reopen the channel," Decival ordered.

"Go ahead, sir," the officer answered.

"Captain, I have credible evidence that you are in league with hostile aliens, and are conspiring against humanity. No more communications will be heard unless they are your complete and utter surrender. Commander Decival out."

"All hands to battle stations!" he continued to his crew. "Comms, get me the *Mosquito*."

"This is the *Mosquito*," Falconi's voice sounded in Decival's implant.

"Falconi, get back to Sol. Tell them we are under attack and are engaging Carter. He's allied with the Bwain and has taken hostile action against the fleet. I'll send another messenger within 24 hours to provide the admiral with an update."

"Yes sir," Falconi acknowledged. "Oh, and Commander Decival?"

"What is it, Falconi?"

"Good luck going after Carter. The last man I saw try it didn't fare so well."

Chapter 12

The Fate's Winds

Aric felt each strand of energy that struck the SSC ships as a violent birth.

"Mine," he thought as the component materials of the four ships were absorbed into the obelisk. *"Mine, mine, mine."*

"There are others," the First Ones said. Images of a flotilla of ships breaking apart into smaller maneuvering groups flashed through Aric's mind.

"These are human too," Aric answered.

"They will be ours. Bring them closer."

"They'll be watching. They'll have seen what happened."

Pain blossomed in what had been Aric's midsection, dropping him to his knees. The First Ones were creators, the engineers of the universe, and they worked in thought and idea, as well as matter. They poured into his ears the last vibrations of atmosphere in the ships the First Ones had consumed, battering him with the final screams of hundreds of crewmen being torn apart.

"They will be us. There is no choice," the First Ones said.

If Aric could have spoken through the misery, he would have told them that he no longer feared their pain. Unable to die, the sensation simply became something to be endured, not feared. Writhing against the deck in schizophrenic disconnect between the part of him that had been Aric and the part the First Ones controlled, he wondered for the first time at their psychology.

The First Ones were intelligent, but almost too much so. Their minds moved in fractals through the dimensions. They were endlessly self-centered, continuously hungry, and constantly searching. Long ago, they had decided that they were the masters of the universe and that it existed to serve them. However, this was when a planet called Earth was still a seething mass of lava, when the Bwain were still growing their feathers in their jungles.

"You will speak to these others. You will make them come," the voice instructed.

"I will make them come," Aric answered, and the tearing within him stopped. He rose, numb, and floated like a ghost through the day room toward engineering. Once there had been a citrus grove here. Once there had been soil and growing things that he had ingested in the same way the obelisk ingested all matter.

Aric passed through the airlocks, which now hung open all over the ship. As he entered his old engineering station and activated the human controls for the radio transmitter, he found his vision had grown blurry. He paused, unsure of what was happening. Then the deeper, still- human part of him remembered, and it horrified him.

*   *   *

The Tranquility

"Atlas, what the hell are we gonna do?" Mephista asked of the Bwain in front of her. She longed to be able to look into her friend's face, but the best she could do for now was to hear his halting words pass through the clacking beak of a Bwain.

"We have to stick to the plan. We don't have any alternatives."

"You know they've informed Earth by now. There's not gonna be any convincing them now that we didn't destroy those ships. They're gonna think you used some kind of Bwain weapon against 'em."

"I know they will, but we can do this. We prepared for this."

She tried to push away her anxiety in an effort to return to the cold calculations that she needed to execute her part of Carter's plan. With so much hanging in the balance though, all she could feel was worry. It'd been easier when she'd only wanted revenge against the SSC, but now the stakes were much higher. The colonists' lives, her own crew, Atlas, and even the Bwain were all depending on this plan working. The more Atlas had told her about the Bwain, the more she stated to understand them, and what motivated them. The only chance for any of them to survive was if the SSC relented, but that was just a pipe dream now that they believed their enemy had drawn first blood. She knew how they thought. She'd been one of them once, a long time ago.

"How are your new crewmen?" Carter asked. In spite of herself, she smiled.

"Your Lieutenant Purcell has them all ship-shape."

"Now I know *that's* an exaggeration. How are the rest of the crew?"

"Julie and Danielle are both doing well. Kaylee is...well, she's just Kaylee, but, they're doing whatever they can to help her adjust, and to feel like she's contributing."

"They're good sailors, and so are you," Carter added.

"I'm gonna have to be to pull off this crazy scheme of yours."

The Bwain suddenly rasped, sounding as if it was trying to clear some obstruction from its throat. It took Mephista a moment to realize that the creature was trying to mimic Carter laughing, and she smiled.

The past few weeks had brought out more of the man that Carter must have been before he'd been exiled to the Swordbelt. In a way, he seemed to enjoy the mental and physically challenges of being the underdog. She could imagine him in the ring, darting from a bigger fighter, and smiling after each near miss, because he knew his time would come. As she sat there thinking about his patient determination, she felt her confidence returning to her.

"I need to get back to the bridge," she said.

"Let's just not make this the last time we talk. You take care of yourself," Carter said.

"You too. Don't spend too much time in the Bwainsong, or you might start growing feathers or somethin'."

"Was that a joke?" he asked.

"Yeah, why?"

"Oh, nothing. I've just never heard you make a joke before. You usually just sound like a pirate," Carter said through the Bwain. This time Mephista recognized the alien's mimicking laughter, and let out a small laugh herself in response.

*   *   *

Gertie

After relaying Captain Carter's messages from the Bwain in the caves to the SSC fleet, Hal had expected something to happen, but it didn't. The hours simply dragged on endlessly, everyone was growing increasingly restless.

Hal had brought his CAD/CAM goggles with him, and while he waited for the Bwain to squawk new orders from Carter, he tapped into his printing station's diagnostics to try and figure out the problem with his factories that Carter had asked him to resolve.

The obelisk had been somehow interfering with his factories, manufacturing odd components that at times seemed like parts for a ship, other times it was a kind of chitin, similar to the exoskeleton of a crab. Then there were the materials that his computers couldn't classify, even though they'd built the stuff. That was what he couldn't figure out. Where had the materials come from?

"Danny, I need to work something out with you," he called. Danny had been napping beside him, his head propped up on a jacket. With so many of the colonists growing more tense by the second, it seemed strange for the boy to be resting. Then again, Danny had been through a lot, so if there was anyone who knew how to handle stress, it would be him.

"Hmmm? Whatcha need?" Danny mumbled as he stretched himself out, and then sat up with his back against the wall.

"Take a look at this," Hal urged. He offered Danny the goggles, and helped the young officer to slip them over his head.

"This looks like a spectrometry analysis," Danny commented.

"Exactly. When the malfunctions started, I ran some of the pieces through spectral analysis."

"There are a lot of unknowns here, Hal. Interference from the obelisk?"

"No, those are elements that humanity has never seen before."

"Well that's to be expected, isn't it? I mean, with the First Ones coming from another dimension and all."

"That's exactly it, Danny. Don't you see? The nanobots didn't gather those materials, but somehow the factories were able to find 'em and then use 'em to make that stuff. What if that's what the obelisk does? What if it draws elements from our universe and other dimensions in order to create physical forms?"

"Then it's *building* the First Ones?" Danny asked, with a puzzled look.

"Exactly. And somehow it was able to communicate with my factories, so there must be a way to talk back."

Danny stripped off the goggles, handed them back to Hal, and then rubbed his eyes.

"You think that could help us?" he asked.

"I'm gonna pump Granger for information. He seems to know more about this than anyone. I need to take some readings at the factories too, but there's a chance."

"Hal, if the navy sees you on the surface, we're done for," Danny cautioned.

"I know kid, but I can help with this. I know I can," Hal insisted. Danny looked at him, his eyes wide.

"Hal, you're the only reason this colony is even still here. The Bwain would have come in, swept it clean, and enslaved every last farmer if you hadn't stood up to Tannin."

For a moment Hal studied the dust, and then he tapped the goggles against the earth and nodded.

"I appreciate that, Danny. You're a good man," he said. This time, it was Danny's turn to be embarrassed.

"I don't think that's true."

"Think about how much you risked to help me, and to help people that you didn't need to care a thing about."

"Things are a lot different now, aren't they?" Danny asked.

"You're damn right they are."

"We'll get you to the factories. Just sit tight for right now though. Captain Carter's gonna pull this off somehow. I know he will."

"I hope so, because I'm gettin' awful tired of sittin' here in the dark smellin' that thing's butt juice. He hasn't eaten that much, so how's he manage to turn a few worms and grubs into that much crap?"

"Talent, Hal. Pure talent," Danny said with a breathy laugh.

*   *   *

The Dauntless

"Fourteen ships from B Wing survived, Commander," his nav officer reported.

Decival stood in front of the main holoscreen, studying his force disposition. The loss of a few ships and Captain Drake was embarrassing, but in spite of Carter's attempt at deception, his tactical situation had changed little. Decival needed to engage the Bwain ship, but with three dozen craft capable of doing so, he wasn't concerned about numbers against such a large ship. He was concerned about trying to understand what Carter would do next.

By the nature of the first engagement, it was clear that Carter had not expected Decival to be so immediately aggressive, and had run from his only protection. Several B wing cruisers had blocked the Bwain ship from returning to the anomaly, and their only concern would be to stay out of range of whatever weapon had taken his ships by surprise. The time and the manner of attack was fully in Decival's hands.

"A Wing, split into two groups. Captain Monderer, you will take command of A Alpha, reform with what remains of B Wing, and re-engage the Bwain vessel. I want that craft destroyed, but be aware of their apparent offensive capabilities."

"Understood, sir," Monderer answered.

"C Wing, you are to remain in orbit around the colony and prepare landing parties. I want a thorough sweep of the town of Landfall. We need to find out where all those people have gone."

"D Wing, you'll remain with the *Dauntless* in reserve. Epsilon, I'd like you to…"

"Commander! We have a new signal at the outskirts of the system," his navigation officer called.

An icon of the system appeared on his holoimage, flashing a familiar color.

"Is that an SSC ship?" he asked.

"Transmission incoming, sir."

"Attention SSC fleet, this is Captain Mephista on the *Tranquility*. We've taken damage from the Bwain and are unable to maneuver. We require immediate assistance."

"Response, sir?" his comms officer asked.

Instead of answering immediately, Decival pulled up the records of the *Tranquility*. The name sounded familiar to him, and he needed to understand its sudden appearance here at the edge of human space.

He looked up, smiling. This Carter was not the strategic genius that Phuri had implied.

"Captain Mephista, this is Commander Decival. I'd be more than happy to send relief. Hold position and we'll be there as soon as we can."

"Thank you, sir. I can't tell you how much this means."

"It will be my pleasure," Decival replied and closed the connection. "Epsilon wing, prepare to engage the *Tranquility*. I expect combat solutions within ten minutes."

"Engage, sir?" Captain Van Stadt's voice questioned through his implant. Van Stadt was a good officer. He had been paying close attention to Decival's transmissions.

"That's right, Captain. The *Tranquility* mutinied against the SSC more than three years ago. You're going to personally clean the pirates from this system."

Decival tapped the data he had on Mephista's defection and the last known position of the *Tranquility* and sent it to Van Stadt.

"You're gonna be left thin if I head out there, Commander. It's 12 hours at full thrust."

"Understood, Captain. But I think I've got the measure of this Carter now. The only ship unaccounted for is the *Fate's Winds*, and I'll still have eight ships to deal with one corvette."

"Copy that, Captain. I'll bring you Mephista's head."

The connection snapped off, leaving Commander Decival alone with his thoughts. On the screen in front of him, his ships spread out like the fingers of a hand that had come to restore order to the system. It would only be a matter of time until the SSC was fully in control. The traitors would never know what hit them.

* * *

Earth

When Capra Falconi entered Earth's orbit, he was surprised to find his atmospheric insertion orders already waiting. He dipped the *Mosquito* toward Earth's blue marble and watched the atmosphere catch fire against his hull. As his craft shook and bucked through the turbulence, it mirrored the feeling he'd had ever since he left Decival and the Swordbelt to deliver his report.

The Captain Carter he had spent nearly a week with on the *Mosquito* hadn't been mutinous. He'd simply been sad. The first thing he had done upon taking up his new position had been to stand up to the pirates, and then he went out of his way to help the prisoners on Judgment.

How did a man like that end up betraying his race? What would drive him to destroy the SSC ships? Carter had to know what he was doing was suicide, and Capra found that he just couldn't understand the man that he thought he had gotten to know during their time together, at least in a small way.

Whatever Lana and Agricourt thought they knew about any political machinations must be wrong. He watched the flames roil his windows as the heat from his reentry grew. Things were often simpler than they seemed. Carter clearly had a death wish, and it was Capra's job to deliver that message.

*   *   *

The *Mosquito* broke low over the Cape, circling once as he waited for other traffic to clear. Nico had given Capra express landing privileges after ordering him to avoid all digital reports that could be intercepted by whoever had the means to spy on him. As Capra entered his landing glide pattern, he saw a strange sight.

The gates to the SSC navy's facility were accessed by a long, manmade causeway that connected to a guardhouse on the mainland. That guardhouse was responsible for protecting the approach. A crowd of hundreds had gathered outside the guardhouse. Capra didn't have time to focus his telescopes as he flashed toward his landing pad, but the image stuck with him as he verified his identity with the port officer and made his way into the SSC headquarters.

Was the base under protest? What exactly was happening?

There was little small talk in the base's corridors. Officers pushed past with tense faces as if they were waiting for some horrible news, and the yellow caution indicators, just below battle stations, flashed at every intersection. Capra had been gone for ten days. In that time, something important had changed. Maybe the Admiral would tell him. That is, if he actually cared to share any of his thinking with an Ensign. Or maybe he could find out something after his briefing from one of the other officers.

Nico's secretary was already standing with the admiral's office door held open as Capra entered the admiral's sanctum. Capra strolled through and nearly froze at the sight of Phuri standing behind the admiral's desk before remembering himself and snapping to attention.

"I'm a civilian, Mr. Falconi," Phuri said.

"Y-Yes, sir. May I ask what's going on?"

"It's a strange thing, Capra. It seems word has leaked of Captain Carter's allegiance with the Bwain. Citizens are protesting at SSC facilities all over the planet. They expect the SSC to take more drastic actions against this threat."

"Do they know about the Battle Group?" Capra asked.

Admiral Nico answered the question as he entered from his private quarters, "That will depend on how successful Commander Decival will be. Please give us your report, Ensign."

Capra told them of the initial engagement and relayed Decival's scenarios as ordered, then he stood at parade rest waiting for either man to speak. Their effort to fight off smiles with so much seemingly wrong on Earth, and within the Swordbelt seemed strange to him.

"I thought you said Carter was smart," Nico said as he turned to Phuri.

"Apparently I misjudged him. At least he's made things easy for us."

"That's true. We'll need to get another progress report."

"I'm ready for your orders, sirs," Capra indicated.

"He's already calling you 'sir,'" Nico said, smiling at Phuri. "Ensign Falconi, you've done your duty. Consider yourself relieved."

"Relieved, sir?" Capra asked. "I don't understand."

Atlas' Flight

"Decival has enough messengers under his command. Go home, son. New orders will come your way soon."

Capra stood there for a moment, stunned by what he'd just heard.

"Is there something else?" Nico asked.

"Admiral, if I may. I've been a part of whatever's going on out there in the Swordbelt. With your permission, I'd like to finish the job, sir."

Phuri's eyes flicked to the admiral. Again, Capra realized that a deeper conversation was happening between the two. He thought he'd done a good thing. He'd risked his life twice in that system to help them understand what was happening. He knew they were trying to do the right thing, so why would they relieve him?

"You certainly have, son. I'll consider your request. Now go home and get some rest," the Admiral said dismissively.

Capra saluted and spun on his heel, but before Nico's secretary closed the office door he heard a last snatch of conversation.

"He *has* been a part of what's been happening, hasn't he?" Phuri noted.

"Yes, and that's knowledge that bears watching," Nico responded.

* * *

Capra changed out of his flight suit at his locker, donning the shorts and light polo shirt that he'd shed what felt like an age ago when he'd made his scanning run to the Swordbelt. As he stood before the mirror tidying his hair, a heavy-muscled man with the single stripe of an SSC Marine Division PFC approached from behind him.

"Ensign Falconi?" the man asked. The private had the trace of what sounded like a Spanish accent, but Capra couldn't tell if his skin tone was from the Florida sun, or if it was genetic.

190

"What can I do for you?"

"The admiral is offering you a ride home."

Capra studied the man a moment, thinking about what Nico had meant when he'd stated Capra had knowledge that bore watching. The private was armed but seemed relaxed, and was looking at him with a friendly smile.

"Well then, if the admiral insists," Capra replied.

Hefting his bag, the courier followed the private into the elevator that led down to the motor pool. Nervous once more, Capra's natural garrulousness spilled out with this strange man whom the admiral may have assigned to spy on him.

"What's the story with the protests outside?" Capra asked. "I saw them on my flight in."

The man's thick eyebrows rose.

"They don't know we keep them safe," he answered.

"That's for sure, but what do they want exactly?"

"They want traitors to be punished," the man replied. The elevator door opened, and Capra tossed his bag into the back of a waiting hover jeep.

"I mean, what does President Kidewange say? He must have released some kind of statement."

The bigger man wrenched the wheel before Capra had belted in, bursting forward in acceleration. Capra held onto the door handle until he could buckle his belt.

"The president wants traitors to be punished too," the private commented nonchalantly. "He says the safety of the human race is his primary concern."

Capra and his driver spilled out from the motor pool into the golden light of Earth's sunset. The air was warm, a mix of citrus and saltwater, and he could hear the gulls calling as they dived in and out of the surf. There was little traffic on the road, and Capra closed his eyes to enjoy the feeling of not being cooped up in the *Mosquito*. There were certainly big pieces moving around him, but he was a small fish, in a big pond, and his involvement in the whole situation was incidental. He had done his duty, and couldn't possibly be in danger.

Soon, a roar reached his ears. The jeep slowed as it approached the spaceport's entrance, and for the first time Capra realized that something more than just protests were happening.

Hundreds of civilians screamed insults about treachery and mutiny, hurling rocks and glass and any other projectiles they could find against the electro fencing that protected the guards. Capra's driver slowed the jeep, leaned out and flashed his credentials. The guard's eyes widened.

"You're goin' out into that?" he asked.

"Admiral's orders," the driver answered.

The guard nodded, reached behind him and grasped a lever.

"You've got three seconds," he warned.

"This doesn't seem right...," Capra began, but then a section of the glowing fence in front of him fell and his driver gunned the acceleration. Capra slid back in the seat, trying to make sense of what was in front of him.

Many of the protestors bore signs, but they weren't what he was expecting.

"*Nico = Traitor*" and "*Kidewange for life*," the signs read.

"Why are they protesting Nico?" he asked.

"Because he's the head of the navy, and because he should have stopped

Carter," the driver said tersely.

There were holocameras everywhere from various news outlets that were reporting on the protestors. Torn between wanting to hide his face and gaping at a sight he had never seen before, Capra gave in to his impulses and scanned the crowd. They seemed incredibly angry, but there were any number of protestors on Earth who could find a reason to be angry. The protestors beat against the jeep, threw water, and screamed. Capra ducked low in his seat, but just before slipping out of sight he saw a familiar face. Lana Delgado was waving both hands at him frantically, shouting something unintelligible from the other side of the jeep's bulletproof glass.

The crowd thinned as the jeep pushed through them, until the driver was building speed. Another group of protestors were making their way toward the scene, marching down the middle of the road a hundred meters distant.

"Hey! What the hell? They're not gettin' out of the way!" Capra called out.

"No, they're not," the driver acknowledged. "Oh well. If they're so lacking in a sense of self-preservation, then that's their problem."

Horrified, Capra watched as the driver cut through the mass of protestors. Bodies bounced off the hood as the tightly-packed crowd fought to get out of the way. It was for a few moments only, but after the driver dropped Capra off at his apartment the image of running down a man and a woman who had been too slow in moving out of the way stayed with Capra.

For a long time he stood at his window, studying the sun-baked streets, and the jeep that hadn't left its parking spot on his corner.

It was ironic that a messenger knew so very little about what was going on. Every time he thought he understood what was happening something changed, and he was getting tired of it. Frustrated beyond words, he picked up his communicator and dialed Lana Delgado's number. It was time to get some answers from someone who would actually be straight with him.

Chapter 13

The Bwainhome

There was a seductive beauty to the Bwainsong. It was a sense of immediate power like no other, and a part of Carter wondered if this was what the First Ones had succumbed to. He remembered the dead anguish in Aric's voice, the hundreds of thousands of Bwain he had slaughtered, and every colonist and crewman who had died in the Swordbelt.

By engaging the SSC navy, his own people, he was simply continuing the cycle that the Bwainsong told him had been going on for millennia. He was no better than the *Narcos*, or the lies that Phuri had spread about him, and yet he had no choice but to continue on his present course if the colony was to survive.

Carter pushed away the subtle whispers of deeper things to focus on what needed to be done. There had been times with Aida that he had marveled at how she could engross herself in potting a plant, or lose herself in a novel for hours on end. Her focus had always impressed him, and he had told her as much on many occasions.

"Yeah, but you always seem to have a strategy," she said to him once when he'd mentioned it. "I see you in the ring, and it's like you don't even feel the hits you're taking. You're always so focused on the end goal that you just seem to brush off all the hits you take until you see an opening to achieve it."

"But I still feel the pain," he told her as he'd stroked her hair. They'd lain with their hands intertwined on the thin strip of sand that had been cleared of ocean's debris near their home.

"Don't worry sweetheart. I'll always be here to ease your pain when you come back home," she promised him, but she was gone now, and Carter felt his body trembling with the weight of what would come.

"Bwainslayer?" the aliens asked.

"I'm here…"

"We do not understand this emotion."

"It doesn't matter."

"It does. We learn from you. We have to know."

"Emotions are irrelevant."

"But humans have them. Humans use them."

"Yes, and we push past them to do our jobs. Show me the fighters."

Another part of Carter's mind filled with a picture of his tactical disposition. It had been a major feat to get the Bwain to understand battlefield intelligence. They lacked critical thinking, but at least now they understood the larger concept of keeping an eye on their enemies.

The obelisk was thousands of kilometers behind the Bwainhome now, and the Bwain's tension at being in such close proximity to their former masters had eased. Another group of SSC ships was approaching the Bwainhome, and Carter had strung his interdimensional fighters in a thin line to intercept. Carter was withdrawing toward the nebula at a deliberate pace, giving the navy the belief that they'd be able to catch him before he reached it.

In a way, he was impressed at the SSC battle group leader's tactical skill. Their commander knew exactly how to deploy his forces, and how to protect his flanks from any approach. His cautious approach, holding some of his ships in reserve while preventing Carter from retreating toward the obelisk was textbook perfect. The commander's mistake however had been thinking that he understood what was happening in the system. He had underestimated just how alien the threat could actually be.

Atlas' Flight

"Mr. Granger, are you ready?" Carter asked through the Bwain beside him.

"I won't know until we try it, but Pandith and I have done everything we can, sir," the Bwain said, echoing Granger's words from the engine room.

"Understood. I'm about to engage. If you have a moment, say a prayer for all of us."

"We'll be ready, Captain."

Carter nodded, and then closed his eyes and gave himself to the Bwainsong once more. He felt the curious expectation emanating from the Bwain in the engine room, felt the harmonic resonance thrumming through the Bwainhome's hull, and then cast his mind out to the line of fighter pilots camouflaged in front of the SSC fleet.

The pilots had yielded themselves completely to Carter's control. Prior to his arrival, they would have flown individually, with little sense of tactics other than to swarm and retreat. It was so birdlike that it would have been comical, if Carter didn't have to expend such an intense level of mental effort to keep them in line.

They had gone too far when rescuing the *Tranquility*. It was crucial that the Bwain minimized casualties and damage in this battle, and the ones to come as well. They would need every possible ship if Carter's plan was going to work.

The first SSC ships slipped past the cloaked fighters. Folded between dimensions, the fighter pilots' minds rose in chorus.

"Attack now," the Bwainsong urged.

"No, we wait."

"Wait for what?" they asked.

In his mind Carter watched the SSC ships slip past. There were ten in the

Vanguard, and another eight in reserve. The vanguard passed by, and then a short time after, the reserve approached. These ships would respond to anything unexpected that hit the first wave. Unless of course, Carter could turn the first wave back.

The reserve ships closed on the fighters, first entering cannon range, then missile range, and then finally laser range. He watched their sleek, carbyne steel hulls rush past his invisible picket line, coming so close that no weapons would be able to track the fighters. Their defensive systems would not buy them any time.

"This is what we've been waiting for. Now, attack!" Carter ordered.

* * *

The Nova

Captain Laura Monderer had captained the *Nova* through seven Bwain engagements and two human insurrections, but she had never experienced chaos like what struck her battle wing's reserve.

"Laser batteries two and seven offline," her weapons officer called.

"Forward magna cannon is disabled."

"What the hell is hitting us? Is it the Bwain? The anomaly?" the captain demanded.

Her holoscreen split into different threat sectors, one showing the bright white lotus of the anomaly, another showing the empty space around her ship, and a third showing the Bwain ship backlit by the Great Orion Nebula. Her crew were flying at their posts, running thousands of simulations a second through the computers, coming up with the most likely probabilities as to what was chipping away at her ships' hulls.

"The best scenario is that we're being hit by small cannon fire, ma'am," her weapons officer reported.

"Small cannon?" she asked in disbelief. "From where?"

"I've lost missile bay two," another of the weapons officers reported.

"Dammit, I want an answer. Get me telescopes and external cameras."

Her holoscreen reconstituted into dozens of views of the *Nova's* shimmering hull as nanobots crawled to restore the damage that was caused by – by streams of plasma and projectiles that seemed to strike her ship from the emptiness of space itself.

"There must be hundreds of them," one of her nav officers speculated.

"Get me a firing solution," Monderer called.

"There's nothing there to shoot at, ma'am! The computer has no targets!"

"Well, something's sure as hell found us!" she snapped, sharing her frustration with the officers on the bridge.

"Laser pods four through eight are inoperative," weapons reported.

"Ma'am, it appears that the hostiles are within our defensive perimeter. Proximity lasers and magna cannons are all we have that'll reach."

"Well bloody fire them then!" she barked. "Helm, prepare evasive solutions."

"Ma'am, at this range, the cannons' projectiles will hit our other ships."

Monderer pounded her chair arm angrily, and then she opened a channel to the rest of the battle wing.

"Alpha wing reserve, separate to a safe distance for magna cannons. I want you to sweep your perimeters until you find whatever it is that…," she said, but then she stopped abruptly as her eyes locked on the screen before her.

"Captain, I see them," the nav officer said needlessly.

Hundreds of small craft that looked like flickering spiders were suddenly just *there,* swarming around her ship. They looked blacker than space itself, but slowly changed color to a glimmering silver as they pulled away.

"Well what are you waiting for? Target those ships and fire!" she ordered. Instantly, as if on cue, the ships once again flickered out of existence.

"Contacts lost, ma'am," the weapons officer reported.

"The nanos are reporting that our hull integrity is at one-hundred percent. We're no longer taking damage."

"Captain, I've got full thrust, no power or inducer damage."

"They're targeting our weapons systems. Comms, send a report to Decival. Nav, bring us to...," she was about to order, but then she Monderer heard an officer call for her attention.

"They're back, Captain! Bearing 23 point 857 point 4."

"That's away from us. They're headed toward the first wave."

"It looks that way, ma'am. Your orders?"

She studied the massive Bwain ship as it lumbered fat and ungainly to try and escape the system. There was a human commanding that thing, a human that was trying to kill her. She'd be damned if she would let Carter get away.

"Alpha wing attack group, accelerate and engage the Bwain ship. Be advised you have numerous small craft at your rear. Reserve group, separate to a safe distance and prepare magna cannons if those fighters return."

Acknowledgements poured into her ear, and she felt the thump as her nav team hurled her ship toward the Bwain.

"Monderer, report," Decival's voice sounded through the communications link.

"I've engaged the Bwain, sir. Minor damage from some kind of fighters deployed to slow us down. They were trying to shield their main ship, but I'm putting the entire wing after it," she answered.

"Are you combat effective?"

"Sixty percent, Commander," she reported just as another voice broke through.

"Sirs, I've got another message from Carter."

"Put it through," Decival ordered.

"That was a warning. You'll never find me in the nebula. You should just give up now," Carter's voice advised.

"Commander, did you copy?" Monderer asked.

"Yes."

"He's on the run, sir. He's desperate. Request permission to catch him."

"You are to proceed with caution, Monderer. We don't know their full capabilities yet."

"I can take a punch, Commander. And I'll make sure to bring you Carter's head."

*　*　*

Gertie

Hal was working a cramp out of his back from sitting on the packed dirt floor when the Bwain fluttered and squawked. It had remained silent in its corner for so long that he'd nearly forgotten that it was in the cave with them. Apparently, so had many of the colonists.

"Hal? Danny?" the creature croaked.

"Here, Captain," Xiao answered.

"They're going for my bait. Get yourselves ready," the Bwain said, echoing Carter's words to them.

"Roger that, sir!" Hal barked. Despite the tension that had surrounded the cave earlier, he saw smiling faces all around. The time had finally come for them to show the arrogant commanders of the SSC just what the people of Gertie were capable of.

* * *

The Fate's Winds

To Aric it felt as if space itself had become pregnant. He had performed his tasks well, had done what he had been asked. His reward was to watch what the increasingly distant part of him that was still human dreaded. The obelisk was peeling itself open like a blossoming flower, and something was emerging.

"We are come!" the voice announced.

As the obelisk split wider, Aric saw the first of his masters' faces.

* * *

The Tranquility

Mephista was on edge. The asteroid field that surrounded her ship limited her ability to see the SSC ships that were on approach, and she worried that even with the thousands of navigation scenarios that were being updated every second, based on the changing conditions around the *Tranquility,* something would go wrong.

"You're out of time, Lieutenant. I need you back at the ship immediately," Mephista ordered.

On a portion of her holoscreen, the enlarged images of two dozen EVO suits skimmed toward the *Tranquility,* but the arcs of the SSC ships behind them were moving much faster, and the countdown above each astronaut's head was shifting into red.

"Understood, ma'am. We're on approach now," marine lieutenant Grayson responded.

Mephista had never done well with the whole waiting thing. It gave her too much time to think. She remembered most of the crew members under her command that had perished. At least the faces, if not the names, and she'd spent time in the early hours of the morning scrolling through the images and information about them all. In doing so, however, it had made her even more leery of this part of the plan's success.

"Ma'am, they're not gonna make it," her nav officer reported.

The captain closed her eyes for a moment and took a deep breath to calm herself.

"Open a channel on the SSC general band," she instructed.

"This is Captain Mephista, to the SSC ships: We're drifting and in need of aid. Please respond."

Only static returned over the channel.

"I'll say again: Please respond to coordinate rescue."

"Ma'am, they're not buying it," her comms officer reported. "They're coming in with their weapons hot."

"Grayson, what is your ETA?" Mephista asked.

"Two minutes," the lieutenant responded.

On her holoscreen the SSC ships loomed larger and larger, picking their way through the asteroids as they approached the *Tranquility*. If she waited two more minutes, those ships would be in line-of-sight weapons range of her still-crippled ship. She had to live to fight another day. There was no other choice.

"Begin the operation," Mephista ordered. "Full thrust aft. Grayson, find what cover you can, and good luck."

"Yes, ma'am," the marine acknowledged.

"Weapons, you are free to launch when ready."

"Ma'am, what about the marines out there?"

"They could use our prayers," she responded uneasily.

"Yes, ma'am. Launching now."

On her holoscreen, all hell broke loose. Mephista turned away for a moment, unwilling to let the bridge crew see her eyes watering for twelve more of her crew that she had little hope of ever seeing again.

*　*　*

The Reichstag

For the life of him, Captain Van Stadt couldn't imagine why Mephista had marooned her ship in an asteroid field. It was the worst tactical position he could possibly think of, and the only explanation he could come up with was that she was trying to sell her lie about her ship being disabled. Either that, or she was telling the truth, in which case the *Reichstag* would be in no danger at all.

"All ships be on the alert for other vessels. The last thing we want is to get caught with our pants down," Van Stadt ordered.

"She's hailing again, sir."

"Ignore it. Thrust to one-third as we enter the asteroid field. I don't want any mistakes."

"Yes sir."

Van Stadt's plan was simple. He only needed to get within laser range, and a concentrated burst from all of his cruisers would gut the *Tranquility*. Missiles and magna cannon were useless in such a densely packed system, and he did not want to risk any of his crew on orbiters. Lasers required only a few seconds of clear space, and he had no doubt that a window of opportunity would open that he could take.

On his holoscreen the asteroids swirled like some kind of maze.

"Captain, I need to elevate above the orbital plane to have a clear shot," his weapons officer called.

"Helm, make it so," Van Stadt stated. "The *Tranquility* still hasn't activated its weapons?"

"No sir. You don't think she could be telling the truth, do you?"

"Captain Mephista led that ship in mutiny and piracy. I wouldn't trust a word she says."

"Lasers are at full charge across the wing," his weapons officer reported.

"Copy that. Are we ...," the captain started to say, but then the ship suddenly lurched sideways, and he had to grab a railing to steady himself.

The ship shook with a scraping, clawing sound. Van Stadt was experienced enough in space to recognize what it meant.

"Damn it, we've hit an asteroid. What's our hull integrity?"

"No sir," the nav officer responded.

"What was that, Ensign?"

"Sir, *we* didn't hit the asteroid. That asteroid hit *us*."

"Captain, we've got a hull breach on deck four. I've lost the inducers in that section."

"Nav, I won't accept excuses," Van Stadt began, but an urgency in the voice of one of his bridge crew caused him to pause.

"Sir, you need to see this."

The image on the main holoscreen took Van Stadt so long to process, that by the time he realized the extent of the trap he had walked into, he knew he was already lost. All around his entire wing of ships, the asteroid field was moving. The massive planetoids seemed to be launching themselves at his ships in a coordinated strike.

"We've lost inducers on decks four through twelve!" engineering called.

"Are those damn things alive?" his weapons officer gasped as the ship bucked and rattled.

"No, they're not alive, but they are being piloted somehow," Van Stadt growled. "All ships, clear those asteroids...now! Use everything you have!" he ordered through clenched teeth.

Magna cannons and lasers opened up all across his battle line, scoring the rocks and breaking them to pieces. With literally thousands of targets, though, his ships couldn't reach them all.

"Hull integrity report," Van Stadt barked.

"We're stable, sir. Deck four is closed off. Minimal casualties."

"A nice try, but not good enough. Where's my firing solution on that ship?"

"Captain, the *Tranquility* is pushing underneath us, full thrust."

"Target and fire. Abandon the asteroids."

"I've got no firing solution, sir. The asteroids are in the way."

"Then, turn us around damn it, and wait until she clears the field!"

"We can't, sir," his nav officer called.

"Why in the hell not?"

"It was the asteroids, sir. They were targeting our inducers. We're down to thirty-five percent thrust. The rest of the wing is even lower, sir."

Van Stadt glared at where the *Tranquility* was slipping away from him on the holoscreen. He had been a fool to let himself be trapped like this.

"It won't be that easy for you next time, Mephista," he muttered. Then he turned and barked orders to his crew. "Engineering, get on those repairs. Comms, inform Decival he has a hostile inbound. And, clear out those damn rocks!"

* * *

The Tranquility

"Atlas, I'm on my way. This plan of yours better work," Mephista relayed to the Bwain who had shuffled onto the bridge.

On her holoscreens, a tight ring of ships guarded Gertie, with another smaller flotilla in reserve. A third wing was spread in disarray near the border of the nebula. They had cut the battle group by two-thirds with just a few hours' worth of fighting. Amazingly, everything had gone according to Carter's plan.

"Nav, what am I seeing near the obelisk?" Mephista asked.

Her helmsman brought up a magnified view of the object, fighting against its strange interference to try and make out exactly what had changed. Where once there had been a single pillar, now the shape had unfolded, with white sheets billowing out into space.

"Ma'am, it looks like something's emerging from the anomoly."

"Oh my god," Mephista whispered. Beside her, the Bwain screeched and tried to flee the bridge. The captain reached out and grabbed the fluttering creature, keeping her holochair balanced against it. She needed her link to Atlas right now more than ever.

On the holoscreen something that looked like a cross between a whale and a giant squid, armored with a hard outer layer of what could have been shimmering electroglass, was squeezing through the obelisk.

"What is that thing?" one of the bridge crew gasped.

"It's one of them. Jesus, they're coming through!" Mephista gasped.

The Bwain tried to wriggle out of her grasp, so she pushed it against the bulkhead with her hover chair.

"Get me Atlas right away!" she instructed it.

*   *   *

Decival
Holding position 50,000 kilometers from Gertie

What had been a perfect plan now lay in tatters. Wing B had taken significant damage to its offensive capabilities, but at least Monderer was still in the fight, chasing after the Bwain ship. Van Stadt was limping after the *Tranquility* at speeds that would put him hours behind the cruiser. It was simply one cruiser, which his remaining ships should be able to handle easily, but still Decival no longer trusted his plan, or his intuition. The uncertainty worried him.

"Send another messenger to Earth. Advise him that we're facing significant asymmetrical tactics and unknown alien weaponry. Casualties are light so far, but progress is slow."

"Yes, Commander," the adjutant acknowledged before he turned and rushed from the bridge.

"Your orders, sir?" his nav officer asked.

On the screen before him, the strange alien weapon that had first struck Captain Drake blinked and jittered, but it did not appear to be moving closer. If the anomaly did move however, it could threaten Monderer's flank.

"Captain Monderer, your system-side flank is exposed to the anomaly."

"Commander, with respect," Monderer's voice came through on a private channel, sounding strained, "I've got the Bwain on the run. I need to reach that thing before it gets to the nebula, or I'll lose him."

Decival zoomed his view, adding course projections and scenarios.

"Captain, you are leaving a gap in our defenses. If anything comes through there, you'll be be cut off, and you're entering a region where communications and sensors will be ineffective at best."

"I am aware, Commander. I'm asking for you to give me another hour, or maybe two. Then we'll have this bastard."

The calm, collected part of Decival instinctively pushed back against the risk, but then he considered Admiral Nico's response if he let Carter get away, and he gave in.

"You have three hours, Captain. At that point, if you have not engaged I will expect your withdrawal. You're already ten hours from the rest of the fleet."

"Understood sir, and thank you."

"The *Tranquility* is four hours out, Commander. All weapons are hot," his tactical officer reported.

"What does she think she's gonna do? Is she planning on taking on twenty ships all by herself?" Decival asked no one in particular.

"I'm scanning for any other ships or anomalies, Commander. Nothing is returning."

"Maybe she's simply suicidal," Decival sneered as he studied the blunt spear of Mephista's ship.

She was making no bones about her course, not even trying to hide or protect herself. Her ship also looked to have suffered extensive damage, but after everything else he had experienced in this system, he fully expected to find traps at every turn.

"All ships outside the command group, enter Gertie's orbit. I want a tight network across that planet. We're not gonna let anything surprise us this time."

"Commander, that will only leave three ships with the *Dauntless*."

"I'm aware of that. I'm more comfortable with the ships' backs to the planet. The command group will act as reserve. But I don't think we'll be needed. The rest of the force should be able to handle things."

* * *

Gertie

Alistair Threed burst through the sod that had hidden him and the other colonists from Judgment, and sprinted toward the set of sharp hills a few dozen meters away. It was hard running in the bulky EVO suit since the suit hadn't been designed for use in a gravity environment, and it chafed against his skin and muscles with every move. Some of the younger colonists had reached the camouflage before him and were already stripping away the green blankets and radar-reflective covering that Hal had printed to conceal the *Tranquility*'s orbiters. Threed bent to help, but instead felt hands guiding him to the ramp.

"We'll take care of this. You just go get yourself settled," someone indicated.

Once he was on board, he dropped himself down into an acceleration couch and fumbled with his restraints while the other suited colonists filed in after him. The man across from him, Thikrit, was sweating and shaking.

"I've never been in space before," the man noted nervously over the intercom when he caught Threed's gaze.

"How the hell do you think you got here?" one of the other former prisoners asked.

A thin smile broke over the man's face.

"A lot of good that did me."

In spite of himself, Threed had to laugh.

"You survived Judgment, you'll survive this," he replied.

Another colonist loaded the orbiter with crates full of Hal's surprises, bolting them to the floor as one of the *Tranquility*'s crew picked her way up the gangway and then made her way to the pilot's seat.

"Belt in, we're about to take off," the woman announced.

"Have they seen us?" Threed asked.

"It's only a matter of time," the pilot answered. "But remember, we want 'em to see the orbiters. *You're* the ones that need to be hidden. Do you remember what you need to do?"

Threed ran through Captain Carter's plan again in his mind. It seemed almost too simple, as if ships shouldn't be designed the way the Captain had explained. When the orbiter's acceleration pressed him back into his couch, Threed realized things weren't that simple after all. He had trained with Danny four different times for this mission, but this was the real thing. This was his chance to strike back against those who'd abandoned him, and all the others.

He let out a battle roar that echoed through the intercom. First one voice, then another, then another picked it up, roaring as gravity pummeled them, and they rode a column of flame up to seek their vengeance.

Hal Yellowknife had been right after all. There wasn't much difference between a criminal, a rebel, and a farmer out on the Swordbelt. He just hoped that he'd live long enough to let Hall know how wise his words had been.

*   *   *

The Dauntless

"The *Space's End* discovered them on sidescan, Commander," one of his nav officers advised. "The orbiters came from Gertie's surface."

"How the hell did they let 'em get into orbit?" Decival barked. He was rapidly losing his calm, and as many deep breaths as he took, they were never enough to relieve his dread that the situation in the Swordbelt was slipping away from him.

"They were scanning for off-planet threats, sir. After your latest order..."

"I know what my order was! Where are those orbiters going?" Decival growled.

"There were eight of 'em, sir, all lifting off from different points on the planet. They're just beyond the battle line now."

"Comms, find out who's on those ships," Decival ordered.

"They claim to be unarmed colonists, sir. They're asking to surrender."

"Tell them to hold their position, and that if they fail to comply with that order, then we *will* destroy them."

"Yes sir."

"Commander, at the absolute most, those orbiters could carry maybe two-hundred people. Where would the rest of 'em have gone?" his science officer asked.

"That's an excellent question. We'll round up whoever's in those orbiters and bring them here for questioning. Monderer, what's your status?" Decival asked as he switched the com link on his station over to the *Nova*.

"Commander, we're nearly in effective weapons range, and I've got quite a package of nukes ready for this Bwain bastard."

"Has he communicated anything?"

"Not since we initially engaged. But I...wait, I'm receiving a transmission."

"It looks like it's coming from the planet. As it did before, sir," his comms officer noted.

"Put it through," Decival said, smiling to himself. Finally, something was going right.

"This is Captain Carter calling Commander Decival. Do you copy?"

"I'm right here, Captain. I'd say it's about time we spoke, wouldn't you?" Decival responded.

"Decival, I need you to listen very carefully. I'm offering you this one and only opportunity to surrender. From this point on, I cannot guarantee what will happen to you and your fleet. Do you understand?"

"Is that a threat, Captain?"

"We're all in this together, Decival, whether you want to believe me or not," Carter replied.

"What I see is a man who has acted in hostility toward the SSC navy at every turn. I believe that the last time we spoke, I advised you that the only communication I wanted to receive from you was your surrender. Are you prepared to deliver yourself and your crews?"

"You have no idea what you're doing."

"On the contrary, Captain. You have inflicted reparable damage, but my battle group is still intact. At this point I see exactly two ships in this system, and neither actually scares me. Unless you'd care to enlighten me?"

"With pleasure, Decival. Just remember, you asked for this. Carter out."

The commander ground his teeth at how Carter treated him. Decival had prepared for years for this moment. He had studied every tactical manual, from the *Art of War* to the *First Bwain Encounters*. Now a disgraced outer-system officer was going to try to threaten him?

"Captain Monderer, I want that Bwain ship destroyed," Decival snapped.

"Yes sir, we're entering firing position now. Oh...wait..."

On his holoscreen, Decival's indicator for the Bwain ship disappeared.

"Monderer, so help me, if you let that Bwain ship reach the nebula..."

Atlas' Flight

Decival snarled.

"No, sir, he was still thousands of kilometers away."

"Then what the hell is happening out there? Someone tell me what's going on!" Decival shouted angrily.

*   *   *

The Bwainhome

"Granger, are you sure you're ready?" Carter asked.

"Of course not, but I'd rather try the drive than be blown to pieces."

Carter let a wry smile slip as he closed his eyes. How many times had his crew looked impossibility in the eye and come out victorious? He was proud to serve with them all.

"What is pride?" the Bwainsong asked as they sensed his thoughts.

"Faith in yourself, and in what you've accomplished," he answered.

"Have fought well," the aliens crowed. *"Have won!"*

"Not yet," Carter cautioned. *"There's a human saying that pride cometh before the fall."*

"What that mean?"

"Basically it means that you shouldn't get so caught up in your own pride that you take everything for granted. If you get too confident about your situation, then you're bound to miss something that could lead to your downfall," he explained.

"So pride not good?" they asked.

"No, pride is good, but too much pride can be bad."

"We not understand," they thought. He could feel their confusion, but he didn't have time to go into it any more than he already had.

"Ask me about it when this is all over. I promise I'll try to explain it to you better," he thought to them. They seemed satisfied with his response, so he turned his attention back to the matter at hand.

He used his mind to reach down into to the bowels of the Bwainhome, where he found Granger standing with Pandith and a group of the Bwain who'd been observing what they'd been doing. He then pushed his perspective outward.

He'd realized something back when he'd initially stood up to the First Ones, something that the Endless Knot had known but the Bwain had forgotten. Their ship had been created by the First Ones, but it was also a part of them. The alien vessel had been made, not built; it may have even been a First One at one point.

Tapping into the dormant heart of the ship that Granger had awakened, he gathered all of the Bwainhome in his mind, and then pushed through what he thought of as the veil of the physical universe, with only his destination in mind. He was looking for a blank field of space that, in certain dimensions and realities, would put him just behind where Commander Decival strode the deck of the *Dauntless*.

"Take me there," he commanded the Bwainhome, and the living ship obeyed.

*   *   *

The Dauntless

"Proximity alert!" the nav officer screamed.

"What in the hell is goin' on?" Decival blurted out as a massive shape just above and behind the *Dauntless* appeared on his holoscreen.

"Nav, get us an escape solution. Weapons, target that ship and fire! Epsilon Wing, this is the *Dauntless*. We're under heavy fire. Peel off the planet and re-form on my position."

"Commander, we have an issue," Captain Werner called, a note of consternation in his voice.

"This isn't the time for *issues*, Captain!"

"My ships are malfunctioning. We're experiencing catastrophic failures of our weapons and propulsion systems," Werner reported.

"That's impossible!"

"Sir, I'm afraid it's more than possible. My science team believes our hull nanos have been reprogrammed."

"Commander, we're taking heavy fire," Decival's weapons officer called.

"Get us away from that ship!" the commander ordered.

"It's not from the ship, sir. It's from everywhere."

Furious, Decival opened a hull schematic and saw rings of fire swirling around the *Dauntless*.

"Well return fire, damn it!"

"Commander, there's nothing there to hit," the weapons officer said as he works the controls on his console furiously, trying to find something to target.

"Get me the other ships. One of them has to at least see *something*. Someone's gotta know what the hell's going on!"

Even as he spoke, the main holoscreen lit with a blinding flash. The *Spacefarer*, his wing vessel to starboard had just been vaporized.

"That blast came from a signature behind us, sir. We've got a computer match, it's…"

"What?"

"It's the Bwain ship, sir. It's Carter."

"What did he just do?" Decival demanded.

"That's a massive ship, sir. Its offensive capabilities easily rival our own. I'd say a planetary bombardment class fusion laser."

"Commander, I've lost the majority of our aft magna cannons and missile bays. I need an order."

"Transmission, sir. It's from Gertie again!" the comms officer called out.

"Put it on speaker," the commander ordered.

"This is your last chance, Decival. Your three task forces are crippled. Your flagship can't fight back against what's hitting it, and I have the tactical advantage. Surrender. The last thing I want is more lives to be lost out here."

"And then what, Carter? You'll sacrifice Earth to the Bwain?" Decival sneered.

"I told you when you first entered the system, Commander. We meant no harm. We could have destroyed your whole fleet but we didn't. We've only done what was necessary to get you to stop and listen. If you want to keep fighting me, then I'll destroy every last ship, and every last crewman you brought out here. If however you choose to surrender, then I'll spare the lives of your crew, and then we can discuss how you can help to save the lives of every single human in the galaxy. It's up to you. I just hope you're more reasonable than the last Commander they sent out here."

Decival closed his eyes. He felt himself trembling, shaking with fury. It had been such a good plan. He'd had so much confidence and strength going into this mission.

"They're hitting our inducers, sir, and I still have no firing solution," his weapons officer called.

"Initiate surrender protocol," Decival ordered, and then he turned and stormed off the bridge.

Chapter 14

Gertie
In Orbit

Threed's helmet visor kept fogging, but as long as he was still breathing and not frozen to death, he considered himself very lucky. He brushed a glove across his face, forgetting that he was in an EVO suit, not back on Judgment, and that he couldn't do anything about the condensation. For a moment, as his suit arm's inducer jetted him off his target, he panicked.

"Remember to relax," Danny Xiao had told him during the training flights. "You can trust the suit. It's a part of you. The less you fight it, the easier it'll be to maneuver."

He smiled as his suit righted him again. Danny was now a far cry from the cocky young kid who had killed a man to get his attention. But then, maybe that was the point. Everyone changed after they killed someone. It was just all too rare to actually see someone change for the better.

The SSC cruiser's hull shimmered before him, stretching away for a quarter of a kilometer. It bristled with weapons pods, sensor arrays, and the white glare of the induction thrusters that could throw the ship halfway across the Swordbelt in just a few hours, which was exactly what Threed and the rest of his colonists were here to prevent.

With his right fist closed, he thrust it toward the hull, directing the suit's primitive guidance system to bring him closer to the ship. Working as quickly as he could, he pulled a coil of spider steel from his waist, activated it with a spark from his glove, and tossed it onto the deck. The gold flow of nanobots, recognizing the electromagnetic signature, withdrew from the circle and gave him a safe landing zone. If he hadn't have cleared a space first, the nanos would have swarmed him in an effort to clean him off of the hull.

Activating his magnetic boots, Threed settled onto the ship's cold steel hull, and then he lifted one of the hundreds of small tubes that Hal's factories had churned out. He twisted the tube between his stiff gloves to activate its electromagnetic broadcast, then tossed the sparking cylinder outside of his ring onto the sheet of nanobots. For a moment, nothing happened. The first two times he had done this, Threed had thought he'd failed, and he had waited for a weapons turret to pivot toward him or an airlock to cycle, releasing a team of marines that would vaporize him in a matter of seconds, but neither of those fears was realized.

Carter and Danny Xiao had been right. The SSC hadn't been looking for boarders. Instead, they had been focused on what was happening at the outer boundary of the system, and Hal's nanobombs had worked like a charm.

A white flash rippled through the tiny robots. For a moment they froze, looking like ice slicked across the black hull. Then the machines flowed toward the white blade of the ship's inducers and the blunt snubs of its weapons turrets and bays. Flashing a tiger-striped combination of gold and silver, the nanobots began dismantling the ship's inducers and weapons with a speed and deviousness that no human weapon could match.

It had been an ingenious plan, one that only could have only come from someone who'd spent the better part of his life with nanobots.

Smiling to himself once again, he triggered his suit to lift off from the ship that would soon be crippled, and left in a state where it was unable to hurt the colony, the Bwain, or anyone else.

He craned his helmet to find the next ship, saw it crouched a few dozen kilometers distant, and closed his fist.

Just as he left the hull, a massive white flame appeared in the black of space above him. It looked like a strange puzzle of a sea creature where the pieces all didn't fit properly.

"Did you see that?" someone cried over their intercom frequency.

"Keep quiet!" Threed hissed. "We can't let them know we're out here."

He tried to keep calm, as Danny had taught him, but the thing was a horrific combination of machine, a living thing, and some other sort of crystalline life. Threed forgot himself for a moment, and in his fear he tried to turn away, causing his inducers to send him into a crazed spin.

When he finally managed to right himself, he saw that the thing, whatever it'd been, was now gone. Now he was facing the largest human ship he had ever seen in his entire life. Flashes and explosions lit what must have been the SSC flagship, until a brilliant lance of plasma fury sliced toward one of the support ships and blew it from the sky.

In the blink of an eye, Threed realized he was hurtling through empty space; a single man in the vast and soundless fury of battle. His breath came faster and faster, fogging his faceshield even more. The ship that was his target was turning, pushing away from him. He could see a few other vessels preparing to leave Gertie's orbit as well. They must have received orders to engage Captain Carter aboard the Bwainhome. He tried to adjust his course, but it was hard to see, and he was so distant that he didn't know if he would ever make it.

Slowly his visor started to fill with a gray fog.

"Help! Someone, please help me! I'm off target, and I can't see. Anyone that can hear me, the ships are headed toward the Bwainhome. There's a lot of 'em, and I think one of the First Ones was here for a minute," he called to whoever happened to pick up his signal. He could feel the panic rising within him, and his heart was pounding hard in his chest.

"Where are you, Threed?"

"I was headed toward my fourth ship, but then something happened and I got tossed out into open space, so I don't know where I am."

"All ships and colonists, this is Captain Carter. Cease hostilities immediately and return to orbit in Gertie. The SSC has surrendered. We did it everyone! We did it!"

Gradually, Threed felt his calm return. He slowly coasted to a stop and turned back toward the planet. Somehow he'd managed to survive, and from the looks of it, so had quite a few others. Once he got his bearings, he realized that he hadn't been lost at all. He was just temporarily blinded by the fog in his helmet, and caught up in the fear of the moment.

He craned his neck upward, looking at the empty part of space where he had seen the apparition, and a sinking feeling suddenly materialized in the pit of his stomach. Things weren't over yet, not by a long shot.

*   *   *

The Tranquility

"Atlas...," Mephista said, but then her emotions caused her throat to tighten. She cleared it softly to allow her just a few more seconds before she had to relay the latest update.

"We did it Mephista! I can't believe it!" Carter said, his voice brimming with emotion.

"Yeah, we did," she managed. What she wanted more than anything was to be next to him in times like this, so she could offer herself, such as she was, for him to lean on. She'd finally learned how not to be alone, and she wondered if he had. It made her sick to dash his elation in this time of celebration, but she had to tell him what she'd seen.

"Atlas..."

"Yeah?"

"Have you seen the *Fate's Winds*?" she asked, her voice trembling with each word.

*   *   *

The Bwainhome

The brief moment of triumph he'd just been enjoying suddenly felt curdled. Carter forced the reluctant Bwain to turn their instruments once more toward the obelisk. The obelisk had changed into a mass of what looked like flexible razor blades, attached to a swollen mouth. Whatever creature was emerging from it was somehow both a ship, and a living thing. It was a massive construct that could only be one of the First Ones.

"MASTERS COME! WE RUN!" the Bwainsong screamed. For a moment they were able to push past his control to seize the interdimensional drive. All they wanted in that moment of fear and terror was to phase the Bwainhome in the opposite direction of the *Fate's Winds*.

"No!" Carter thought, trying to reassert his will over them. *"You can't run!"*

"Must live! Must be free! Must run!"

He was losing them, and in so doing he was losing the only vessel that would be big enough to hold the majority of the colonists, allowing them to escape from the Swordbelt before the First Ones could assert themselves. For a moment, Carter was back in the helicopter watching Aida disappear in a cloud of smoke as his house imploded, and feeling the weight of failure absolutely crushed him.

He had lost his wife because he had given up. It was the only time in his life that he hadn't fought, and it had ruined him.

He seized the Bwainsong as tightly as he could, forcing the aliens' minds to focus on him.

"Running is for the weak! The Bwain are strong!" Carter told the Bwain as forcefully as he could.

Here the Bwain paused, thrumming with tension and what, in a human at least, would have been panicked adrenaline.

"The Bwain are weak. The Bwain are slaves," they thought.

"No! You're only as weak as you think you are, and no one can make you a slave unless you let them," Carter replied.

He felt the energy draining from the interdimensional drive, felt their thoughts of food supplies and other factors rise once more to the surface.

"You have to stand for something, or there's no point in being alive," Carter continued, maintaining his strong resolve through the Bwainsong.

"What does Carter stand for?" the Bwain asked.

"I stand for life," he answered.

*   *   *

Earth

"YOU SWORE TO ME THAT THIS WOULDN'T HAPPEN! YOU TOLD ME THAT CARTER ONLY HAD ONE SHIP!" Nico screamed, his face contorted into a mask of absolute rage.

"Lower your voice," Phuri said as calmly as he could. "Others may be listening."

Nico's heavy chest heaved. Sweat coated his hairline, and the buttons of his uniform had sprung open at his throat. The man was like an animal bashing himself against his cage, and Phuri had only a little longer to wait before releasing him.

"President Kidewange will be learning the news of Decival's fleet soon. There are those who believe he will offer to negotiate with Carter," Phuri said slyly.

"And what of it?" Nico asked.

"There are those who fear the Bwain more than anything."

Nico snorted, stomping to his office window and staring at the ocean's molten caps.

"What do you want, Phuri? What happens now? I'm a soldier, not a politician. I have no experience with coups."

"What I want is revenge," Phuri answered. "And what I'd like you to do is to remain the same, well-respected soldier that you've always been. At least for now. Resist Carter at every turn. Project your strength as the bulwark for humanity against the aliens, and let me handle the rest."

"What do you mean *handle the rest?*" Nico asked, eyeing him warily.

"I'll be the timekeeper. I'll tell you when to be ready, and when it's time for that *good soldier* persona of yours to change into something else."

*　*　*

The Dauntless

Commander Decival stood at attention, a quiet fury burning alongside the humiliation he felt standing there in the shuttle bay before his senior officers. He fully expected to be spaced, or shot on sight; but he had to respect Carter's demands, or who knew what else would happen to his fleet? His crippled ships were still hours from Gertie, and with the capacity that Carter's alien ship possessed to appear anywhere, there was little chance of fighting back.

Part of him even hoped Carter would tell him how he had turned an entire solar system into a massive trap.

The orbiter that arrived was a strangely bulbous purple mess that looked as if it would have been at home on the sea floor. Dozens of crude modifications scarred a hull that seemed to glisten and throb as it settled to the surface of the cargo deck. The bay doors sealed shut, an oddly shaped door irised open, and a gaggle of Bwain poured from the orbiter.

Decival's marines cried out, grabbing their plasma rifles and taking up whatever strategic positions they could find.

"Hold your fire! I said hold your fire, damn it!!!" Decival shouted at the top of his lungs.

The Bwain that scuttled across the deck were grotesque, mangy things, though their stumped limbs seemed oddly muscular. To see them up close and alive like this, Decival was surprised. How had these pathetic creatures terrorized all of Sol Space Command for so long?

His interest shifted as a tall man followed the Bwain down the shuttle's hatchway. The man wore a battered flight suit, and the star insignia of an SSC captain. His face was a mass of cuts and scars, and his nose had been shifted more than once in his youth. What gave Decival the most pause was the incredible sadness in Carter's eyes, as if he bore a wound that would never heal.

"Captain Atlas Carter, I presume," the commander said, raising his chin slightly as a subconscious sign of both defiance, and superiority of rank.

"Commander Decival," Carter said as he crossed the deck and extended his hand, but Decival pointedly refused to shake hands with him.

"I hope you'll understand if I don't shake hands with a man who's betrayed his whole race," Decival snarled indignantly. Carter stared at him for a moment, and then shook his head as he let out a sigh.

"Is that what you think this is about? You thought I came here to take your scalp myself?"

"What else would it be about, Captain?"

"The entire universe is at risk. I'm here to ask for your help."

"My help in *what*, exactly?"

"Escaping this system before the thing that destroyed the first of your ships consumes us all. What the Bwain and the colonists did to your ships can be reversed or repaired. But we need to make Alcubierre jumps sooner rather than later if we're gonna survive what's coming out of that damned anomaly."

"And what is coming out of it, Captain?" Decival asked.

Frustrated, Carter glanced at the Bwain on either side of him. Then he reached into his pocket and held out a twisted yellow mushroom.

"Here, eat this, and then I'll show you," he replied.

* * *

Decival came to his senses in a cold sweat, panting and exhausted.

"My god, we have to hurry!" he said urgently. Carter nodded at him from where he sat next to the bunk. His expression was as grim as his mood.

"I'll need every one of your drop ships to make as many trips to the surface as they can. My science officer believes it'll take about fifteen hours if we run at maximum efficiency. Once we're done, we'll jump from the system and warn the Earth about what's coming."

Decival reached up and took Carter's hand to help himself stand.

"It won't work, Captain," he said as he rose unsteadily to his feet.

"Why not?"

"Because I ordered every ship in the fleet to vent its antimatter the moment we surrendered. I couldn't risk the Bwain having a way to get back to Earth."

*   *   *

Gertie

Hal looked at the list on the tablet in front of him, and then glanced up the compound's landing pad. Long lines of colonists were filing into the rows of orbiters from the dozens of ships that were helping. Hunched farther down, away from the others, were the strange bulbous Bwain ships. Many of the aliens fluttered and bobbed through the sky. They seemed almost like children lost in play, lifting their wings and scratching in the dirt, bending to snatch bites of grass within their beaks.

The beeps and warnings of the colony's heavy equipment sounded all around them. Front-end loaders were filling the Bwain's orbiters with the stuff of life: soil, seed stock, compost, and everything else on Hal's list. A long row of hovercarts carried what at first looked like mounds of dust, but if he slipped on his goggles Hal would see the glowing signatures of trillions of nanobots that were about to make the longest journey they had ever traveled in their entire existence.

One of the Bwain landed beside him in a fluttering squawk. It cocked its head, blinked its eyes, and then croaked at him.

"Danny?" it said, the D sound softened by its hard beak.

"Captain? I'm here," Lieutenant Xiao acknowledged as he came walking over to stand next to Hal.

"How much more time do we need?" the alien transmitted.

"Just a few more hours, Captain, and then we'll be finished."

"Need to hurry."

"We'll do our best, sir," Danny said. With the transmission ended, suddenly the creature shook its head, and then fluttered off to join its brethren.

Hal looked down once more at his list, ticking off the number of hovercarts, the last scrapings of soil, and carts of harvested vegetables. He frowned, scanning up and down as a breeze kicked up around him. The grass swept coolly against the hills, and the clouds curled in tawny ribbons.

"Something wrong?" Danny asked.

"There's no Nightcrawler on the manifest," he noted.

"I'm sure someone will end up smuggling some on board. Do you really want some though?" Danny asked.

"No. Never again," Hal answered as he started toward the Bwain ship.

*   *   *

The Fate's Winds

"*Faster,*" the First Ones groaned. They floated inside of Aric, around him, and above him, pulsing with an energy drawn from the cords that strained between the twelve dimensions. They hungered for the life force and heavy matter that the physical world offered, and as such, they clawed at the ships that were now leaving the Swordbelt, their tentacles just missing the final few vessels. When they realized they had failed, the First Ones' rage howled through him like the tearing of the empty vacuum ripping through his soul.

Aric was learning to endure, and he bore the pain stoically. Standing at the edge of the *Fate's Winds'* torn hull, he stared with eyes that had once been human. Everything that he had ever known was dwindling away from him. The First Ones would follow Captain Carter of course, gaining in speed and strength. Already, they had reached Judgment, and a part of him felt their joy as they sunk their cabled arms through the fissures in the planet's atoms, absorbing the heavy molecules that only existed in these dimensions. They were feeding on the planet, and growing ever stronger.

"*Aric Keith, why do they run?*" the First Ones asked.

"Because they aren't strong enough to fight."

"They never will be. Why would they fight?"

The distant part of him that had once sat with Danny Xiao on Judgment. They both thought at the time that their lives were about to end, but things didn't turn out that way. After a few moments, he answered them, the words slipping out before his mutilated other self could stop them.

"Because fighting is better than giving up," Aric responded.

He cringed, expecting the pain of their punishment, but this time there was no pain. There was nothing. Nothing but a message from the First Ones.

"We will fight them, then. We will fight all," the First Ones replied.

Aric watched them emerge into the universe one by one, writhing like fallen angels who had come to claim their vengeance.

About the Author

J. Channing is an engineer and manager for a semiconductor company in Boise, Idaho by day and a dedicated entrepreneur and freelance writer by night. Born in Butte, Montana, he spent most of his childhood roaming around the northwest, living in eighteen different locations before getting through high school. When not at his day or night job, Channing is also actively involved in the community, with his church, and as a small business owner. He utilizes his business ties and proceeds to give back to the local community, having raised funds for Boise area charities.

J. Channing has been interested in military history, time travel, World War II, and weapons technology since he was a small child. The original story concept for *Forever* was outlined on one of his many solo bus rides from the Seattle area to Helena, Montana. It was adjusted and improved over decades and was finally, as a labor of love, completed. The book is a fulfillment of a story that has played out in his head hundreds of times; he hopes the world enjoys it as much as he always has.